Whitney & Freddy

a

Boyfriend Dilemma

George Beckman

Published by Books from Graestone

Dedication

For all the kids who feel they aren't seen for who they are.

Acknowledgments

Thanks to our son Matthew, who said, "Dad, why don't you write something?"

Ruth, who has spent hours on this book.

I'm grateful for my critique partners, Rachel, Harlow, Abby, Rawchel, and Mark, who have supported me and taught me a great deal.

Thanks to Donna, who tries to clean up the messy grammar parts.

And to all my #LineByLineTime friends on Twitter—thanks for helping polish the rough places.

Other Books by George Beckman

Members of the Cast

Partway to Wolfskill (Poetry)

The Wolfskill Trilogy:
The Ship from Wolfskill
Airships from the North
The Air Loom

Content Warning

I write clean and wholesome books. However, *Whitney and Freddy a Boyfriend Dilemma* has scenes involving alcohol and domestic violence. (Non-Sexual) In addition, Freddy gets in a fight with a bully at school.

Table of Contents

Haiku

Bubble bath wholesome

Falling deep under her spell

Dating Whitney Tate

Whitney- First Day

"The new girl is stacked!" And so it begins.

The comment is followed by guy noises, and I hurry past them.

What if I just walked away? Teachers aren't expecting me.

I keep going beyond the last wing of classrooms and stop at a parking lot. A street leading away from the school is lined with houses with green yards. An older gentleman is getting ready to mow his lawn.

I look back and move to my right, between the office and the sidewalk.

It's peaceful.

I put my back against the cool marble school sign and slip down out of sight. I should be used to the comments. I look down and wish this wasn't the first thing kids notice about me.

The mower starts, a cloud of smoke wisping across the grass.

"Hey, you OK?"

My breath catches, and I stand quickly. It's a boy's voice, and I don't want to see any more boys. I slide my hand along the back hem of my sweater.

"Do you have a dentist appointment or something?"

With the mower, I should pretend I don't hear him, but I shake my head. *Why is he out here? Why am I responding?*

"First day?" he calls.

I refuse to turn. Let him look at my normal side.

"The warning bell is about to ring. You don't want to get a tardy."

I'm suddenly exhausted. "I may just leave," I say to my shoulder.

There's a pause while a school bus rumbles past, blocking my view of the lane.

"I wish you wouldn't."

Kind words from a stranger. Tender words. Caring words.

A lady kneels to work in her flower bed. It's so normal, and I'm

1

stuck. Between the school and the sidewalk. Between Ohio and California. Between having friends and no one. Between this voice and escape.

Freddy- The Back of Her Lap

The first time I see her, Paul Evans makes a crude comment and gestures toward his chest with both hands. I'm pretty sure she heard him.

She has jet-black hair just below her ears, not like the other girls. If the boys weren't so busy gawking, they might have noticed her big blue eyes—almost transparent.

She hurries past the history wing toward the street, ducking behind the offices. Off limits.

I shouldn't follow her, but she's lovely and doesn't deserve Paul's mouth.

I find her on the grass, staring across the street. She's kinda tall for a girl but looks small. Lost. I keep my distance.

She puts her back against the school sign and slips out of sight. Should I get someone? Miss Gill, my counselor?

When I call to her, she pops up and moves toward the sidewalk.

She has grass clippings on her skirt.

Aw, man—how do I tell her? She's gonna think I'm checking her out, which I guess I am. I stall with small talk.

She tells me she's thinking of leaving, her voice so tiny I hardly hear her. Discouraged? No—sad.

I scramble for the right words and tell her I wish she wouldn't. At first I don't think she hears me, but she takes a half step toward the sidewalk.

"Hey—there's grass on—on the back of your lap."

She brushes with her right hand.

"Other side. Sorry."

Her hands are small, delicate, and the clump falls away.

"Got it."

She hugs her books, not moving.

"You gonna be OK?"

She speaks to her left shoulder. "Go away, please."

I step back. "OK, I'm going."

"Wait?"

She's quiet.

"I'm here."

"Where are the history rooms? I don't know where my next class is." Her voice is reduced to a squeak. "Room 206."

3

"Right behind you, to your left. Street side, third door."

"Thanks." She lets her notebook down. "Please let me be."

Whitney—Lunch

A bell rings.

The man's mower stalls, and he fiddles with the motor. He reminds me of Mr. Paulson, in Ohio. If that was his house, mine would be next door, and Joanie's would be six streets over. We could climb up to her brother's treehouse and talk as we had so many times. Like we did three weeks ago when my heart was breaking.

Three weeks. Forever. The ache is overpowering.

The mower starts again, and I steal a glance over my shoulder. He's gone, and I'm not sure I would have minded if he stayed.

After a longing look at the restful scene, I turn toward the classrooms.

The doors are closed, and I stop in front of Room 206.

I'm already late and decide it doesn't really matter. I double back to the Girls' at the end of the wing and lay my books and purse on a sink. I spin my skirt around and check for grass stains.

I tuck and straighten. My lightweight black pullover sweater is cute over a white blouse.

I sigh. Apparently, black didn't "minimize."

I adjust my sweater one last time and gather my things.

At the classroom, I slip in as quietly as possible, but eyes watch —except the teacher, who has his head in a cupboard.

I don't want to be on display in front of everyone, so I take an empty seat. The guy next to me whispers, "Hey." I nod and arrange my binder, pencil, and pen.

The pencil sharpener stops scraping, and a skinny kid with dirty hair comes too close. "I sit there."

"Oh, sorry." I gather my things and wish the desk had an exit on the right. I slide out, his arm brushing my shoulder. "Excuse me?"

He steps back, eyes roving, and I escape to the front of the room among whispers.

The teacher is piling books on a small table. "What's going on over there?"

"I'm new. I have an admit slip?" I check my sweater to make sure it didn't ride up.

"John, one of these on each desk." The teacher finally turns and holds out his hand. "I'm Mr. Tompkins."

For a second, I think he wants to shake, but he gives his

5

upturned palm an impatient wiggle, and I hand him the admit slip.

"Take any empty seat."

I could be strolling down that street now, maybe calling "Good morning" to the woman working with her flowers. She would turn and wave her little shovel.

A girl sitting in the row on the door side wiggles her fingers and pats an empty desk. I clutch my binder to my chest and hurry down the row.

"I'm Laura."

Grateful, I smile. "Whitney."

Laura's thin and cute in that way some girls are. Each part of her face doesn't quite fit, but it all works somehow. The sum is greater than the parts?

The cafeteria lady is all happiness, and I smile and nod to brownish rice with anemic ham squares.

The tables are well identified: Jocks, Cheer, Showoffs, Readers, and Nondescript. A girl with pointy glasses glances up and says, "There's room here."

She looks kind, and I sit.

"I'm Minnie." She wrinkles one corner of her mouth. "After my grandmother, who is nice, but—Minnie Vaughn."

"Whitney," my mother's maiden name, but I don't tell Minnie.

She doesn't take a breath. "What subjects do you like?"

"I like math and English."

And choir. I have a hall pass to try out during fifth period. I want advanced choir.

Minnie gestures to the girl across from me. "This is my friend, Loretta."

"Hi, Loretta."

Loretta smiles a "Hi," and continues peeling a tangerine.

There is a commotion at the Showoffs table, but I ignore them. Eventually, the room begins to clear, and Loretta says, "Good to meet you, Whitney," and she's gone.

Minnie breaks our silence. "So, are you interested in science because there's a group of science kids in a club? Well, four of us." She blushes. "Sorry. I guess you landed next to a science enthusiast." Minnie inspects my eyes.

She's throwing me a bone in a room that didn't seem ready to offer anything but looks—some disapproving from Cheer.

"Science is OK, too."

Minnie leans against my shoulder. "So the Science Club meets on Tuesdays. In the Physics room. Mr. Coulter is the advisor. We're doing fun physics experiments."

I know moping in my bedroom doesn't help anything. "I'll ask my mom."

Minnie beams and the bell jangles my ears.

At my locker, a big guy kicks off the wall and moves too close. I lean forward to keep him from watching me work the combination and feel his breath on my neck. I turn, giving him a cold stare.

"Hey, you're new."

I should write this stuff down.

"So what's your name?" His eyes do a slow sweep up and down. He curls his lip like he has a toothpick in his mouth, but he doesn't.

"Whitney, and I'm late for class."

"Hey, *Whitney*. I'm Taylor." He leans closer.

I move to my right, but he puts his other arm out, hemming me in.

"Listen, Taylor. Good to meet you, but I have to go." I make a quick duck under his arm and move away.

"See you around, *Whitney*." He finishes with a "Mmm, Mmm, MMMM."

I don't look back.

Freddy- Bubble Bath

First period, and I can't believe my luck. Mr. Sanchez puts the new girl in the seat in front of me. Whitney Tate.

She's out of my league—punching above my weight, Dad would say—but it never hurts to look—and dream. I thought a lot about her gazing across the street. So straight and slim.

Kids are arguing about the time change, and I lean forward. "It's not for two weeks, but then it'll be getting darker earlier than it stays lighter later longer."

Whitney turns halfway in her chair, and the scent of bubble bath surrounds me. "True." Her bright eyes roll toward me. "But in summer, it stays lighter later longer than it gets dark early."

I could have talked to her for a month, but Jim comes up our row handing out a pop quiz. His eyes linger on Whitney and it makes me jealous, which is silly because Whitney doesn't even know my name.

Whitney works fast—and it's her first five minutes in this class.

I scan my paper to find questions with answers I know. Mom's going to kill me.

Whitney is the first to finish. I'm almost last to turn in what I hope is a C.

After class, I try to stay close to Whitney, but Tom is homing in on her. In the hall, she looks up and smiles at something he says, but when he brushes her arm, she jerks away and trots three steps.

Chris comes alongside. "Freddy, can I have a ride after school?"

"Meet me at the car right after." I lose sight of Whitney, and I slip into a dream, imagining giving Whitney a ride home.

Whitney- Yellow Marks

I made advanced choir! Mrs. Albertson is everything I could hope for, and singing sixth period gives me something to look forward to all day.

When I walk in, she has a small group around the piano. She plays and leads with an effortless grace. She's a contralto, although I wouldn't be surprised if she could sing high C's all day.

She notices me. "Laura? This is Whitney. Please get her music, and she can sit by you."

Laura, from History, hops to the task and brings me a black binder of music, and a concert folder. "Hi. Glad you're here."

Other kids are finding their places, and Mrs. Albertson stands at the piano. "Miss Wayland is out today. Yellow tab in your binder, 'Christmas Song.'"

She plays a rich introduction, and we sing. The harmonies are scrumptious, and with each note the troubles of the day melt. It breaks into six parts, and Laura points to the second soprano.

Goose bumps run up my arms, and my eyes are damp. I only muff one note, and when we sing the last chord, Mrs. Albertson holds us. Laura and I stagger breathe as the notes fade.

Confidence swells in me. I can survive this school, this move.

I notice, "Arr. M. L. Albertson." I flip the sheet back and forth. Lorenz Music. Our teacher is a published arranger!

"Altos, measure twenty-five…." Mrs. Albertson plays and sings the line. "With me now." The third try, the notes are true.

After supper, Joey is in my room again. I take his arm and lead him out gently. Well, gently until he begins to buck.

"I was just look-ee-ee-eeng," he whines.

From the hall, I glance back at the piles I *didn't* leave on my desk. "You were playing with my schoolwork again." I feel the pouch of his sweatshirt and pull out a yellow highlighter with no lid. "Joey!"

I kneel and see a yellow stain showing through. "Mama's gonna kill you." *If I don't beat her to it.* "Where's the lid?" *If he marked my school papers….*

He gives me his cherub look.

"Off it comes. Up, up." I tug on the sweatshirt sleeves, and he puts his hands over his head. "Where is your tee shirt?" Actually, it's good he isn't wearing a tee, because there's a yellow blob on his stomach.

I haul him into the bathroom and scrub the yellow without much success. I lift him by the armpits and kiss his belly button, making him giggle.

When the sweatshirt is in the sink to soak, I call, "Mama!"

I know she's in her room. Since Daddy died, she's up in the morning to get breakfast, but after checking at Safeway, she lies on her bed, red eyes staring at nothing.

I pull a shirt over Joey's head and crouch on my heels. "Stay out of my room, *please.*"

He's already engrossed with some plastic army men, and I leave him.

My trigonometry solutions have what might be a cat in the middle of tomorrow's assignment. Then I spot *Anne of Green Gables* on the floor. Joey has filled in the embossed title in yellow, and I sink down, tears blurring my sight.

It's not just that Daddy gave me the book—his Mom's book—the grandmother I never met. And it's not just missing Joanie. And it's not having a boy comment on my bustline the first day of school or the eagerness of the others to join in at my expense. I put my head against the side of my mattress, shoulders shaking.

Or maybe it is? The sum is greater than the parts?

Freddy- Fix That Grade

Mom puts my English quiz at her place at the table. "Silverware and napkins, please."

Dad's not here. He's at Stucky's Bar and Grill, and he didn't go there for supper.

After I pour the milk, we sit. I take her outstretched hand, and we say grace.

She doesn't pick up her fork, and I wait. "Freddy, this D is unacceptable." She sighs. "Your teacher had to call me. There's a quiz next week. You are to get at least a B."

She takes a bite of meatloaf. "I don't understand you, Freddy. If you can make A's and B's in your other classes—you can do it in English." She takes a swallow of milk. "No grade, no car. *Gaige?*"

She's Georgian, not the state, and I understand. "Yes, Ma'am."

"You can Ma'am me all you want, but I'm not kidding, Mister."

"I'll do better."

"Yes, you will." She grabs my hand. "Freddy, look at me."

Her dark eyes are serious. "I went down to the school with you to help in Kindergarten and the lower grades. Don't think I won't come and sit by you in your English class."

"I know."

She lets go of my hand and pushes a piece of meatloaf in a little circle. "So, other than your English grade, are you being a good boy? Polite?"

"Always."

"To your teachers—everyone?"

Thoughts of Whitney Tate flood my mind. Her hair. Eyes. Back. Hands. Figure. She's fun when she's not sad. I can tell almost at a glance when she's having a hard time.

I wish I could tell Mom about her, but with my English grade, I'm pretty sure boy and girl stuff isn't a suitable topic.

And, who am I fooling? I have no chance with a girl as special as Whitney Tate.

I wash, and Mom dries.

Whitney- Track

The PE uniforms are dull blue. We tried, but the blouse pulls at the buttons and bags everywhere else.

The blouse might have worked, but I have two bras on because we're doing a track unit. I'm a fast runner, but it can be pretty awful.

After we attempt a mile in eight minutes, the coach lets us walk the track to "cool down." I'm hot, and my chest feels smothered, and I regret promising Minnie I would go to Science Club.

Laura comes up beside me. "Hey." She has long legs with muscles.

Glad for someone to talk to, I say, "Yeah, what was your time?"

"Seven-two."

Laura can *run*. "Seven fifty-four."

"You qualified! There's a fitness test—have to be under eight."

Smog has turned the mountains dirty gray. It hurts to take a deep breath, and I tap my windpipe.

"It's the air. Bad but not critical. We don't dress for PE when it's really bad."

The boys are playing basketball on the lower courts. *Oh, good. We get to parade by on the way to our locker room.* I'm dying for a cool shower, but I'm not anxious to be *in* the showers.

I'm glad to see that some girls wrap in towels. It doesn't help when showering, and I try not to notice other girls noticing.

I reach for my towel, but a pouty girl who hasn't dressed out is holding it between two fingers as if it smells—staring at my chest. "Are you kidding?"

She lets my towel slip from her fingers, and I snatch it before it hits the wet cement, hug it to me, and hurry away—but not before I hear, "Well, she's not stuffing." Another girl who hadn't dressed for PE says something I'm glad I can't hear.

How do these girls get away with not dressing out? I scramble into my clothes.

No one has ever, ever said anything in the locker room before. Thoughts of them gossiping closes my throat.

Freddy- Ride, Anyone?

I squint toward the track. Whitney's walking with her hands on her hips, and the ball bounces off my shoulder.

"Get your head in the game, Sanders!" Coach's tenor is piercing.

I race down the court after Cooper and manage to dribble the ball out of his hands. I circle, dribbling hard, chuck it to Mouse, and he puts it in.

Nothing, Coach?

I hustle through the showers and into my street clothes. Outside, I search the groups of girls but don't see Whitney. As if I ever would have the nerve to say, "Hey, Whitney. How 'bout a shake at Daisy's?"

I've never asked a girl to anything. Well, I managed to ask June to a dance freshman year, but that was only after Sam said he was thinking about asking her. I hated myself for that.

After Trig, I hurry to Mr. Coulter's room. Today, we are talking about the solar system. Howard Stickney has a telescope, and the club is meeting at his house next week to view Comet Ikeya–Seki. It's a pretty big deal, and Howard has seen it.

I'm watching oxygen and hydrogen, bubbling into two long test tubes, when Minnie says, "Hi, Freddy." I look up, and there's Whitney.

"Hi." I remember to include Minnie.

"This is my friend, Whitney. Whitney, this is Fredrick—but we all call him Freddy."

Whitney gives me a shy smile with big, reassuring eyes. "We have English together. Hi, Freddy."

And PE the same hour. I wonder if she's noticed. I straighten up, and gesture weakly at the test tubes. "Electrolysis." *Slick, Sanders.*

Mr. Coulter gathers everyone around the front chalkboard. He has drawn several stars and the position of the comet. Whitney is standing one foot away, and I want to edge closer.

Mr. Coulter has Howard talk about the comet and what to expect. Howard passes mimeographed half-sheets with directions to his house.

"If anyone needs a ride, I can pick you up," I blurt, stealing a look at Whitney and Minnie. Tim Rodriquez takes me up on the ride.

13

Room for two more. The thought of Whitney in my car makes my stomach tingle.

"Minnie? Whitney?"

"Oh, thanks, Freddy. My mom's taking us," Minnie says.

Whitney gives me a half smile and mouths, "Thank you."

Whitney- Minnie & Loretta

The weekend was so lonely. You can only read so much and play with army men on the floor so long. Sunday was a bad day for Mama, and I know she spent most of the afternoon crying in her room. She doesn't sob but that evening her eyes looked like two burnt holes in a blanket. So, I'm glad to be back in school.

Freddy has great hair. Black, wavy. He's one of those wiry guys —quick. When we passed the boys playing basketball Friday, he darted around on strong, hairy legs.

I've never had a boyfriend. I'm not sure I want a boyfriend. I want to be kissed. Never having been kissed is sort of stupid for a junior. Especially when every guy on the planet seems to think I should go behind the bleachers with him.

Philip Peterson in English is bugging me. He sits beside Freddy, but I notice him pushing his row forward before class. He's almost sitting beside me.

He cheated on last week's quiz. It was grammar stuff—true-false and multiple choice. The guy doesn't listen in class, makes crass jokes, and got the same one-hundred I did, and it was my first day in class.

I think Mr. Sanchez suspects something, but Philip's sneaky. Now, I try to cover my work, but if I sit up to even take a breath, he must memorize five answers at a time. Mr. Sanchez should do a writing unit. Philip probably can't spell his name.

At lunch, I go to my table—I guess it's my table, and Minnie is genuinely sweet. I decided to bring my lunch like Loretta. It may be juvenile, but I like peanut butter and jelly sandwiches.

"Howard said after we see the comet, he will train the instrument on the moon." Minnie turns pink. "Instrument—doesn't that sound more technical than telescope?"

I grin and take a bite of my sandwich. The bread has gone dry near the crust. Mama gets day old at the store.

"So, my mom will come by your house at seven. We don't want to be late. When I showed her the address, she said she knows right where it is."

Minnie hasn't touched her food.

"Better eat, Friend." *Friend?* Yeah, she's officially a friend. So far, my best friend at this school.

15

Minnie pokes at her food. "Howard's house is pretty fancy—I hear." She leans in. "My sister drove me—drove by there one time."

Loretta has stopped peeling her tangerine and rolls her eyes. "She's a goner."

Minnie is flustered but recovers. "We have very similar interests."

Similar interests? Is Freddy interested in anything I'm interested in?

This puzzles me because since the move, other than reading in my room and watching Jeopardy! with Mama, what interests me? Freddy didn't do well on the English quiz, and I like school, especially Trig. I love choir, but I'm not sure Freddy wants to talk about singing and breath support.

It would be nice to know what I am doing when I am kissed. I tried putting on Mama's red lipstick and kissing a napkin, hoping for one of those perfect red lip shapes. It wasn't perfect.

"Whitney, where are you?" Minnie's waving her hand in front of my eyes. The lunch room is emptying, and I grab my papers, shoving them and the rest of the sandwich into the bag. The sliced carrots are still moist, so I pop two in my mouth.

Minnie is bouncing on her toes. "So, I'll see you at seven." Not sure whether Minnie is more excited about seeing the comet or Howard.

Freddy- English Leather

I wash my car after studying in the school library. It's not the coolest, but I got it from Mom's best friend, Polly. She was careful, and there isn't a scratch on it. I got some wax and shined it again last week. Sort of a blue-grey coupe. The chrome is still great.

Mom stops me when I come in. "Freddy, the quiz is tomorrow. Get home at a decent hour."

"I will." I smile down at her. "I've been studying."

I spend extra time in the shower. At breakfast, Dad said I could try some of his English Leather aftershave. My morning dad is much easier than my night dad.

I shave carefully and put a little aftershave on my neck.

I'm sorta scrawny, but I can grow a beard. I let it go last summer while we were camping, and it's black and thick. I put on jeans and a plain shirt. It isn't cold, but I wear my Pendleton, like a light jacket.

It's a short drive to Howard's, and I roll the window down, enjoying the fresh air.

Tim! I circle back three blocks and stop in front of Tim's. He bounces down the steps and jogs to the car. "Thanks," he says as he slides in.

Tim's OK. He's not extra cool. Like me, I guess we are just regular.

"Have you checked out the new girl, Whitney?" he asks.

Maybe I spoke too soon. "Yeah. She seems nice."

He chuckles. "*Real* nice."

I am officially jealous. Tim goes with Suzie Blakely and has for a while. I feel like he has more to say, so I click on the radio. Tim thinks twice, and we wait for it to warm up.

K-POP is playing a Beach Boys song. I tap my hand on the wheel.

"You don't have to take me home. Suzie's coming to get me."

Suzie drives her dad's '55 T-Bird. She's blonde and looks so cool in the car. Maybe Tim should be jealous of me?

Nah. Girls like Suzie don't waste precious time on guys like me. Which gets me to wondering—Tim is good-looking, but there are guys up the ladder who flirt with Suzie all the time.

Whitney comes to mind, and I feel unfaithful for a moment,

which is crazy because we hardly know each other.

Three cars are in Howard's circle drive, and I park behind a Chevy.

A sign says, "Use the Side Gate," with an arrow. I follow Tim, hands in my pockets.

One of those little dogs with hair in his eyes meets us, and I make sure the gate clicks shut.

Whitney is wearing a V-neck sweater over her blouse. She's talking to Mrs. Stickney but gives me a glance.

The telescope is a reflector, and it must be an eight-inch. I don't know that much about telescopes, but this one is expensive. Howard is standing near as Minnie stoops, looking through the eyepiece. Her head comes up. "Howard, that's amazing!"

Howard takes a quick look and adjusts the mount. "OK, the comet only stays in the field for a short time, so queue up."

Whitney is next, and she puts her hand to the neck of her blouse and leans in.

"See it? Is it still centered?" Howard asks.

"My!" Whitney is breathy. "It's come all this way."

Howard's dad is pointing to the comet. I look in the direction he's pointing, and I see it—a tiny streak.

"You want to look?" Whitney's asking me.

"Sure." I come quickly to her side. She doesn't move away while Howard aligns the telescope. "Thanks." I love her eyes in the moonlight.

"Ready." Howard steps away, and I lean in.

The comet almost takes up the whole circle. I watch, unmoving, until it begins to slip out of sight. When I stand, Whitney is still there. "Thanks, Howard. That's incredible."

Howard reorients the scope, and Tim takes a turn. I'm not sure how interested he is; he's been watching the gate.

Mr. Coulter is being cool, letting Howard do his thing.

"You like it?" I ask Whitney.

"Yes." She leans slightly toward me. "Minnie's in heaven."

Minnie's back at the scope, and Howard is extra close, whispering in her ear.

Whitney hasn't moved away. "Are you going to stay until we see the moon?"

"Yeah. I don't have to be anywhere," which is not entirely true. I'm determined to study my English notes again, but I'm not leaving Whitney's side even if I have to study 'til midnight.

18

"Have you been to Howard's before?"

"No." I search for something clever and settle for a crooked smile.

I'm desperate to ask her to a movie or for a coke. Anything, but Howard has swung the telescope to the moon.

Mr. Coulter laughs at something Mr. Stickney says.

"The visual plane cannot encompass the entire lunar surface, so I will train it on the crater Copernicus. You can look a little longer as other lunar formations move into the field. You will see other fascinating features."

Minnie's bouncing around so much that she can hardly focus on the eyepiece. I smile, catch Whitney's eye, and gesture with my head.

She comes closer. "She's so excited about the moon missions—gobbles up any news." Whitney still smells fresh.

"How about you?"

Whitney rubs the sleeves of her sweater. "I came because Minnie is so kind, and the comet was—impressive." She hugs herself tighter.

"You cold?" A breeze chases dry leaves across the patio. "You can have my Pendleton."

"Oh, no. I'm fine." Whitney puts her arms down, but they are back up in moments.

It's cooler than I thought it would be, and I take off the shirt. "Here. You're shivering."

Whitney meets my gaze. "Thanks." She slips into the shirt, two sizes too big for her. She gives me that corner-of-the-eye look. "You're nice, Freddy."

Nice. Is nice like she likes me or nice like a polite boy? She's stunning in my Pendleton. "I try."

She gives me a half smile.

When it's Whitney's turn, she's still, staring into the eyepiece. "You have to see this. Quick, it's moving."

I bend in, and the crater is perfectly centered. She's right at my ear. "See it?"

"It's like you can touch it." I stand. "Don't lose your whole turn." I glance back into the eyepiece. "Look. A new one is coming into view."

Minnie is standing so close to Howard that I think their shoulders are touching. "The article on Grumman's work on the lunar lander is good. You've read it, right?"

"Yes, but I thought they would stick with fuel cells for power."

19

Whitney straightens and steps back.

I'd rather stand under the moon with Whitney than look at it through a telescope. "Go ahead, Tim. Take a gander."

Tim has come back from the gate. "Suzie will be here any minute."

"I think he wants to see Suzie more than the moon," I say out of the side of my mouth. Whitney nods.

She tilts her head toward Howard and Minnie. They are holding hands. When he moves to adjust the scope, their fingers trail as they pull apart.

I bend around and look into Whitney's face. Her lips are turned in a slight smile. "I think you're a romantic."

Whitney doesn't react. I was hoping for a "Yes" with a big smile—her gazing into my eyes.

When Mr. Coulter finishes his last look, Mrs. Stickney comes with a tray of cups. "We have hot chocolate. Howard, there is another tray on the counter."

Minnie follows him inside. When Mrs. Stickney brings her tray to us, Whitney takes two and hands one to me. My heart is flipping in my chest like in the cartoons. "Thanks," I manage.

She holds her mug in both hands, taking a sip. "Hmmm."

Hmmm indeed. I'm one of six Americans who aren't crazy for chocolate, but standing in the moonlight next to Whitney Tate, drinking the cocoa she handed to me, is about the best thing I can remember.

Whitney- Tangled

Minnie and Howard are cute. Awkward as all get out, but darling. Who am I to think that? I'm standing, drinking chocolate, which is not my favorite beverage, with Freddy, and I'm wearing his plaid shirt. It's heavy—warm.

I have a light sweater over my brown patterned blouse, and I'm not sure I like the look of the V-neck.

Why is it cold? I thought California was balmy.

Is Minnie wearing contacts? I thought she took her glasses off for the eyepiece, but they are nowhere to be seen.

Howard and Minnie are looking in a tidy shed by the house.

Freddy seems to like me, and the thought makes my stomach do a little flip. Is it a like-like or a friend-like? He doesn't give me the up-and-down eye scan with a long pause like most of the boys. Maybe he doesn't like girls shaped like me. Is that why he offered his shirt? Is he trying to cover me up?

I'm so bad at this. I wouldn't know how to be a girlfriend. Don't think I want a boyfriend here if they are like the guys I've met so far. Would I want Freddy for a boyfriend? His shirt smells like the cologne he has on tonight. I don't know what it is, but it's heavenly.

Minnie and Howard start rolling the telescope into a shed. The patio lights are on, and I see it's built onto the back of the house.

"Come, look at the storage unit Howard built."

I'm not sure how interesting this could be, but Minnie's billing it as if Howard just built the lunar lander thingy himself.

I follow her over and look inside. Minnie has proudly turned on the light. I duck in to see shelves and star charts on the wall. It's very nice—for a shed.

Minnie waves her hand. "These are the celestial seasons, and there—star locators."

I step back and realize I almost stepped on Freddy's foot. "Sorry."

"Missed by a mile." He reaches down and rubs the dog's ears with both hands. "Hey, Feckets."

"His name is Charlie," Minnie offers.

Freddy is still working on Charlie's ears. "OK, Feckets, go on. I can't rub your old ears all night."

Suzie, in a low-cut white dress, swoops into the yard.

"You're here," Tim says. Seems pretty obvious. He turns to me. "This is Whitney. She's new."

Now, *Suzie's* bent over, rubbing the dog's ears, and she's putting on quite the display. She looks up, still petting, and says, "Yes. She's in my typing class."

I muster a, "Good to see you." If I didn't know any better, I'd think she's giving me the stink eye.

"We have to jet if we're going to get to the thing." Suzie reaches for Tim.

Tim looks over his shoulder. "Thanks, Howard. Tell your mom thanks for the chocolate."

Suzie tows him toward the gate.

"Didn't he come with you?" I ask Freddy.

"Yes, but I knew Suzie was taking him home."

Mrs. Vaughn is at the gate. "Minnie, Honey. Time to go."

I start toward the gate. *Freddy—ask me if I want a ride. I think I do. Maybe not.* I've never been alone in a car with a boy. Do I want to be in a car, alone, with a boy? I think it should be OK with Freddy. He seems safe. Would Mama care if a boy brought me home?

Freddy, I'm halfway to the gate. Ask, Freddy. I'll say yes—I think.

At the gate, I pull the shirt close so it won't catch on anything. *Freddy's shirt!* "I'll be there in a sec," I call.

I run back to Freddy. He has the sweetest eyes. "Here." I pull my arm out of the left sleeve and tug the shirt around. The other sleeve bunches up around my wrist and stops. Who thinks up this stuff? I'm standing in front of a boy with his shirt in one hand, the other snarled in the inside-out sleeve.

Freddy reaches to help, reconsiders and takes his hand back. I pull harder but don't want to rip a seam. The only thing to do is start again. I work the shirt up on my shoulder, feeling totally exposed.

Freddy says, "Here," holding out his hand.

I extend my arm to him, and he inspects the cuff. It's still rolled, and he straightens it while I stand mortified.

He undoes the button and gently tugs the sleeve down my arm. He's so close. I catch the shirt as it slides off my shoulder and hand him the wad. "Thank you."

"It looks good on you. You could have brought it tomorrow."

My heart does that thing when it feels like it is in your stomach and throat at the same time. "Thanks."

I almost pat his arm. I want to pat. Would he like me to pat? "Gotta go."

22

"See you tomorrow."

It wasn't a question. Does he mean he's looking forward to seeing me, or is he stating the obvious?

I'm quiet on the way home, but it doesn't matter because Minnie is giving her mother a moment-by-moment description of the evening. Mrs. Vaughn is uh-huhing at the appropriate times. She's good, tossing in an occasional "Oh?" Minnie wouldn't notice if her mom fell asleep. Minnie's in her element, and it's kind of endearing. Innocent.

I sit in the back seat, wishing the heater was on higher. I cross my arms.

Freddy- Cheating

Whitney is on my brain. I force myself to study. Having her see me get a good grade on this test drives me.

I thought it was sexy when she put her hand at the top of her blouse to look in the telescope. Her hand was so delicate.

I force my eyes to focus. Study. I make it through the review sheet, and start again.

When Suzie was petting the dog, her dress fell open. It was low-cut and didn't leave much to the imagination. I'd looked at Howard, afraid Whitney would see me gawking.

Whitney's modest hand to her neck was so much more.

I go through the sheets two more times and fall asleep. I jerk awake at six with them half under my face. I haven't drooled. I scan the questions again. I have this. I'm in the shower, dressed, and eating cereal by six-thirty.

"You're up early," Dad says. He's OK this morning.

"Studying for English."

Mom gives me a look, and I assure her I'm ready for the test.

At seven-thirty, I start the car and drive to school. It's cold, and the heater is starting to work when I pull into the student parking lot.

I can't wait to see Whitney and take this unit test. This is a do-or-die moment. Mom has enough trouble without me fouling the waters.

I review my notes again. A ripple of excitement goes through me. This test will finish the grammar unit, and we are moving to poetry and then, finally, writing. I hurry up the walk and wait at the corner of the English wing.

Whitney is walking with a senior, Carter Watkins. How did she get here before me? The guy's quite entertaining, apparently. I am so jealous I can hardly watch.

Last night was so—peaceful—easy. I didn't feel like I had to try, and Whitney seemed to be herself. Not that I know who she really is, but if last night was it, I like it.

They stop for a moment. She stares up at him. Listening to every word. Fascinated? Her back is to me, but she's concentrating on him. She shifts her books. His hand goes out, and she turns away. I pull back around the corner.

Who am I kidding? Carter's hitting homers and I'm whiffing.

In the room, I go over my review again. Whitney is almost late and plops down heavily. I want to tap her shoulder, but I'm not sure I should, and I need to ace this test. It counts one-third, for the unit.

Today, Philip has Lucy Talbert sitting half a seat beyond the other rows, and Mr. Sanchez tells everyone in her row to slide back. "Give Lucy some room."

Philip says something under his breath, and Whitney turns the other way. He rams Jimmy's desk. "Move up, fool!"

We start the test, and Philip is eying my paper. Whitney is crouched over hers, and Philip probably thinks a C- is better than what *he* can do.

Is Mr. Sanchez really this dense? I look up. Not dense—reading a book. Must be nice to get paid to read while kids cheat right under your nose. I mark the rest of the answers wrong.

I turn to the second page. I know all the answers, but Philip is poised, so I mark the last twenty wrong.

I look up, and Mr. Sanchez glances back down at his book.

I turn the paper over and stretch. Philip flips his closed and pulls out a miniature deck of cards. The guy is playing solitaire.

Whitney takes her paper forward with thirty-five minutes left.

Finally, Philip swaggers up like he's king, and slaps his paper on Mr. Sanchez's desk. He can't wait to get back to his game, and I erase like crazy.

I guard my paper, elbow out so there is no way Philip can see, and fill in the right answers, but he's concentrating on his game.

Six minutes left. I spend another two minutes cleaning up any former marks, and take the test to Mr. Sanchez. Does he know what I did?

I go back, but Whitney doesn't look up. She's engrossed in a book.

So close, yet so far.

After class, I catch Whitney's eye. She's hugging her books close. "That was fun last night," I say.

Her smile is shadowed. "Yes. Thank you again for letting me wear your shirt."

Something's off. I feel a chasm between us and want to jump the distance. I want to say something, anything. But I turn and walk out. I don't check to see if she's behind me.

25

Whitney- The Jerk

Dear Joanie,

I've made some friends. No one like you- I miss you so much!

The kids here seem nice but I have gotten some rude comments about- well you know.

Happier note: last night, I went to a Science Club (I know. Who would have thought?) to look at comet Ikeya–Seki. I don't know if you have heard of it. I probably wouldn't if I wasn't here.

Anyway, there's this boy, Freddy. He seems different than other guys. I think I <u>like</u> him. But it may be too early to know.

Tell me how things are. I miss you and the gang so much. Tell everyone I said Hi.

Love,

Whitney

I thought of Freddy a lot last night. I could see myself dating Freddy. Not like Suzie and Tim. I don't want to lead a guy around by the nose. But with Freddy, I could be myself—I can tell. Even if it didn't work out, maybe I could have a first kiss. A tender kiss.

After A Cappella, I hurry toward English, hoping to find Freddy. Maybe we could talk before class.

Then along comes a senior. He's tall and walks me toward English, and he seems genuine. Sorta funny, even if he's pretty full of himself and has almost crowded me off the sidewalk. Then he stops, so I stop.

"Hey, you want to come to my house after school? We have a pool—heated."

I stare like a dodo bird.

"Come on, it'll be fun. You have a suit, don't you? Of course,

26

girls in California wear bikinis."

Why am I standing here, heart pounding?

Because he's staring and not at my face. I bring my books to my chest, and he steps closer. Before tears can push at my eyes, I blink. I may be shaking my head.

"No? I bet you look *hot* in a bikini." He acts like he's going to put his hand on my upper arm.

I turn away onto the grass. It takes a moment to get my bearings. *English.* I take two steps on the grass and am back on the sidewalk, moving fast.

Laughter. "I knew you couldn't get her," some guy howls. "You owe me five bucks, man." echoes in my ears.

Now I'm a bet! I hug my books and walk faster. There's a Girls' at the end of the English wing. At the mirror, I wipe both eyes. Red. No one can see me like this. Not Freddy. Not anyone.

Freddy. Is he for real? Sincere? I'm not sure I want to test the theory.

I'm almost late for class and keep my head down. *Don't look up.*

I'm first to finish the test and take it to Mr. Sanchez. I pull out *Pride and Prejudice*, and when Freddy walks by, I pretend I'm engrossed.

I've read and reread *Pride and Prejudice*. I brought it because I knew I would have time after the test, but I'm not even looking at the words. I turn the page when I think of it.

The lines are blurring, and I keep telling myself, *don't cry, do not let them see you cry.*

I know I'm prettyish and have a figure. I don't think I am prideful, but I keep running into prejudice. "Pre-judge." I'm being prejudged. By boys. Sometimes girls.

No, it's boys. I grind my eyes closed to keep the tears back. Boys are a bad lot. Freddy Sanders can go fly a kite.

I almost slam the book closed, but remember I'm supposed to be reading.

I'm done with boys and their one-track minds.

Somehow, I make it to lunch, and Minnie is all happiness, giving Loretta a minute-by-minute retelling of the evening with Howard sprinkled in like some exotic seasoning.

Loretta is digging into the stem end of her tangerine, nodding from time to time. I'm not sure what Loretta's thing is, but I'm guessing it's not telescopes.

Minnie takes a breath, and scrunches up her eyes at me. "Hey, you OK? You haven't said a word."

27

"Just tired." Frustration mounts, and I'm tempted to say, "Couldn't get one in edgewise," but Minnie doesn't deserve that. She's been nothing but kind.

Minnie picks up the story, glowing when she gets to Howard holding her hand.

A few minutes before the bell, Loretta folds up her sack and holds it to the side of her mouth. "You've got a spot."

It takes me a moment, and then I look down. Jelly! This day just keeps getting better. "Thanks," I whisper.

I pick up my bag, check it for any errant food, and sorta hug it until I can get to a restroom. Naturally, the paper towel dispenser is empty, so I dab with toilet paper. It's not as bad as I feared. The light pullover is dark blue, which helps. I spend more time brushing lint off than cleaning.

Karen from Typing comes in and says, "You too?"

"Yeah. Par for the course."

Daddy had explained that one to me the week before he died. He loved golf. Nice way to go—doing what you love. Sudden Cardiac Arrest. Ugly diagnosis.

Very efficient.

Karen is blotting a spot on her sleeve. "Laid it right in the lasagna I spilled. This sweater is new."

My eyes are swelling with tears. Daddy. What the jerks said this morning. Not talking to Freddy. I don't mean to let go of a sob.

"Hey, Whitney." Karen gives me a kind smile. "Ah, come here." She envelopes me in a hug. She's pleasantly plump and smells like mint. She pats my shoulders, and the dam breaks. "Awww."

I sob. I'm not sure why. I miss Joanie. I miss my old house. I miss my dad. I take a shaky breath. Not everyone has an agenda: Minnie. Loretta. Laura. Karen.

Karen digs in her purse and produces a paper towel. "This school never has towels."

I blot my red eyes. "Thanks."

The spot is drying. Maybe Karen blotted it with her hug. The hug has blotted my sadness. Daddy. The jerks. Freddy?

Oh, Freddy—are you genuine or are you playing the long game?

Karen and I walk across the quad together. We aren't talking, and that's OK. When we get to the first sidewalk, I start left.

"I'm this way."

Karen pauses. "It gets better."

I turn toward her.

"I'm new, too. About a month before you."

I don't trust my voice, but give her my first real smile since A Capella.

Freddy- Cheater?

"Excellent work, Freddy. One hundred percent. Quite an improvement." Mr. Sanchez adjusts his glasses. "I need to see you, Whitney, and Philip after school."

"Today?" Philip moans.

"Today, Philip."

Whitney shifts in her seat, and I'm getting a bad feeling.

It takes about two weeks for the day to be over. When I get to the room, Whitney is standing, hugging her books. She's not near her desk, and her eyes show no expression.

Mr. Sanchez taps his pencil and looks at his watch. He confirms what he sees by checking the wall clock. "We'll wait a couple more minutes."

Whitney puts her books down and sits. I sit as well.

After four minutes, Mr. Sanchez says, "Well, let's start."

Whitney won't look at me for more than a split second, and her eyes are cold.

"Freddy, you seemed to have erased most of your answers." Mr. Sanchez holds my paper for both of us to see. "You put in new answers and got one hundred percent, just like Whitney—the only other one hundred. Only Whitney didn't change any of her answers."

Whitney's eyes are shooting daggers, arms folded.

Why do I feel guilty? I look over my shoulder. Philip is nowhere in sight.

"What do you have to say for yourself, Freddy?"

"My answers are my work." Whitney makes a noise in her throat that shakes me, but I keep going. "I studied the review work over and over." My voice fades to a sliver at the end.

Now Mr. Sanchez has *his* arms folded. "Whitney, what do you know about this? Did you share your answers with Freddy?"

Whitney gasps, "NO! Sorry. No. I kept my test covered with my arm and hand, except for the part I was answering."

Mr. Sanchez looks at me with wide eyes. It's a question.

"I know the answers. I studied, Mr. Sanchez. Ask me any of the questions. I really did study."

Philip saunters in.

"I will, Freddy." Mr. Sanchez unfolds his arms. "Philip—glad you are here. We're talking about last week's test. The one you failed."

"Yeah, I wasn't feeling good that day." He glares at me, one eye squinting.

"Weren't feeling well? Do you feel better today? Do you feel like retaking a part of the test?"

Philip shrugs. "I may have forgotten some of the answers."

"Mr. Sanchez, I have Science Club," Whitney says. "I don't want to miss it."

"Mr. Coulter knows you're here."

"I ain't in the club. Some of us work." Philip drums quietly on his desk.

"I called the store and told them you had an important meeting because of your work in English."

Philip's head jerks up. "You know where I work?"

"You've bagged my groceries."

"Oh—yeah."

"Mr. Sanchez walks to the left of the room. "Whitney, would you please sit here." He puts a paper on a desk. "Please leave all your things there. Only bring a pencil."

He goes to the center of the room. "Philip, this is where you will work."

"I don't have a pencil."

Mr. Sanchez goes to his middle drawer and takes a pencil to the desk. Philip slouches over and sits.

Whitney works fast and lays down her pencil.

"Freddy, you work here."

The test is easy. Three questions are from the original test, with the order changed. Five easy questions, and I sit up straight when I am finished. Whitney has her elbows on the desk, head bowed.

Philip finally marks the last answer.

"Please stay; this won't take long." Mr. Sanchez gathers our papers, scans the tests, and writes at the top of two sheets. "Congratulations, Whitney. One hundred percent."

Whitney starts to get up.

"One more minute, please. Philip, you didn't get one right. I'll call you into Mr. Tyler's office in the morning."

Whitney gives me a questioning look. I mouth, "Vice-principal," but I'm not sure she understands.

"Philip, you better get on to the store."

When Philip is gone, Mr. Sanchez takes off his glasses. "I think I know what's happening here. Does this have anything to do with

Philip moving his row forward? Whitney? Any ideas?"

"He copies. I try to keep my answers hidden, but it is hard to stay hunched over my work all the time." She pauses. "I guess he copied Freddy this time."

"Yes, but his answers were the wrong answers. His answers are the answers Freddy erased."

Whitney looks at me, her eyebrows asking the same question.

Mr. Sanchez moves to the side of his desk. "Freddy, why did you erase your answers and put new answers? Answers that match Whitney's answers perfectly." He leans against the front of his desk,

Whitney's eyes move to mine, and I try for a smile but keep it small. She watches and turns away, her eyes the last thing to leave.

"OK, I saw he was copying my answers, so I marked them wrong and waited until he handed in his paper and then changed them to the right answers."

Whitney is sitting up straighter. I don't lock eyes with her even though I want to. "I studied, Mr. Sanchez. The review sheet. My notes, the text. I went over and over them." Whitney's still watching.

"Really. My mom was going to take my car away." I swallow. "And I'm tired of getting bad grades." I look right at Whitney. "I'm not dumb and don't want people to think I am." The words "I am" are almost a whisper.

Whitney's eyes are on me, but she's looking right through me.

I turn to Mr. Sanchez. "I'm not good at grammar. I'm looking forward to poetry." Then it dawns on me.

"Wait a minute—I couldn't have copied Whitney. Whitney was the first one to turn in her test. Philip didn't hand in his paper for twenty minutes."

Whitney is staring toward the front of the room, but I'm not sure she's seeing anything.

Mr. Sanchez stands. "I want to believe you, Freddy." He walks behind his desk and studies all three of the tests. He smiles.

"On today's impromptu quiz, you got one hundred percent. And two of the questions I gave you today were not on the original quiz and not on Philip or Whitney's test. Congratulations."

I am relieved and a little mad. Before I can stop myself, I say, "You didn't believe me." I lock on to Mr. Sanchez's eyes. "I studied...."

"Maybe I didn't handle this perfectly, but I wanted to hear it from you. I've suspected Philip for a while, and I wasn't sure you would —well, own up to what's been going on—tell on him."

Whitney's flipping through her notebook. I wish I could see her face. I'm still upset. I study for the test, and Mr. Sanchez assumes I cheated. What's Whitney thinking?

When Mr. Sanchez excuses us, I hurry out and wait for Whitney. She comes around the corner and stops. She hugs her notebook, chin down.

"Can we talk for a second? Are you going to Science Club? There are a few minutes left."

She doesn't raise her head.

"Whitney, what have I done?" I sense she's like a skittish cat. I step back two steps, and her head comes up. "I'm not a cheater," I say.

She gazes to her right, staring at the math building. I look but don't see anyone or anything to see.

"If I did something, I didn't mean to."

She keeps staring, her eyes filling.

I hate what is happening. "I don't want to make you cry."

She makes a quick swipe. "Oh, Freddy. I'm not crying. I'm just —so—frustrated."

"With me? 'cause I will leave you alone if that will help."

She finally turns toward me, hugging her books harder. "It's not you, Freddy," she whispers. "It's not you."

"So, you're not mad at me?"

She's looking at the math wing again, more tears building. "You seem like a good guy, Freddy. I just..."

"Wha—"

She's still looking away but interrupts with a whisper. "Freddy, I don't want to be so—close." A tear runs down her cheek, and she doesn't wipe it away.

My stomach quivers, and for a second, I can't speak. "Should I ask Mr. Sanchez to change my seat in English?"

Now the tears are flowing, but there's no sound. I want to comfort her. I want to pull her face to my shoulder and hold her hair. I want to be more than friends.

"I have to go." She turns, trotting away, clutching her books.

Whitney- Dinner Guest

I'm happy when Mr. Sanchez tells us Freddy got all the answers correct on the five questions. Relieved. I didn't want Freddy to be a cheater.

When he tries to talk, I get emotional. Freddy's concerned and I run away. His questions are questions I don't have answers to.

When he helped me get my sleeve untangled, he was so tender —leaning down, concentrating on helping me.

But the jerk senior—I don't even remember his name—trying to get me to his house, hoping for a *bikini*. And it was a bet.

I'm not sure if I should walk home. Minnie's mother has been picking us up, but should I wait in the parking lot?

I don't want Freddy to come looking for me.

Yes, I *do* want Freddy to come back. I want him to be different than those other guys. I want him to take me home.

Why can't I trust Freddy?

I stand with my back against the wall, facing the street. Stuck. Again.

A gray car passes, and I catch a glimpse of Freddy. The car is older but shiny. He doesn't look, and a wave of disappointment swallows me.

Maybe Freddy is just less crude but thinking the same thing other boys think. I lay my books down. I'm sick of everything. Sick of not being seen for *me*. I'm so tired.

Minnie comes around the corner, stopping short. "Where were you? I've been worried."

I should have told her I might be late. "Mr. Sanchez needed to see some of us about a test. I didn't know he would keep us so long."

"Some of us? Freddy wasn't at Science Club either."

I turn away. "Freddy was here."

"Good." Minnie pauses a half beat. "I wondered if you had gone somewhere with Freddy."

"It was just about a test."

Minnie's mother pulls up to the curb. *Saved.*

Mrs. Vaughn is excited about a new dish she's cooking. "Would you like to stay for supper, Whitney? We would love to have you."

"Say yes, Whitney, say yes."

I just want to go home. Put on my PJs and hide.

I know Mama's lonesome, but I'm not sure I can help with that.

34

"I can ask my mom."

"Yay."

I sit in back and put my notebook in my lap.

"I'm making Steak Diane. I've pounded the meat until it's tender as a maiden's heart. It will only take twenty minutes or so."

I ride, thoughts scattered, and follow Minnie up the walk in a dream. She leads me to the kitchen phone.

"Mama? I've been invited for dinner at Minnie's. Is it alright if I stay?"

"Of course, Honey. I'm glad you're making friends."

I don't want to worry Mama. "I am, too." I almost say it's been a long day, but I settle for, "Mrs. Vaughn will bring me home at eight." I usually kiss Joey goodnight when he goes to bed.

Minnie's room is cozy. Not big. She has a bookcase full of science books, and I run my finger along one of the shelves. Minnie sits on her bed, hugging a blue stuffed bear.

"I think Howard wanted to kiss me last night!" she whispers. She gets up and pushes the door almost closed.

Does Freddy want to kiss me? Why am I thinking about kissing Freddy?

Minnie sighs. "I've never been kissed. I don't think Howard has ever had a girlfriend."

Has Freddy ever had a girlfriend? I'm not sure I want to know. He was thoughtful today, offering to move in English. "I've never been kissed either."

Why am I telling Minnie this? Maybe she brings out the best in me? Or is it the worst?

Minnie hugs the bear. "You're so pretty, I thought you would have had lots of kisses."

It wasn't that I hadn't had the chance, but I didn't want to be kissed by Sid Grant who cornered me in the hall at Felicia Jones' birthday party, or Lance Latimer who kept pulling me close in eighth-grade dance class. Miss Hough moved through the dancers, tapping couples on the shoulder and saying, "Proper foxtrot position." She tapped Lance three times.

Minnie is still waiting.

I settle for, "Just not the right time."

"Howard is getting his driver's license this week." Minnie puts the bear aside. "You and Freddy seem—well, it would be fun to go on a double date." Minnie props the bear against the headboard, fixing his legs to hold him in place.

"I don't know if Freddy is going to work out. I mean, I don't think I want to go out."

Minnie's mouth twitches.

"I don't mean I don't want to double date." This isn't what I want to say. "It's complicated." It would be so good to let it all out. To have someone here who understands, but Mrs. Vaughn calls us for supper.

Mr. Vaughn is a tall man in horn-rimmed glasses. He's one of those guys with three pens and a mechanical pencil in a plastic pouch in his shirt pocket. He tells us about the computer room air conditioning system going down at Aerojet. Stacks of computer cards are on the sideboard.

After we eat, I offer to help in the kitchen, but Mrs. Vaughn says I'm company, so Minnie and I sit on the couch. I wish we could continue our conversation, but Minnie is in Lunar Excursion mode, showing me an article in a magazine.

If I don't trust Freddy, why do I like him so much?

Freddy- The Workout

By the time I get home, I'm frustrated. Whitney is unhappy and that makes me unhappy. But what really makes me unhappy is that she doesn't like me the way I like her.

Does she like that senior, Carter? He's always corralling girls. Blackwater High's gift to women. Something inside me burns.

In the garage, I lower the bag Dad set up for me. I slip on my speed bag gloves and punch, starting with quick light jabs. Dad is pretty sure I need to "toughen up." I'm not sure I want to be tough, but I punch harder and harder.

After ten minutes, I break a sweat, and the blows are solid thumpers. I feel the drive in my shoulders. "Don't be a wimp. Stand up for yourself."

I have never felt the need to stand up for myself, but it's a big deal with Dad.

I'm glad Mr. Sanchez kept the cheating problem between us kids. *Punch.* This is the kind of thing that would send Drunk Dad sailing down to school. *Punch, Punch.*

When I was in fifth, Dad was pretty sure Mr. Grover was picking on me, and I thought Dad was going to choose him off at a teacher conference, because I got a C in English. *Punch, punch, PUNCH.* Mr. Grover was one of my favorite teachers. Dad's still fighting the wrongs he thinks he suffered when *he* was in school.

Three quick jabs.

Dad hasn't hit Mom for months, but it's only a matter of time. *Punch.* Most of the time, he's too drunk by the time he gets home.

Adrenalin flows, and I pop the bag up high. Head high. Right, left, right. Left, right, left. *Punch, punch, punch.* Right, right—short jabs. *Punch, punch.* I'm sweating hard when the timer from the kitchen rattles.

I give the bag an uppercut and pull it up to the rafters. I do forty sits, and forty pushups, the last ten with a clap. After marking my workout on the wall calendar, I return the timer.

Whitney and I were getting close Tuesday evening, weren't we? She was having fun—enjoying herself? Enjoying being with me? What caused the change? I've been over every word I said, every move I made. Was it when I helped her get her arm untangled?

Who am I kidding? A scrawny guy with a five o'clock shadow by one o'clock. A guy scraping by in English. I do have good hair—hair

37

that behaves.

In the kitchen, Mom says, "Hungry, Honey?"

"Sure. Let me get a quick shower." We don't wait for Dad anymore. Mom's a good cook—Dad doesn't know what he's missing.

I look at my red knuckles—bag work isn't good for piano hands. Dad doesn't understand.

'Piano's for girls.' That's why we don't have a piano. But, the moment I touched the keys of the old upright in the church basement, I knew piano wasn't just for girls. My Sunday School teacher, Mrs. Simons, let me fiddle around while the other kids ate cookies. I played quietly, not mashing clusters of keys down with my palms like Ted.

It wasn't long before I picked out "Jesus Loves Me" and found lower notes that went with the melody. I lived for those times.

Mrs. Simons paused her cleanup one Sunday and said, "Freddy, I believe you have a talent. Maybe I could give you lessons—after church. I'll talk to your mother." And for thirty glorious minutes after Sunday services, I sat at that piano with Mrs. Simons. Sometimes even longer. Dad would be down at Stumpy's Bar and Grill by then anyway.

After supper, I go to the giant pinboard near the wall. It's so big, it covers part of my window. I have clippings of boxers and articles about matches arranged with thumbtacks. It keeps Dad off my back.

I don't box down at the gym. Mom won that battle. Sammy Girolami took a right cross and doesn't see out of that eye. Dad's bluster didn't win that argument. He tried to backhand her, but she was quick, ducking away.

The walls of this old house are made of lath and plaster, and he broke his ring finger with that swing. The wall didn't have a mark. He lost two weeks of work, and I smiled inside.

Mom babied him as if it was her fault. She even bought him a bottle of Jim Beam and brought him ice for his hand. He said bourbon was a gentleman's drink, but gentlemen don't knock women around.

I squirm behind the poster board to the bench of my hidden Wurlitzer 120. I run silent scales as the tubes warm. It's not a real piano, but the upper register has a pleasant tinkle, even if the bass notes distort. My friend Gary installed a jack for Ham Radio earphones so no one will hear. I leave one earphone against my temple so Dad won't surprise me.

For the next hour, I am where I am meant to be. My teacher, Mr. Blackwater, has a beautiful grand, but here, working on my arrangements, I may as well be playing a concert grand piano. I add an A minor seven-flat-five into the progression. 'Separates the men from the boys,' Mr. Blackwater says.

I try to sleep but it is a fitful night so in the morning I shower and shave again, and leave early to gas up the car.

Who am I fooling? I want to see Whitney, even if she doesn't want to see me. I'm not spying on her. Well, maybe I am, but I hope to figure out a chance meeting. Fat chance.

I put in a dollar's worth because I only get a few hours at the hardware on Saturdays. It takes the gauge to three-quarters. Maybe Clarence will give me more hours. He says I can work Sunday mornings, but I play for the youth choir at church. Lessons are barter —I mow the lawns, front and back.

I shove the keys in my pocket and walk onto campus. There aren't many kids around. A few football players, probably going to the weight room. Most classrooms are dark. I'm shivering, wandering up and down the front of school, watching kids get out of cars. I hustle to the student parking every few minutes, but I don't think she drives.

At ten till eight, I head for English. She didn't ask me to have Mr. Sanchez move my seat. Maybe she plans to move? Or switch classes?

And then she appears—coming from the north buildings? She's wearing a cute white blouse with a cardigan. I slip into the room and pretend to read today's poems. I read them four times last night.

A wave of bubble bath envelops me as she takes her seat. She doesn't look back, arranging her notebook, textbook, and pencil. She's very particular.

The three-minute bell rings, and she turns, looking right at me. She starts to say something, gives a flick of a smile, and turns forward. This time, her eyes leave first. She settles in her chair.

I lean close. "I'm thinking about circulating a petition to have the school serve doughnuts and milk first period." She may have laughed.

Whitney doesn't turn but, head down, says over her shoulder, "I'll only sign if they have crullers."

"I'll have to run that by the committee. There's a hardliner glazed camp."

She puts her chin close to her shoulder. "Well, no crullers, no signature."

"That's a lot of pressure, and I need that signature. When you're famous, your signature will be worth millions."

"What if I sign Janice Kellogg?" She finally turns halfway, meeting my eyes. "I always sign Janice Kellogg on petitions. I knew her at my grammar school. She's not from the cereal company."

"Ah, one of the lesser Kelloggs."

Whitney nods and turns as far as she can. "I'm sorry about yesterday. I—I don't want to be—I don't know—unfriendly...."

She's doing that staring at nothing thing. She has a beautiful profile, and her eyes aren't misty. "I'm—can we be friends—but not—I'm sorry." She swallows hard. "You're a good guy, but right now, I need to just be friends?"

"OK." I want to pat her shoulder, but don't. This seems hard for her, and I suppose it is. "I think you're fun." It's true, and it seems harmless.

"Thanks." This time, her eyes are the last to leave as she turns to the front.

She makes me giddy. I sit back, open the book to the correct page, and find the notes I made because I'm about to start getting A's in English.

Mr. Sanchez lights a candle on a TV tray. "A candle isn't very bright." He nods toward the door, and the lights go off.

"Watch, kids, as the candle seems to get brighter."

My eyes adjust to the dimness, the candle glow increasing.

"As we begin our poetry unit, poems we will read may have been written by candlelight. You might give it a try." The room is quiet. "Even a small light is significant in a dark world."

There is complete quiet. I'm not sure how many are listening, but I cling to every word as if golden. The thought strikes me, and I put "she clings to every word as if golden" in my little notebook for future use.

Mr. Sanchez takes time to look up and down the rows. "Kids, never think you have nothing to say because brighter, more famous words have been written."

He gestures to the candle. "Be careful writing poetry by candle light. We don't want any fires started due to careless night poets."

The lights flickering on jars me.

Whitney is facing the candle. Mr. Sanchez blows it out, and she watches until the last of the smoke has trailed away.

For the past few minutes, I had almost forgotten about Whitney

40

Tate, but we are once again gazing at this marvelous universe that surrounds us. I must have made a sound because she breathes, "Yeah," to her shoulder—and me.

Whitney- The Musical

A Cappella is heaven. Now I start the day and end the day with singing —not only the singing but voices blending, vibrating my being. During "I'm Dreaming of a White Christmas," I see Freddy in my mind. I'm not sure why, but it's a sparkly moment—like when they put a silk stocking over the lens to capture Doris Day gazing into the camera. I know it won't snow here for Christmas, and I won't be home, but I'm suddenly thinking of Freddy—about the poem I wrote last night.

> Dark eyes these days
> Lingering in repose
> Drawing my gaze
> Loving it's me he chose
>
> Something, something....

I muff the Second Soprano, and I know better. I half raise my hand—it's what we do—to let Mrs. Albertson know we know our mistake and will fix it without her having to one finger the part. I pull myself away from Freddy thoughts and lean closer to Laura.

Laura says I'm lucky to have been invited to A Cappella, and I know I am. This is one thing I can do well—love to do.

Mrs. Albertson stops at a quarter till eight, gives us a big smile, and says, "I like how this concert is shaping up, singers. You will make the school proud."

I want to make Mrs. Albertson proud—not because I want her to think I'm better than the others, but because I know she's feeling the harmonies in her soul.

"Whitney, can you wait a minute?" she asks.

I hold my binder to my chest.

"We're doing a short Christmas musical. I'd like you to consider joining us. There's a character you would enjoy."

I'm new and don't want to step on toes. Laura sings in my range. Not as strong, but her voice is like crystal. She can sing a straight tone like a boy in an English choir.

"Have the parts been assigned? I don't want to...."

Laura slips up beside me. "I suggested you, Whitney. I tried the part and can do it, but—I'm more of a chorus person." She fiddles with her ring. "The part is the lead, and you would be perfect." She gives me a nervous look. "Really. I tried the part for two rehearsals. There's a quartet—that's where I belong."

I'm so flattered I don't speak.

Laura gives me a nudge. "It's only two acts. Mrs. A wrote it. Think about it?"

Mrs. A hands me a red binder. "Season's Memories."

"Turn to page seventeen to Sarah's song 'Homesick.'" Mrs. A plays and begins to sing.

Sarah's melody is haunting, and I join her. I could sing with Mrs. A forever. ♪"How I long to be by the fire, with snow at the window, surrounded by you...."♪

I sing the last line of the solo with tears forming, but I tighten my stomach and finish without a quaver.

"You like it, don't you," Mrs. A says gently.

I'm Sarah, and a tear escapes. "Yes. You write beautiful music."

Mrs. A smiles. "I have a beautiful life." She closes the fallboard. "Take that with you. We can talk tomorrow."

I know I have a beautiful life but wish I wasn't so miserable trying to live it.

On the sidewalk, I walk toward English with the melody floating in my mind. I see Philip homing in on me, and I walk faster, holding my sweater closed. The senior—I've learned his name is Carter —is with some buddies. I watch out of the corner of my eye in case he sidles up to me. I'm glad I can't hear what the guys are laughing about.

I've known Freddy for two weeks, and not once has he treated me any differently than the other girls. Not that I am different, other than the obvious. His focus isn't on what others seem to focus on. I pull the sweater away from me and hurry down the sidewalk.

Freddy's already in the room. I need to explain. I want to explain. I don't want to have hurt his feelings—but I can't remember exactly what I said to him.

I want to be friends; I know that part. But he has to understand I'm not looking for a boyfriend.

I really like him, but I'm scared of what being a girlfriend might mean. I want to be kissed. I want to feel his arms around me, but that would mean us squeezed together. That's the part that worries me. I didn't mind when Karen hugged me. She's a girl, and she was comforting. I long to be comforted.

I have to find a middle ground. I want to keep Freddy close—but not too close. I sigh. Even I know the voice in my head sounds crazy. There should be an instruction booklet for this stuff. *Navigating High School Without Making a Fool of Yourself.* Will I ever know enough to write such a book? That change would create a monumental shift in the tectonic plates, shaking the entire state.

Freddy- Piano Man

A man wants twelve sacks of concrete in the back of his station wagon. I can handle them, but getting them all in the car is another thing. I put three on the tailgate, climb over, and move them forward. These things are more than half my weight. I repeat the process, and the guy pretends he doesn't see me shifting them forward. Maybe he has a kid who will unload them.

I bump my head on the ceiling each time I stack a second bag. When I have the twelfth loaded and the gate closed, the guy says, "Thanks, Kid." I'm polite and tell him he's welcome.

I'm putting up sheetrock tools when Clarence calls me. The guy is back. He doesn't look like he's even broken a sweat. "Making a pad for my camper trailer." I nod and start loading. I'll sleep tonight, but I notice the burn in my biceps. Maybe I will grow some muscles.

Whitney Tate. I really need to think about something else, but loading concrete is mindless work. I let an arrangement of "Christmas Song" play in my mind—an assignment from Mr. Blackwater: "Don't rush the progression. Watch for chances to make subtle changes in the middle of the chords." I would love to play it for her.

I crack my head on the upper gate. I'm more tired than I realized. Three more sacks.

When I'm finished, he says, "You do OK, Kid, take a rest. This is the last of them. Clarence has more coming, Monday. I'll come by at four."

I smile for more than one reason. "Have a good day."

Clarence is drinking coffee in the back. "Freddy, want a couple of hours Monday?" I want the hours and agree.

At least it's not Tuesday. We will be working on the speed of sound on Tuesday. A chance to be around Whitney—out of class.

Monday, I get a note to go to the office at eleven-fifteen. I find Miss Gill, my counselor, in her office with Mrs. Albertson. Mrs. Albertson has her right arm in a sling, a white cast sticking out. Her fingers are swollen and purple.

"Fredrick, I have been telling Mrs. Albertson about our talks about music programs in colleges."

I smile. Miss Gill is a good egg.

Mrs. Albertson returns the smile with lots of white teeth. "Fredrick, I've seen you on campus. I'm glad to meet you in person." She wiggles her bad arm as if to shake and chuckles. "You see what ice skating backward can do."

I start to smile and then don't. She catches me and says, "Oh, it's OK to be amused. I'll live."

She fumbles a thick binder onto the corner of the desk. "We are putting on a Christmas musical. We've known for some time our regular accompanist, Miss Wayland, will be in San Francisco that weekend. I'd planned to play."

Mrs. Albertson is a fun lady, already laughing at herself, flapping the sling like a bird wing. "So, you see, I am in a *bind*. It's December second, third, and fourth—a Thursday, Friday, and Saturday."

She twirls the notebook so it faces me. "Take a look, please? Rehearsals are Mondays, Wednesdays, and Thursdays—days we all could meet. Thursday has to be at seven in the evening—Debate. The other days are after school." She's leaning toward me. "We really don't want to cancel."

The choirs are lucky to have Mrs. Albertson as their teacher. Enthusiasm for music flows from her like a cool river. I open the binder: "Season's Memories," M. L. Albertson. I look up. "You wrote this?"

She doesn't blush and is not full of herself. "Frustrated composer, I suppose."

Maybe there *is* a touch of pink.

I hear the Introduction in my head, fingers tingling in anticipation. I may have been humming because something makes me look up.

Mrs. Albertson's eyes are dancing. "Oh, Fredrick, you hear it, don't you? What do you think? I made this binder up for you last night. Well, my husband had to do the punching."

I flip through several pages. "You want me to play for the play." I smile when I think how dumb I just sounded. "—musical?"

"Is this something you can handle?" She bites the side of her lip. "I have a confession. I called your piano teacher, Mr. Blackwater, to see if he could step in. He recommended you."

She turns to Miss Gill, who says, "I gave Mrs. Albertson his number. I met Mr. Blackwater a few years ago when his grand-niece attended here. I hope that is all right. We're in a tight spot here."

"Not a problem," I say quickly. I'm flipping pages, melodies dancing in my head. The accompaniment shows a good sense of chord voicing, although I imagine she doesn't have my reach. I look up. "Yes, this looks great."

"Oh, Fredrick, I could just hug you." The cast is flapping again. "You're saving the day."

"You can call me Freddy, but maybe Fredrick would sound better on the program." *If* there's a program, I think too late. Things are moving very fast.

"Fredrick," Miss Gill says, "I got a good report from Mr. Sanchez, but you know you must continue to do well in your classes."

"Yes, Ma'am."

"So, Fredrick—Freddy, because of this," Mrs. Albertson points to her sling, "we aren't meeting today, so the next rehearsal will be on Wednesday."

"I'll be there."

I hurry to lunch, feeling very honored.

Whitney- Pensive

Minnie is expounding in detail about the speed of sound and sonic booms, with a bit of Howard to add extra interest—at least for her. She can't help herself, and I realize Loretta is amused—in a deadpan way. "You're coming, aren't you, Whitney?" She doesn't wait for an answer. "Loretta, you might find this interesting."

Loretta is eating a sliced apple. "I have Blackwater Times paste up on Tuesdays." Minnie knows Loretta is the school paper photographer.

Freddy is across the room, reading from a thick binder. I understand about cats and curiosity. We have decided to be friends, but I'm not sure that means me walking across the lunch room to be friendly.

His table is crowded, so I would have to stand. Freddy's so polite that he would offer me his seat. It doesn't matter because I'm not parading across the room. So, I'll think friendly thoughts from here.

Loretta tosses her apple in her lunch sack with disgust. "An apple a day doesn't keep my love of tangerines away." She notices Minnie has stopped to listen.

Loretta gives her eyes a twirl. "My mother says we don't have to eat fruit shipped from who knows where when there is perfectly good fruit on the West Coast." She folds her sack, waiting for Minnie to revive her monologue.

Freddy is engrossed, tapping his foot as he turns the page. I've never seen Freddy act nervous.

"So, we get to use stopwatches, like watching a runner cross the finish line—even though you can't see sound coming." Minnie is pleased with her effort at humor, and Loretta pulls out carrot slices.

Minnie rubs my shoulder with hers. "Glad you are enjoying the club."

I can hardly admit to myself that Freddy is the main attraction for me, which I don't understand. I can't seem to decide—and it's a simple decision. Yes or No. I'm pretty sure Freddy likes me. Wants to be more than friends.

On the way to PE, Freddy walks beside me. "Will I see you at Science Club?" he asks, and I give him a genuine smile, "Yes." I glance over, and he's watching my eyes.

I'm pretty enthralled with *his* charcoal eyes, but right now, I'm noticing his lips. He has nice lips. Not chapped, and they turn up when he smiles. Standing on my tiptoes would put me at the perfect kissing level.

Eyes, Whitney, eyes. Fair's fair—he gives my eyes lots of attention.

Does he look in other places when I'm not looking? Even Minnie has given a curious glance more than once, so I suppose he does. I'm uncomfortable not with the thought, but with admitting to myself that I have looked at his shoulders and waist. I even like his hairy legs.

"Hey, you going to follow me this way?" he asks.

I've been so busy mooning, I'm halfway down the sidewalk toward the boys' locker room. "No. I…" and I'm at a loss for words. "I was thinking, that's all."

"Yes, very pensive today."

"Yeah, see ya." I turn back to where the sidewalk splits.

Pensive? Was I gawking? Doing the very thing that makes me mad when boys do it to me?

I was in such a daydream, I can't remember. Probably not. I'm not a gawker. Am I?

PE helps me get my mind off my wishy-washy feelings, except when I gawk down to the basketball courts. I decide that a distant gawk is acceptable.

Charlie Gonzalez from History is also playing. I'm trying to concentrate on Charlie when Laura says, "Our turn after this." We are running hundred-yard dashes. "Watching Freddy?"

Of course, every drop of blood in my body decides to rush to my cheeks. "We've decided to just be friends."

"Why? You like him, and he *likes* you."

I must be pretty obvious.

Choir is excellent for getting rid of my gawking worries.

We have our music memorized, and it's beautiful. "Winter Wonderland" is perfect, and I am not thinking about Freddy other than trying not to think about him.

Mrs. A directs with her left hand. Sometimes, her cast tries to jump into action, and she winces once. Her fingers are still pretty swollen and purple.

I wish I could kiss her booboo, like I do Joey when he's hurt, and make it all better.

Singing with Laura is such a pleasure. We sense each other's breathing, and I can match her vibrato perfectly, but I will never have the clarity of her straight tone. It's magical.

My voice has more power. The words 'fat lady sings' flicker across my thoughts. I'm not fat, and pray no one sees me in a choir robe and thinks I am.

I don't think I'm vain, but maybe I am? Is that why I am so self-conscious? I hope not, because I remember Jane telling Lizzy in *Pride and Prejudice* that "our vanity deceives us," and the thought isn't flattering.

Freddy- Speed of Sound

Mr. Coulter gives us each a stopwatch, and tells us to put the lanyard around our necks and not to take them off. He's pretty serious.

We walk to the end of the 220, and Whitney is peering at the secondhand twirling around her dial. She starts and stops the watch. "Why does yours have two reset buttons?"

I'm not completely sure, but say, "This is the split button. It somehow lets you keep the first time, while the clock is still running. I think it's for timing laps or something."

Whitney starts and stops her watch several more times. "OK, let's start at the same time."

We reset, and I say, "Ready, set, go."

"OK, do the split thing." Her head is very near my shoulder, and my heart is going faster than the second hand.

We put our watches close together. "OK, I'm clicking the split."

"Cute," Whitney says. "One hand stops at that moment, but the other one is still going." When I press it again, she almost squeals. "It caught up! Hiding behind the black pointer."

I am so head over heels about this girl.

Mr. Coulter gathers us close. "I see most of you have figured out the button at the top starts and stops the watch. Let's all make sure the watches are wound. We let them run down when stored, so give the knurled knob at the top a few turns. When it stops, don't force it."

I have already wound mine, so I watch Whitney give hers a few turns.

Mr. Coulter tells us to take notes, and Whitney lets the watch hang. I stare and then look away. I vow to keep my eyes to myself.

"You are going to record the time between seeing the smoke and hearing the sound. On your notepad, number from one to five." He holds up a pistol. "This is a starting gun. It doesn't have a barrel for a bullet, so no one is going to get shot." He smiles.

I lean close and quote W.C. Fields. "Did I kill ya? Did I kill ya? Ooooh, goood, I didn't kill ya."

Whitney rolls her eyes up to mine.

"W. C. Fieeelds. The Man on the Flying Trapeeeze."

She laughs, but it has no music. "My dad used to like him."

Used to?

Minnie is bouncing on her toes, eager for the experiment.

"OK, I'm going to the edge of the far basketball court, a quarter of a mile from here. That's four hundred forty yards. Stand here at the edge of the track. You will hold up one hand, so I know you are ready.

"I will put the gun up for three seconds and pull the trigger. Start your watch the moment you see the smoke. The instant you hear the sound, stop your watch. After recording your time, punch the reset button and raise your hand. Keep them up high."

Mr. Coulter is in slacks, but he runs with the speed and ease of an athlete—long, powerful strides. I'm impressed.

He stops, turns, and gives us a wave. I feel the excitement—I want to get this right. I check my reset and raise my hand.

The smoke appears and I'm aware how long it took to click. The pop is there almost instantly, and Whitney gives a little, "Oh. I wasn't ready."

"Alas, I was a late clicker as well." I tear my eyes away from her and write a second and a half.

Minnie waves her stopwatch toward us. "Mr. Coulter is ready."

I remember to put my arm up. Whitney turns her back to me and raises her hand, and I am fascinated by her shoulders.

The gun goes off, and I'm not looking. I don't start or stop my watch.

The next time, the group holds the watches out in front of them. The gun goes up, the smoke appears, and the sound comes. I record one and a third of a second.

Whitney leans in. "You missed number two?"

"Yeah, I was—I was somewhere else." We both have the same time for three. Maybe I'm doing better than I thought.

She points to her number two. "I missed it too."

In the fourth round, we lean toward the gun in unison. Smoke —pop. I'm a little slow and get closer to one and a half. Whitney puts her watch near mine, and we compare. She's at a little more than a second again.

When our hands are up, Mr. Coulter puts up the gun and shoots. Whitney and I agree on a tad over one second. I decide on one point three.

Mr. Coulter jogs back, and we start to the classroom.

I move close to Whitney. "I read my history by candlelight."

This gets a smile. "I tried a poem by candlelight."

I want to say, 'You would be beautiful in candlelight,' but if I were honest, I would say, 'You are pretty no matter what.'

She gazes at the foothills and sighs. "The feeling of the moment was beautiful."

"Do I get to see the poem?"

Whitney is quiet for the rest of the way to the room.

At the chalkboard, Howard is being a know-it-all, going on about the speed of sound in other mediums. Minnie is eating it up, but Whitney goes to the chalkboard with him. They both record everyone's times. Whitney and I aren't the only ones to have missed a time.

Whitney beats Howard to an average of 1,944 feet per second. Howard is looking at Minnie, and Whitney is still working. She rounds the speed to 746 miles per hour. I'm impressed, and I'm pretty sure Mr. Coulter is, too. Howard mumbles something, but Minnie says, "Wow, Whitney, you're fast!"

Whitney returns to her seat, and I wink. She doesn't look away.

Whitney- Agony

I'm nervous about singing my solo in front of the group. I can do it. I'm good. I almost don't want to be too good. Vanity? Maybe it's just nerves.

Laura swings open the auditorium door for me, and I go in first. Freddy is sitting at the piano!

Freddy Sanders is in the auditorium, sitting on the piano bench! He's talking to Mrs. A, and his right hand reaches out easily without looking and ripples a bit of Jim's melody.

I realize I've stopped, and Laura nudges me. "Don't be nervous. You'll be great."

Freddy Sanders plays the piano? The binder! It's open on the music rack. Mrs. A points to a line, and Freddy plays instantly, full, beautiful chords. He points, says something, she nods, and he makes a note on the music.

I find a seat but can't stop staring. The grand piano faces the stage, so Freddy hasn't seen me. He looks as if he has been playing that piano all his life. Maybe he has. What do I know?

"All right, on stage everyone. Quartet, in the wings, stage left."

"Jim, stage right. The art department is still working on the set, but you will sing through a window." Mrs. A is moving quickly along the foot of the stage.

"Lois, you will be knitting upstage and will join Jim for the duet. Whitney, start in the chair. It will eventually be a bench."

Freddy has been making notes in the binder, but his head comes up, he sees me, and the biggest smile spreads across his face.

"All right, cast. Let's try this from the top."

Freddy plays my intro every bit as well as Mrs. A, but the bass seems richer. He's doing something different. Mrs. A is smiling—and I miss my cue.

"Sorry." I raise my hand part way. "Won't happen again. Can I have it from measure six, please?"

Freddy doesn't look at the music and plays, giving me a nod at my entrance, and I sing.

I keep my focus on the middle of the auditorium, but I sense Freddy is watching, taking cues. He seems to anticipate my every move, and I am free to sing, confidence and tears fighting for top billing.

I don't belt the last note, and Freddy lends it just the right touch as if he's breathing with me.

The cast claps, and Freddy gives me a tiny reassuring nod.

I can do this. With Freddy there, coaxing magic out of the piano, I can do this.

Later, during the patter song, Freddy lends a rhythmical, almost comical percussive counterpoint to the accompaniment. He plays with absolute ease, and Mrs. A can't smile wide enough.

Near the end of rehearsal, Mrs. A calls me aside and walks me through my movements in the last number. She's so good, I hang on her every word.

When she moves on to Jim, I notice Freddy and Laura at the piano. He's laughing and plays quiet chords. He pats the bench, and she sits by him. He leans down for a sheet of music and puts it on the rack. He gives her a confidence-building fist on the shoulder, and Laura lights up.

I should be so happy for my friend. For Freddy. And yet, I am beyond jealous, accompanied by a feeling of grinding hopelessness. This is my doing, and Laura is lovely.

I told Freddy I didn't want to get serious, and he's keeping his end of the bargain. And I am in absolute agony.

Freddy- Matchmaker

Whitney is in the musical! She has a beautiful voice. I know I'm prejudiced, but seeing her on stage, standing simply, casting her voice through the auditorium adds to her charm. I'm under the Whitney Tate spell.

I am surprised when Laura comes to the piano. I know her from Chemistry, and she's sweet. I'm quietly playing "Frosty the Snowman," and she sings along, her voice clear.

"Thank you for saving our production, Freddy. When you said you were taking piano lessons, I had no idea." She leans her hip on the grand.

"Glad to do it. I have to say, I'm impressed with Mrs. Albertson's composition. She's really very good—Mrs. A, as you all call her."

"I think so, too. And the story is touching."

"You have a lovely voice. Why aren't you doing any solos?" Laura puts her head down, and I say, "You'd be great."

"I think I don't want the pressure—you know, singing in front of everyone."

"You sang for *me* just now."

"But you weren't depending on me. If I had a key part, everyone would be depending on me, and I don't want that."

I pat the bench, and she sits. "The quartet would be empty without the soprano. They're depending on you."

"Safety in numbers?"

The cast is leaving, and Whitney was one of the first to go. I play the introduction to 'Rudolph.' "Come on, try it." Laura starts to sing, and I say, "Up there, on stage."

She turns away. "I couldn't."

Mrs. A leans against the stage proscenium, her good hand rubbing her fingers at the end of the cast.

"Sure you can. I turn toward the auditorium, and only one person is sitting behind us. Hey, Jeremy, would you like to hear Laura sing 'Rudolph'?"

Laura gasps. "Freddy," she hisses.

I look at Jeremy. "What do you think?"

Jeremy gives us a ripple of applause.

"Go on, it's OK," I whisper, and she stirs on the bench. "Your

56

fans are waiting."

"There's only Jeremy and Mrs. A."

"And me. An audience of three."

I play a subtle progression. "Jeremy, go up and help her get started. Do the echo parts."

Jeremy is up the aisle in several bounds and leaps onto the stage. He goes to the side steps and holds out his hand.

I nudge her. "Go on, it'll be fun. I've been vamping forever here."

Laura goes up and manages to allow Jeremy to take her hand and lead her up the steps. I play the introduction, singing the reindeer names, and Laura joins. Jeremy watches, and I think there is something in the way he looks at her.

By the second verse, Laura's singing is strong, and Jeremy adds percussive echoes. Before stopping, I loop back, play a jazzed-up bridge, and start them on the third verse again. Mrs. A joins, and we end in four-part harmony.

Mrs. A. begins switching off the stage lights, and I close the keyboard lid.

Laura comes close, Jeremy standing back after the stage lights are down. "Thanks, Freddy." The room holds the red glow of the exit lights.

"I tell you, you're keeping your light under a bushel."

I think she blushes, but it may be the lighting, and we start up the aisle. Mrs. A. and I slow a bit, so Jeremy and Laura are side by side, and I'm quite pleased with myself. Matchmaker.

Whitney- Boyfriend Requirements

Dear Whitney,

Just a short note to say, it was so good to get your letter. I rode my bike by your house the other day. The new folks seem to be taking good care of it, but it made me cry.

A boy! Look at you. I hope he keeps being nice. I had a sorta date with William Clarke. I love his English accent. I say sorta date because there wasn't even hand-holding. So, here I am, still Joanie-who's-never-been-kissed.

The big news is I cut my hair! Just shoulder length, but a pretty big step for me.

<u>Please</u> keep writing.

Love,

Joanie

I am so excited, I read Joanie's letter three times. Joey has an earache, and I put in the drops the doctor had Mama get. We didn't need the expense of an appointment and the medicine. Plus, Mama had to leave work. Whitey, her boss, was good about it and told her not to punch out. He would do it for her later. Mama almost cried when she told the story.

"Read to me?"

"What do you want to hear?"

"*Adventures of a Brownie.*"

I knew the answer before I asked. The book is ancient, from Daddy's uncle. We take a few moments with the one color plate in the front. "Which story?"

"When they pick cherries."

I've read this adventure so many times that I can read and think about other things without missing a beat—things like Freddy.

Joey is asleep in moments, but I'm not moving until he's really gone.

I like Freddy. Let's face it, I more than like him. He's charming. Even though he may be interested in Laura, I allow myself to daydream. He meets all the boyfriend requirements if I had a list—which I do. It's a bit stale because I made it in eighth. I sneak away and pull the shoebox from under my bed:

1. Gallant. *During my knights phase.*
2. Musical. *Wow, he checked that box today!*
3. Funny. *His W. C. Fields imitation was perfect.*
4. Has hair like Little Joe on Bonanza. *Yes, but shorter.*
5. Clean. *Freddy smells so good.*
6. Taller than me. *Yes.*
7. Doesn't untie my shoes in class. *Doubt Freddy will do that.*
8. Can ride a bike. *Hmm?*
9. Likes Strawberry Ice Cream. *Like Joanie.*
10. Wears a belt. *Where did that come from?*

There's so much I don't know about Freddy, but it would be such fun to find out. As friends.

It's sad to have a shoebox under your bed with things like this list, ticket stubs from a movie I can't remember, a picture of Joanie and me in dress-up clothes in the fifth grade, the flower Daddy gave me for my twelfth birthd.... Frustration envelops me.

I jam the lid back on the box. It takes three tries to get it to settle, and I cram it under my bed. I bury my nose in my pillow and scream.

With a long sigh, I put on my pajamas, drag a blanket off the bed, and curl up on the floor next to Joey. Mama is bone tired.

Joey wakes up three times, and I put more drops in his ear each time. At two-seventeen, the real question is: why can't I let myself trust Freddy? Daddy was a good guy. All boys aren't jerks.

At four-thirty, I write:

Dear Joanie,

It's the middle of the night. Joey's sick, and I just put drops in his ear.

You cut your hair! I'm so proud of you. We've talked about it forever. If you can, send a picture.

59

I sit with two girls at lunch, Minnie (she hates her name) and Loretta. Minnie is a complete science enthusiast but a kind soul. She invited me to sit at her table the first day when I was feeling lost. Loretta is one of those "watchers" who comes up with wise sayings. You would really like her.

Pretty fed up with boys. My second day, a guy, Tom, came up and walked me toward History. He's good-looking, and he was paying attention to what I was saying. He asked if he could talk for a moment and when I said sure, he took my upper arm to lead me to the side. The backs of his fingers were more than brushing the side of my bra! Then he straightened his fingers, pushing in before I could jerk away. I'd talked to him for two minutes, and he was feeling me up on the way to History.

I am so frustrated, that I decided I want nothing to do with boys. Maybe boys in college are more mature.

So, I have put Freddy at arm's length. I told him I wanted to just be friends and am so upset with myself. I am still so hung up about the whole hugging thing. I wonder if something is wrong with me? I wish I could be more trusting- Freddy is a gentleman and doesn't constantly give me the eye treatment.

I wish you could click your heels and be here. You could meet Freddy and give me advice. I am sorta lost without my wise friend.

Exhausted.

I Love You,

Whitney

I spend extra time on my hair, and I'm not sure why. If Laura likes Freddy, then that's that. I would never go against a friend over a boy, but I don't want Freddy to stop noticing me. Talking to me. But—

Last year, Mrs. Collins talked about words in language that reverse the meaning. I can compliment a person and add "but" and the person will think, "Here it comes."

I like Freddy, *but* I act like I don't like him. Maybe I like him *but* wish I didn't? Or I want him to like me, *but* not too much. Maybe I want him to like me, *but* let me keep my distance. Am I parking him until I make up my mind?

It says something when you're alone and blushing. I check on Joey and re-read the poems for today.

Freddy- She Fled

Whitney smiles when she sees me, and we walk into English together. It isn't an accident that I arrive when she does. She's wearing a dark blue sweater over a white blouse.

I haven't told my dad about playing for the Christmas musical. I'm not afraid of him anymore but don't want to hear his drunken diatribe.

I lean forward. "You have a beautiful voice." She smells so good.

She turns. "Thank you, Freddy. You play with such authority."

"Like a cop? Or like the principal?"

She smiles. "You know what I mean." Whitney has those lips that turn up at the corners even when she's not smiling. When she smiles—wow.

Mr. Sanchez is talking to Philip. Philip is slouching, but he's listening.

I lean toward Whitney's left ear. "How many sopranos does it take to screw in a lightbulb?"

She shrugs.

"One. She holds up her hand, and the world revolves around her."

Her shoulders shake.

"I have more, but I need to focus on today's poems." It's not true—I've practically memorized them, but Mr. Sanchez is picking up the roll sheet.

When class starts, Whitney reads Milton's "Sonnet 23" with the phrasing of a singer, and I feel a lump grow in my throat. Her voice is strong, without a fault. There is silence and an audible sigh from Mr. Sanchez—and me.

"Beautiful," I whisper.

The class must be half asleep. Philip is rubbing his pencil over and over under his printed name.

Mr. Sanchez leads a discussion, and Whitney and I are the main participants. We get to the last line, "I wak'd, she fled, and day brought back my night," and Mr. Sanchez asks, "What do we learn in this line?"

Whitney whispers to her left shoulder, "Go ahead if you want."

I look at Mr. Sanchez, and he gives me a nod.

"Milton is blind." I say it with simplicity, thinking of the way

62

Whitney sang yesterday.

I can't see Whitney's eyes, but I'm pretty sure the three of us are sharing the beauty of this moment.

My mind is swirling. It's as if I wak'd, Whitney fled, and that day brought back my....

I'm not blind, but there's night, and there is night.

Whitney- There Isn't A Me and Freddy

Freddy acts as if nothing has changed, but everything he says is "distant." Distant may not be right, but he's speaking over the wall I have built. Frost says, "Good fences make good neighbors." I'm not feeling like a good neighbor, but I make good walls.

Laura didn't say anything about Freddy in A Capella this morning, but Laura doesn't go on about boys. I lose Freddy in the mob of students crossing and crisscrossing their way to second period. When I get to History, Laura isn't there.

I'm so bad at this. I leave my books and walk back outside. To spy? *No? Yes?* I don't know. I start back inside when I notice Laura and Jeremy are talking near the crepe myrtle. I spin and go to my seat.

I'm a green-eyed woman—well, I have blue eyes, but I'm covetous of Laura. I sigh. I was jealous and now I'm glad I may have no reason to be jealous.

Laura comes in and fiddles with her bangs. Were they talking about the musical, or were they *talking* talking? First steps of flirting kind of talk?

Do I flirt with Freddy? I think I did those first days. I turned around in my seat more than I needed to. I gave him the eye. I know I have big eyes. I knew my sweater had pulled tight. I saw him glance, and I liked it.

I was flirting!

I'm two-faced. A fake. A fraud. A phony. A hypocrite.

"You OK, Whitney?" Laura wonders.

"Yes," I lie, "just tired." Class is in session for ten minutes before I get a grip on myself.

Minnie is in overdrive. She went to Howard's to study, and they watched "Science All-Stars."

"Howard and I are going to work up an experiment and send it in. We're both creating a list of ten ideas and then we'll compare. I think we will come up with at least three similar ideas."

I gesture to Loretta's tangerine. "Your mom relent?"

"My dad got a bag. He works at Market Basket." She grimaces.

"These are hard to peel." She chips back one tiny piece at a time.

"Howard has an advanced chemistry set, so we might do something with acids and bases. Your tangerine is acidic."

"Yes," Loretta says.

I don't think this was a news flash to her. "Why don't you invite Howard to eat with us?"

Loretta's eyes do a quick flick left and right.

Minnie nods toward the football and cheer tables. "Howard and I don't flaunt our affection in public."

Loretta gets the peel started. "Minnie, you were practically Siamese twins walking up the sidewalk before school."

Minnie doesn't miss a beat. "We weren't officially on campus yet. We were just glad to see each other."

Loretta tilts her head and gives Minnie an unbelieving look.

"It's true." Minnie pivots. "What about Freddy, Whitney? You like him. Don't deny it."

Loretta pauses, tangerine slice mid-air, and waits.

"Well—we're just friends. Freddy may like Laura Grayson."

Loretta gives me the look she gave Minnie but doesn't say anything.

"I—well—"

Now, they are both waiting. It would be better if they laughed or teased, but they look at me like I have an "I Like Freddy" sign around my neck.

I try to think of a clever comeback. A deflection. Loretta still hasn't eaten the bite, and we lean our heads together. "I may have goofed it up," I whisper.

Loretta lays the slice back on her napkin, Minnie studying my face.

"OK. Guys sometimes—like me for the wrong reason." They wait. "Guys make one part of me," I gesture with my chin, "the only thing about me."

For the first time, I notice Loretta isn't exactly flat-chested. She pops the tangerine slice in her mouth, chews, and says, "Billy Fellini and I went to the movies last summer. He walked me to my door, kissed me, and he reached for—" Loretta waves a hand.

"What did you do?"

"I slapped his fat little face. He was a sloppy kisser anyway, and the movie was worse than the second feature."

I have to know more. "And that was the end of it?"

"No, we went out for the rest of the summer."

Minnie is nodding. Apparently, this is not news.

I can't believe what I'm hearing. "Did he try it again?"

Loretta says, "I taught him to kiss better," and pops another slice in her mouth.

Will Freddy think I'm a sloppy kisser? Freddy or some other boy? Will I be a sloppy kisser if I've never kissed a boy? Maybe it was Billy's first kiss. Maybe I need a practice boyfriend, so I'll be a good kisser when I kiss Freddy.

Why does every kiss thought that comes into my brain involve Freddy?

Loretta is done with the Billy Fellini story. "So—you and Freddy?"

I'm heartsick. "I don't think there *is* a me and Freddy."

Freddy- Right Jab

After my bag work and supper, I sit behind the tack board, playing through the show. It's going to be good. Jim and Lois's duet is becoming more balanced, and I no longer have to play their notes. When not on stage, Whitney sits to my right—not close, but I feel her watching me.

Is she watching me or my piano playing? I suppose I'm just happy to have her nearby. I run the accompaniment to the duet and look to my right, pretending she's there. Of course, there would be no room for her because the piano touches the wall.

I pull off the earphones, hit the switch, and slide out from behind the piano. I'm sitting on my bed when Dad opens my door, none too gently.

"You putting in your time with the bag?"

"Yes. Every day." I don't know why I even bother to mark the calendar in the garage.

"We'll see about that." He's in a mood. "Let's see some pushups. Give me twenty."

I am boiling and decide to clap on each one. I pop my hands together so hard the sound echoes in my room. At twenty, I don't stop. My pecks are burning, but I do forty. When I look up, he's not even there. My door is open to the hall.

He's ready for a fight. Sore about something. I move quickly toward the kitchen.

Mom is at the stove. "Let me heat this up for you, it won't take a sec." She's acting like he's the center of the universe.

He sways, looking over her shoulder. "The pork chops look dry."

"Would you like some gravy? I have some in the fridge. I can —"

"Oh, aren't you sweet? An answer for everything. What I want is a little quiet respect! I see on the bank statement you wrote a check to Market Basket for twenty-two dollars. What's that for?"

"Food, Arthur. Pork chops, potatoes. Mil—"

"Did I ask you for the grocery list?"

Yes. You just asked. I move nearer the table.

"I don't know what you want me to do. You're mad when I make pork chops, you're mad when I—"

Dad grabs her arm, and a pork chop slips off the fork before she can put it on the plate. He sways, staring at Mom. She picks up the meat and brushes it off. "Do you still want it?"

It's a chancy thing to say, but also a perfectly fair question. He has her arm again.

"That hurts, Arthur." She pulls free.

I see it coming; he crosses over to give her the back of his hand.

I grab his left elbow, and he comes around, the right moving toward my face. "You stay out of this!" he roars.

The fist glances off my shoulder, but now he's jabbing with the left. I duck sideways, and the right comes back up. I jab once, hitting him under the eye. His head snaps back, he stumbles and goes down hard.

"You little—"

"No!" I'm so loud Mom makes a little whimper. I stand over him. "No. You touch her again, I'll break your jaw." Tears are burning my eyes. "Sober up. You're making a fool of yourself. Get up!" My throat feels raw.

He stares dully at me.

"Get up!" I'm roaring. "You heard me. Get up and go to bed."

It takes a couple of tries. Mom starts to reach for him, and I wave her back, shaking my head. She's crying.

When he's on his feet, I follow him down the hall, and he starts to open their bedroom door.

"Oh, no. Guest room for you tonight." He turns like he's going to argue. It takes two wobbling shuffles to square off in front of me.

"You've got your nerve," he growls.

"So do you. Go to bed. I don't want another word out of you until you're sober."

He opens his mouth, and I think of a fish out of water gulping for air. He goes into the room, and I shut the door behind him.

"Freddy, you can't treat your father like that."

I hear him in the bathroom. "I can't watch him hurt you." She's crying again.

I stand at the end of the hall to make sure he goes back into the guest room. In my room I jerk the blankets off my bed in one angry pull, and lie across the doorway to the guest room.

It's a terrible night. I can't get comfortable, and my hand is throbbing. I try not to think about Whitney. How would I ever explain something like slugging your dad so hard you knock him down? I can't explain it to myself, but I go around and around trying.

68

I'm sure of one thing: I probably will have to do it again.

I hear him rustling around in the morning and am wide awake when he opens the door.

"What are you doing here?"

I'm on my feet instantly. "You know what I'm doing." It's my turn to growl.

All the steam goes out of him. He starts to rub his cheek where a swollen bruise has formed, but thinks better of it. I'm guessing his cheek is as sore as my knuckle.

At breakfast, he's quiet. After he eats, he looks at me, coffee in both hands. "I never want to hear you talk to me like that again. I'm not a kid."

I'm on my feet. "No!" I don't want to fight, but I'm at the end of my rope. I lower my voice. "No. Last night is the last time you're coming in late and drunk and acting like it's *our* fault. Come home drunk, but no more acting like it's *Mom's* fault." I'm still standing over him. "How much did you lose on the fight last night?"

His jaw muscle twitches.

"You bet on Johnson again, didn't you? He's a lightweight punk. How much?"

When he doesn't answer, I don't stop. "Look at Mom's dress."

He just sits, staring at the coffee cup.

"Look at it. She took two dresses back to Penney's after you lost on Galliano."

I throw a card on the table with the meeting times of AA at our church. "No, Dad, if you don't want me telling you what to do, knocking you flat, then grow up. You're a grown man, and there's nothing about your life that's any tougher than Mom's or mine, except we don't come home late, drunk, and broke." The voice I hear grinding in my throat sounds too familiar.

The punch left a knot on my middle knuckle. It's sad how easily he went down. I know he was drunk, but I pulled the jab. If I had hit him hard, we would both have broken bones.

69

Whitney- Ice

Dear Joanie,

I seem to be in a revolving door.

I'm still eating lunch with Minnie and Loretta. I guess I was gawking at Freddy across the cafeteria, and Loretta flat out asked if there was a Freddy and me. I said no, and it seemed as if Loretta was surprised- or maybe thought there should be a Freddy and me.

I'm in a Christmas musical. Not bragging, but I have the lead. But would you believe Freddy is playing the piano for it? Our choir teacher, Mrs. A. (who is wonderful), broke her arm and can't play. I walk into the auditorium for practice and there he is! Who knew? And he's such a good pianist, and I find that hard to ignore.

Anyway, I'm a mess, but what's new?

Love,

Whitney

Freddy isn't waiting for me. I like it when he waits for me, but I keep pushing him away only to wish he was closer. He's hunched over today's poems, but he meets my eyes. "Morning," he says.

"Hi." My voice sounds small, and I don't know why. Why can't I just be normal? I'd decided to say, "Freddy, I've been distant. I've been giving you mixed signals." The last part sounds grown up. Am I grown up? I don't feel grown up—I feel mixed up.

Then I planned to say, "Can we start over—you and me?" I would pause and watch his eyes.

This would work better in the hall.

He could say yes, and we could hug.

70

Well, probably not. But it would be nice if we *could* hug—if I wasn't so hung up on hugging, I would kiss him on the cheek, and he....

But I leave it at "Hi."

Very romantic, Whitney. And I *am* romantic. I just do better reading about someone else's romance. Will I grow old and read about Thor, bare-chested on a sea cliff with his arms around a damsel in a diaphanous gown like the books Auntie Barbara reads? I lay out my notepad, pencil, and pen. Mr. Sanchez is going over Mary's paper with her.

I turn, not in that leaning flirty way, but spin around in my seat. Freddy's knuckle looks awful.

"Freddy!" I hiss. "What happened to your hand?"

He covers his right hand with his left, and I reach out and lift his hand. The middle knuckle is purple and swollen, and the two beside it are pretty red.

"Does it hurt?"

He looks at me with clouded eyes. He's tired. "It's nothing. I banged it on something."

I'm whispering, "Hurt it? Freddy, that could be broken."

"Nah." He slowly opens and closes his fist. "It's just a little stiff." I catch the hint of a grimace.

I put both hands on his desk, and he pulls his hand back. "Did you put ice on it? Ice is good for swelling."

He gives me a crooked half-grin. "Didn't think of it."

I want to pat his left hand gently. "Did you like Byron's poem?"

Freddy recites softly:

> She walks in beauty, like the night
> Of cloudless climes and starry skies;
> And all that's best of dark and bright
> Meet in her aspect and her eyes;

My breath catches, and he holds my gaze. "Wow."

"True story." He hasn't stopped looking into my eyes, and I find myself short of breath.

"Alright, class, let's see who is here on time."

I face the front of the classroom. I'm more than charmed. I'm moonstruck.

71

When the lunch bell rings, I hurry to the nurse's office. Miss Odegaard's Norwegian accent is darling, but she has questions.

"What do you need ice for? You're not planning some mischief, are you?"

I can't stop a smile. "No. I have a friend who hurt his hand, and I thought ice would help."

"Well, if he's injured, he should come see me, don't you know? He may need a doctor's attention."

"He's being a he-man about it, I'm afraid." I'm not sure that's true, but Freddy's not going to talk about what happened.

Was he in a fight? He didn't have any marks on his face. I looked —on the sly.

Is Freddy a fighter? A tough guy? Alarm fills my chest. He doesn't seem like a tough guy. His tender concentration on the tangled shirt sleeve flickers in my mind. He's gentle.

Miss Odegaard hands me a little decorated vinyl bag. "I put some ice wrapped in a washcloth. Maybe you can talk your friend into dropping the tote and the washcloth off here." She winks. "Don't tell him, but maybe I can get a look at his hand."

"Thank you so much."

At the lunch table, I arrange the washcloth and put the bag on the bench. I don't want Freddy to have to carry a "tote" sprinkled with pink tulips across campus. I take a deep breath, remember to let it out, and walk across the cafeteria.

"Hey, if you're looking for a place to sit, you can sit on my lap," says a kid who should have more sense. *This is such a bad idea.* I weave through tables to where Freddy is sitting.

"Freddy? I got this for you."

He looks up—surprised.

I hold out the washcloth. "It's ice—for your hand." I wish both hands were free so I could pull my sweater closed. Freddy's not moving, so I shake the washcloth in front of him.

When he takes it, he keeps his right hand in his lap. "Thanks— thank you."

"I hope it helps." I start to turn away. "Oh, the nurse asked that you take the cloth back—or if you give it to me, I'll do it."

He rests his hand on the table.

My face can't hold a candle to the color of his knuckle. "Oh,

Freddy, will you be able to play?"

He flexes his fingers. "Not broken. I'll make out." He's looking up with sad?—yes, sad eyes. "This is really thoughtful." He slides over. "You want to sit?"

I feel the whole room watching. Probably my imagination. Should I sit? I want to sit. What would sitting mean?

I better not. How long have I been standing here not answering? "I'm sitting with Minnie and Loretta." Duh, that's obvious. I sit in the same place every day. Maybe Freddy hasn't noticed.

Having used every single red blood cell in my body for my cheeks, I wind my way back to my seat. I'm almost there when a guy says, "Hey, looks like you got rejected. I can squeeze you in," he leers, patting an empty place on his bench.

No wonder it's empty.

"That guy's a nobody. Come sit with some of the team."

Someone snorts. I think it was me.

Freddy- Pain

My hand is throbbing. I keep flexing my fingers, which ends in a pain that continues even when I hold still. I'm pretty sure it's a bone bruise, but I don't want to have to explain it to Whitney. I would love to talk about anything but my Dad to Whitney—or anyone. 'Grow up!' keeps echoing over and over, even when I am doing other things. *Grow up.*

*Well, Dad, I'm trying. Are **you**?*

The anger that swells with that question worries me. I've read about this at the Pasadena City College library. I know enough that there is a time when a reversal of roles between a child and a parent happens. I never dreamed it would begin when I was seventeen.

Grow up. If I'm going to tell him to grow up, I need to be responsible for growing up as well. And this is the tricky part. I don't want to—can't allow myself to become my dad. Controlling. Angry. Physical. Especially with those who can't defend themselves. Women.

People talk about women being strong, not being dominated by a man. Mom is strong, inside. But she weighs one hundred ten. Dad weighs two ten. Some of it is a booze gut, but he boxed. Barrel chested. And she was brought up to obey.

I flex my hand, glad it's lunch. And then Whitney is here. I look up, and she's lovely. This is a new angle, and I study her chin. She's holding out a tan washrag.

She's one foot away, looking right at me, with a washcloth in her hand. Guys in here hassle her, and I doubt she likes it, and she just walked across the cafeteria.

I take the cold rag, not sure what to say. I'm not sure I want her to see the sore hand. I wish I had an aspirin. She's talking, and I should be responding, but exhaustion has set in. The fight. Sleeping on the floor. Of talking to Dad this morning.

I put the ice against my hand, but she doesn't want to sit down. By me. That's pretty obvious. I need to face facts, and the main fact is, Whitney doesn't like me like I like her. She's a friend. I would rather have her as a friend than not have her around at all.

She's been here three weeks, and I cannot imagine a world without a Whitney. How did this happen?

The ice makes my knuckle throb, but I leave it pressed firmly and watch her walk back to her seat. Thomas What's-His-Face makes a crack, and if my hand wasn't sore I would go over there and tell him to keep his mouth shut.

No. That's Dad's way.

I've sparred with Dad for years, but I don't want to fight. Plus, Thomas is a dolt. Never argue with an unarmed man.

I've talked to Reverend Potter about my dad. Preachers are like doctors—they can't talk about things people tell them. About the drinking. I've asked about the meetings. I can't make my dad go to meetings; I know that.

Whitney is watching me. I hold up the ice and give her a weak smile. I could look at those eyes forever—but I don't.

I have to adapt part of the right hand of Whitney's solo. It comes out OK, but it hurts pretty bad. She moves easily downstage, and the effect is lovely. I do the arpeggio without a hitch; the pain is worth it.

Mrs. A's watching, and finally she says, "Cast, take a minute. Get some water. Don't go far." She sits on the bench. "Freddy, have you hurt your right hand?"

I take my hand from under the keyboard. "Yes, Ma'am." It takes me a moment to look up, and the kindness in her eyes causes me to look back at my hand.

"I knew something was off—your usual flow is missing. Can I?" She puts out her good hand, and I lay my hand in hers. "Oh, my, how did this happen?"

"I work out with a boxing bag. I was hitting high and smacked the chain fastener. I wasn't concentrating."

She's looking with great concern, and I hate the lie. I hate that I hit my dad. I hate that if Whitney found out, she wouldn't want anything to do with me. I don't want to end up like *him*.

But I can't let him hit Mom. He has split her lip before. Then, the next day, he's sorry. Always sorry when he's not drunk. He'll never do it again.

Don't trust him. It's the oldest gag in the world.

Mrs. A is saying, "You need to put ice on this."

"I did."

Whitney has come close. Not eavesdropping close. Concerned close? Why am I such a wimp?

I want Mrs. A to put her arm around me. I glance at Whitney. I

75

want Whitney to sit by me with another ice pack and hold it on my hand. I could lie down under this piano and sleep for a month.

"Whitney got me some ice at lunch." My eyes catch Whitney's, and she's looking into my soul.

"Whitney, what a lovely thing to do. It's encouraging when students watch out for each other."

She's testing the knot on my knuckle and the bone underneath. "I don't think it's broken. You probably bruised the joint." She gives me a sad smile. "I was a Biology minor. I thought about training to be a nurse." She runs her hand along the finger. "Can you straighten your fingers?"

"Yes. It's mostly stiff. It aches when I move it—but it aches when I keep it still." Whitney has come closer.

Mrs. A turns my hand over, peering at my palm. "If this is not feeling much better by tomorrow, I want you to see the nurse."

"Miss Odegaard is very nice," Whitney offers.

Nice. Everybody is nice, even Dad, except when he's drinking. I finally take my hand back, reach out, and run a blues scale with a little reverse twiddle in the middle. "I'll be OK."

"Alright, Cast. Set and places for the quartet."

Whitney is still watching me. I mouth, "Thank you," and am rewarded with a lovely Whitney smile.

76

Whitney- TR3

I wander around the car—Daddy's car. I haven't uncovered it, but sometimes I do, partway. It's a 1960 Triumph TR3. He was so cute when he drove it. It cost a lot to ship it to California, but neither Mama nor I could part with it. Not yet, which is silly because it's just metal.

I lift the cover off the driver's side and get in. Mama and I can't drive a stick. It doesn't matter because the battery's in the little trunk. Mr. Paulson said we needed to put the car in *mothballs* if we weren't going to drive it.

I stretch out my hands and grip the wheel. *Oh, Daddy. I'm in your little car—but I wish you were in it, and I was waiting for you to pick me up at school.*

I like a boy, Freddy—and you would like him. He plays the piano and is polite. You always told me not to hang around boys who weren't gentlemen.

I know enough to push the left pedal before moving the gear shift. I pull the lever back and forth, remembering the wind in my hair when we drove together. I make an engine noise and glance at the door to the house to be sure no one heard. Like Joey, playing with his cars on the floor.

Do they have golf in heaven? I hope you get to play every day, but I hope you get to think about Mama and Joey—and me. I don't want to be forgotten.

We don't go to church anymore, and I don't know much about heaven. I think Mama was—is—pretty mad at God. I hope God understands these things 'cause she was only thirty-three when Daddy left.

Someone once used the phrase, "When God took your father." I can't believe that. God didn't take my daddy away. God wouldn't be that mean. I was thirteen. Joey was only two.

No. Daddy's heart failed, and God welcomed him into heaven.

I pretend to shift the gears but don't make a motor noise. Mama opens the door from the house, and says, "Oh, Honey. I didn't know you were home."

"I just got here." I don't look up because I know we will both be crying, but she comes and stands by the car, running her finger up the chrome windshield frame.

"It's sure a cute little car."

And we both are crying. Not sobbing. Just that deep aching cry that whispers in your throat.

She takes a deep breath. "Do you think you would like to learn to drive it?"

I have my California license. It was the first thing Mama and I did when we arrived. Maybe it would be better to have the car out, whirring around town. Wind in my hair. "I think about it sometimes."

"Your daddy would like that. He would love to be able to teach you to driv—"

I wish she hadn't said that, and I know she wishes she had left it unsaid because the last word *drive* died suddenly.

The thought *died suddenly* irritates me, and I slam the shifter forward, but it doesn't protest. It clicks into place with a satisfying sound somewhere under the car.

"How's Joey?"

"Better. Sleeping."

He didn't sleep well last night.

"You ready for supper?"

I give Mama a big, natural smile, holding her red eyes.

"Come on in when you are ready. We're having spaghetti."

I sit for long minutes, looking at nothing. *Maybe Freddy knows how to drive a stick.*

Even with the cover, the car is getting dusty. I will get a bucket, water and towels and wash it. Daddy always kept it clean. Shiny. How do you polish a car?

I whisper, "I'll get smarter, Daddy. I'll make your little car shine again." I pull the cover gently over the car, straightening it over the windshield, and go into the house.

I lie in bed for a long time, nowhere near sleep. Loretta and I found ourselves alone after lunch. Minnie left early, so we went outside and sat on a bench under an oak. She's not Joanie, but Loretta listens.

"You OK?" she asked.

"Everything is a mess."

"What's the first—biggest mess?"

Somehow, I felt safe. "I'm so sick of the constant references to my figure." I looked down in disgust. "I don't try to dress sexy. I try to downplay *things*. I can't wear dresses because if it fits on top the rest is a tent. But, at my old school and now, this school, since the first day, I hate changing classes." I sighed. "Maybe I'm just imagining part of it."

"Oh, you've been a topic of conversation." Loretta stopped suddenly, putting out a hand. "Not me, Whitney. Not me." Her eyes showed concern.

"But, yeah, it's real. One day, David Chambers was gesturing and wisecracking about you from across the quad. I walked right in the middle of his buddies and said, 'Shut up, David. You're such a child.' I surprised myself."

"Thanks."

She patted my knee and got up to go. "All of us have things about ourselves we would change."

I didn't know what to say. I thought I would cry but didn't.

Now, lying in bed, I do a little. I turn on my side and just sniffle for a minute.

Freddy- Squishy

When I get home, Dad is waiting in the garage. He doesn't tell me to get started with my workout. He doesn't even look at the bag, still hanging high. He has a purple goose egg on his cheek.

"How's the hand?"

I'm caught off guard. I didn't know he noticed. I don't have the energy to lie. "Sore."

"Let's see." He's surprisingly gentle, and I don't mind him moving my fingers back and forth. "We need to put ice on it once an hour. I don't think anything is broken, but the ice will take the swelling down.

I'm done hiding. "I play the piano. I'm good. I'm playing for a musical at school."

The words hang between us, and he takes a deep breath. "I know about the piano."

I wait. Will he bluster? Go to Stumpy's?

"How?"

"Your mom told me. I've been home all afternoon. I told Jim I had an important meeting. And I did." Dad starts up the steps to the house. "Let's get some ice on that."

He gets out a tray and wraps ice in a dishtowel. As before, the knuckle throbs and then numbs. The swelling is going down.

"When your hand is better, I want to hear you play. Your mother says that piano in there isn't a very good one."

"Best I could do. It didn't work when I got it, but I put a new tube in it. Better than nothing."

He's quiet. Thinking. He gets up and pours a cup of tea. I've never seen my dad drink tea. I didn't know we had any tea in the house.

Mom comes in and takes a casserole out of the oven.

Dad eyes the clock. "I have to go out at seven."

I tense inside and hope he doesn't notice. I don't want to fight with him.

"Al, can you set the table? Freddy, pour the milk."

Dad arranges the silver and pours more tea for himself. I've had about two swallows of tea in my life, but I get a cup.

Mom doesn't have much to say, but she seems content. It's the first time we have had an evening meal together—in peace—in a long time.

When Dad leaves, I dread him getting back. I unplug the earphones and go through the music. My hand is definitely better. At eight-thirty, I plug in the earphones, one on my ear and one against my hair. I'm not getting caught if he comes back in a mood.

I work on all the music but spend extra time on Whitney's solos, playing with my eyes closed, seeing her in my mind. She's lovely when she's singing; she's lovely in repose.

I have to get over this. Whitney isn't interested in being my girlfriend. I ache inside, but...

I review my Chemistry notes.

I hear Dad come in, but he and Mom talk quietly in the living room. I leave them alone and sleep well.

Thursday, Alice Thomas is looking at her rear tire when I pull into the student lot. When I get out, she says, "Freddy, do you think my tire is going down?"

"I think it will be flat by the time school is out."

She puts her hands on her hips. "Mom said I should drive her car this morning. I don't want her to think I'm incompetent."

"Not sure a flat tire means you're incompetent."

"Well, when I came out, I thought it looked squishy, but didn't tell her. I guess I hoped it wouldn't get worse." She sighs. "It's worse. Way worse."

Squishy tickles me. "Do you have a spare?"

Alice dangles a set of keys at me. "I think so, but I've never looked."

I take the keys and open the trunk. The car is a boat, a 1959 Chevy. The spare, jack, and lug wrench are all in place. I rap on the tire. "The spare sounds like it has air."

"Oh, I never thought about the spare not being blown up." She laughs at herself. "That doesn't sound right, does it? It sounds like it's exploding."

I laugh. "Yeah, maybe inflated? I have a cousin who says, 'aired-up.'"

"I'm not going to get to a station after school, am I?"

"I doubt it. I could change it for you at noon."

She brightens. "Oh, really? That would be great."

"No problem. Shall we meet here?" She's cute. A little elf-like girl, thin, quick, and lithe.

We walk to the classrooms together.

I pause. "I have to go this way. English."

"OK, I'll see you in History." She's off, almost lifting into the air with each step, hair bouncing.

I take my seat behind Whitney. *Alice Thomas.*

Whitney turns. "Good morning, Freddy."

Her voice sounds low—kind of sultry.

I had more of the doughnut routine in mind, but I just say, "Morning."

I put some brightness in my voice, but I'm irritated with Whitney. All friendly, but keeping me at arm's length. Getting ice for me was thoughtful, and I have the washcloth laundered and folded in my coat pocket.

I'll be friendly, but I've decided Whitney is a tease. I'm not sure she knows she's doing it, but I'm pretty tired of it.

Whitney- Zoom Bass

Dear Whitney,

A quick note to tell you I wish you were here. I still eat with Mary Ann and Paula.

I am across the country, but the Freddy fellow seems to have your attention. If my Whitney has any special talents it's being a good judge of people. Think about it. Please.

Mrs. Lawson is pregnant. She's stopping mid-year. She looks cute in her maternity clothes. I've waited two years to have her as a teacher, and now she's leaving.

Big news! Carl Smith called. I think he was trying to ask me out, but he never got the nerve. The poor guy is so shy. Should I ask him? We know he's liked me forever. Help!

Love,

Joanie

I was going to write to Joanie, but my throat is scratchy, and I woke up with a voice about half an octave down. I'm pretty sure it's sinus because the kid from down the street was mowing our lawn, and I made the mistake of walking through a cloud of Bermuda dust.

Freddy is quiet, so I turn halfway in my seat and say, "Hi, Freddy."

He greets me and sounds happy enough, but he doesn't look at me for more than a second, and I face forward.

I want to remind him to return the washcloth but don't want to sound like I'm his mother, so I decide not to turn and talk again.

Maybe his hand still hurts. I should have asked him about it.

We're doing Frost, and I love Frost. I want to partner with Freddy, but when I turn around he has his head together with Alan

Simms. I scan the room, and only Philip doesn't have a partner. "Want to work together on the meaning of the poems?"

Philip shrugs. "Sure." He scoots his desk closer but keeps his distance. His book is open to "After Apple Picking."

We discuss the poem and it turns out Philip has picked apples at his grandma's for years. He's almost eager to tell me about how hard the apples hang on when you try to pick them. This is about as animated as I've ever seen Philip.

I ask if Philip has felt the "ladder round" when going to sleep, but he says nowadays ladders have flat steps. We write up our comments, and I help Philip spell. I feel as if I know a little more about picking apples from the poem, which is lovely, and from Philip's experience.

I walk to History alone. Fred Hanson tries to talk, but I tell him I have to get to class. The sidewalks are damp, but it must have been a short shower during English because I hadn't noticed.

I see Laura, but she's with Jeremy, so I slow to give them some room.

"Whitney, hi!" Laura and Jeremy are both smiling, so I join them.

"Is your voice getting better?" She turns to Jeremy. "She was a Zoom Bass this morning."

I look puzzled, and Jeremy is quick to say, "The new Rolling Stones album—they use a Zoom Bass." He pauses. "Not sure what it is, but it's low."

"Jeremy has a really good stereo in the living room. His mom doesn't like it on too loud, but when she was in the garage doing laundry, we turned it up." Laura puts her hand to her chest. "You can feel it."

I've only heard of the Rolling Stones, but I love that Laura is having a good time. "Nice," I offer. I should try to sound more enthusiastic, but I don't want to have a conversation about the Rolling Stones.

Jeremy peels off for Spanish, and I notice they've been holding hands. Laura and I cut across the quad.

I've never held hands with a boy. Well, Joey doesn't count. Daddy used to hold my hand when we shopped together. I imagine he's beside me, and I put my hand a little further out, grasping at air, and bump a girl. "Sorry," I mumble over my shoulder.

Laura laughs. "Sorry," she says as low as she can.

I am a Zoom Bass. I could sing an F.

84

I know it's silly, but I keep scanning the kids for Freddy. *Make up your mind, Whitney. It's not that hard.*

Then I see him coming out of the nurse's office. I shouldn't have doubted. I should have asked how his hand was. I *should* do a lot of things.

After History, a guy tries to walk with me. "Hey, Whitney. How ya doing?"

I glance around, but most kids are in class. "Hi." I try for a smile, but can't place this guy. I have to pay more attention to kids around me.

"I'm Pete."

I make an effort. "Nice to meet you, Pete." Very civil, but I'm wary that he will shift into leering mode, but he doesn't. He's just walking, looking across the quad.

"Well, I'll see you in typing."

Typing. I really have to pay more attention. "Yes—yeah." The guy must think I'm a clod. *Nice to meet you, Pete? Good job.*

I wish I didn't create this push-pull world. But I know why. Because the assumption is that I'm a coquette. I just learned that word, a flirt—a tease. Apparently, I look the way I do on purpose.

So, my figure pulls, and I push, and I'm not happy about either.

Will I say something to Freddy at lunch? I can't say, "I see you took the washcloth back," because that would sound like I'm watching him, which I am, but I don't want him to know that.

How many times can you say, "Hi." Maybe I could ask if he noticed the rain during English. This is so pitiful.

Minnie is watching for me. Loretta hasn't started her tangerine. Is she dieting? No, she's nibbling on a potato chip from a little snack bag.

"Whitney, you won't guess. Howard got his license. He got a perfect score on the written *and* the driving portions of the test."

Loretta winks at me. She's a good winker. Just a flick that's gone almost before you notice. Joey has to pull up his whole cheek.

I'm a winker with medium skills. Joanie and I stood side by side and practiced in the mirror. I haven't had the nerve to try it out on anyone yet, but feel it is a skill that will come in handy. It would be cool to be able to give Freddy a Loretta wink.

"He's the best driver. He has the DMV Manual memorized, and I quizzed him between classes."

"Sounds like you could pass," Loretta says.

Freddy isn't where he usually sits.

"Oh, I don't think so," Minnie is quick to say. "I mean the test, sure, but—the driving part...." Minnie's hands flutter. "There's a lot to do, and both our cars are standards." She works an imaginary gearshift by the steering wheel she's gripping. "Howard can drive both a standard and an automatic."

She slumps. "My dad tried to teach me in the Safeway parking lot. It was after closing, and I had the whole place to myself. I only got going once. I'm either racing the engine or stalling it." She sighs. "I'm doomed to my bicycle—and the handlebar grips are the kind with little colored streamers." Minnie turns but can't meet my eyes. "I haven't grown much since sixth."

"Cut 'em off." Loretta starts to work on her tangerine.

"Oh, I couldn't cut them off." Minnie laughs at herself. "They're cute." And *she's* cute, caressing an imaginary streamer.

Where's Freddy?

Freddy- Two-Fisted Soap

Alice is waiting on the sidewalk. "Are you going to get dirty, 'cause if you think you'll get dirty, I know a bathroom that has paper towels. I can run and get some. I'll bring damp and dry."

"I have a dust rag in the car."

"So, what should I do?" She makes a muscle. "I'm pretty strong."

She gets the trunk open and I loosen the wingnut that holds the tire upright. Alice is right there. "Lemme get that out."

She grabs the tire and gives a mighty tug. I give it a little help, and she manages to roll it over the lip, and down it goes.

It bounces as high as her shoulder, and she gives a little squeal but is not about to let a tire get the best of her. She keeps it at arm's length, legs splayed, but captures the thing, flops it over, and puts her foot on it. "Gotcha."

I get the jack set and pop the hubcap. I get two wooden blocks from my car.

The lug nuts are pretty tight, and my hand protests. I have three loose, when Alice says, "Let me try one."

I stand up to give her room. She's tiny but determined. She really bucks up and then blows her bangs up in exasperation. "I hate being a weakling."

"You're not a weakling. I thought you were about to get it. Mind if I help?"

I crouch opposite her and let her get started. I give a little pull, my hand touching hers, and with a squeak, the nut turns.

She looks up with victory on her face. "We did it!"

"You were almost there—I only helped a little."

"Really, or are you just saying that?"

"Really. Try the last one."

I have to help her, and she's disgusted. "If I was by myself, I couldn't even change a tire. My older sister is five-ten."

"You need to carry a cheater—a short piece of pipe to slip on the end of the wrench for leverage."

"I'm asking my dad tonight."

I show her how the up-and-down switch on the jack works. The car is heavy, and she has to bounce on the handle to make the last few clicks. When the lug nuts are off, she tries to pull the tire off. It

87

slips down and tips toward her. I catch it before it bumps her head.

She bends over, brushing her skirt with the backs of her hands. "If you weren't here, they would find me buried under this dirty tire."

Getting the spare hung on the studs is a struggle for her. I show her how to lift it while standing, catching the upper rim with her fingers. She can't get the holes lined up but refuses help. Finally, she has success. "I'm never driving off on a squishy tire again. Look at my skirt!" she declares.

Alice starts the nuts and gets them tight enough to let the car down.

She jumps, landing her whole weight on straight arms three times before the first click. Once it's easier she works the handle like crazy, and the jack almost falls on her foot. She's quick, I'll say that.

I lay the flat tire in the trunk, and we decide to leave the hubcap off until she gets to the service station.

She inspects the spare. "I think it's a little squishy."

"You're not going far. Just take it easy."

Alice grabs a little duffle bag. We stop at the bathrooms on the English wing. Naturally, the boys' restroom doesn't have any soap. I rub my hands together hard, my knuckle throbbing, and give up.

In the hall, I'm looking at the dirt, when Alice appears in a new skirt. She looks good.

"No soap," I say.

"Oh, here." Alice runs into her restroom and comes back with her fists closed. "Hands out! Hands out!"

I obediently put my palms up and she rubs both hands with soap. I'm back at the sink, scrubbing, when Alice hollers in, "You need more? I can get more." For a second I believe she would prance right in with soap. "Nope, getting clean."

"Towels?"

"Yes, please," and I go to the door. She brings a huge wad. I'm guessing girls don't spend their time trying to stick wet wads on the ceiling. Between that and 'seat walkers,' some guys don't have enough to do.

Alice inspects my hands and gives a nod of approval. "I can't send you to lunch with dirty hands." She flips my right palm down. "What's that?" She leans close. "Looks sorta bad."

I've developed a number of explanations and choose the "I banged it on something" version.

She takes another look, and we start to the cafeteria—not particularly hurrying.

"So, do you go to football games? Friday is the championship. I haven't seen you at any games."

She's noticed! "I haven't been going."

"It's pretty exciting—I mean, the team's pretty good. The dance after is fun, too."

She's half inviting me. We sit by each other in History this year. We kid around. She's cute. This may be a good way to get Whitney out of my head. "Sure, we could meet up and watch the game—or we could take my car."

We stop at her locker. "We can't sit together at the game." She tosses the duffle in and slams the door. "I'm a flag girl with the band, but we could go to the dance. It's a home game."

Would Whitney go to a game with me if I asked? Do I want to go to a football game? Nah, she's not interested.

Whitney- Tinkerbell

Minnie is winding down about her lack of driving confidence, and Loretta is almost finished with her second tangerine when Freddy comes in with a cute girl. She's talking a mile a minute. She's slim— petite. Freddy laughs and says something, and she bats at his arm.

Even I know the bat-the-arm trick. I've never had the nerve to bat. Never thought I wanted to bat, but it makes Freddy smile.

I like it when I make Freddy smile.

Yup, he sits in his regular place but makes room, like he did for me, and she sits. He doesn't even have to pat the bench. She just slides in, jabbering away.

I am double jealous.

First, she's so natural. She probably wears size minus one, and yet she has a lovely figure. She's darling. She has that shoulder-length, almost frizzy hair that bounces when she moves.

Second, she's with Freddy, and she finds him charming. And why not? I'm charmed by Freddy, and I'm halfway across the room.

I finally look away, but Minnie has noticed. Loretta glances in Freddy's direction and gives me a look.

Minnie leans close. "Who's Freddy with?"

Loretta doesn't even blink. "Alice Thomas. Flag girl. She's in Spanish with me."

Alice Thomas. If she had wings, Alice Thomas could flutter up and out of the cafeteria like Tinkerbell.

Dear Joanie,

I wish you could meet Loretta. She's so matter-of-fact. She would tell you to talk to Carl. You deserve a Carl Smith.

I don't think I should be giving you advice. I think I REALLY like Freddy but have "parked" him. He's such a great guy, but I think I messed that up. He's just being friends like I asked, and I'm heartsick.

Today he was eating lunch with a lovely girl, Alice Thomas. She's like Sherry Morris—petite and as cute as she can be. They were laughing and talking. And she's very good at the bat-the-arm trick! Oh, and to top it off, she has bouncy hair! Grrr.

At the rate I'm going, you are going to be first to get a kiss.

I would give anything to hear your voice, but even a three-minute call is so expensive. Write when you get time. Thank you for your letters- they are lifesavers.

Love,

Whitney

Freddy- Toodle-oo

I decide to follow Alice to the Texaco station. She says her mother has an account there. The spare tire is about the same amount of "squishy."

She's a careful driver but has to sit with a little pillow under her and another behind her. She peers over the steering wheel when she pulls out of the student parking lot. She's cute as a button but doesn't need to be in a car as big as the Chevy.

When we get to the station, she eases up to the building and parks about five feet away. She gets out, goes to the front, gives me a goofy grin, gets back in, and pulls forward—straining her neck to see over the hood. When she's satisfied, she gets out and gives me a "come on" with her left hand and a head nod.

Inside, a guy with "Chet" on his coveralls comes to the counter. "Hey, Alice." He looks over her head. "Your mom not with you?"

She places both hands on the counter and squares her shoulders. "I have her Chevy. The left rear tire was squishy this morning, and by noon it was flat."

Chet's lips twitch when she says squishy. "You know, we have a cure for squishy tires. Let's take a look."

She hands him the keys and steps back as he hauls the tire out. "Pretty squishy," he says. "But only on one side."

"Oh, Chet, you think you are soooo funny." She steps closer. "Chet, this is my friend, Freddy. He helped me change the tire and followed me—in case."

"Nice to meet you, Freddy." He holds up dirty hands.

I hold up my palm to let him know we don't need to shake. "Good to meet you, Sir."

Alice gives me another head come-on and leads me to a Coke machine. "Your choice. My treat."

"I'm OK."

"Nope! Not gonna stand for that. You helped change the tire and you're gonna have a *refreshing beverage*." She's already sliding in a coin. "What's it gonna be?"

"Root beer."

She pulls up the lid. "Nope. Coke, Orange," she leans into the machine, "or Royal Crown."

"I guess I'm drinking Coke."

She stands on her toes, struggles to slide the bottle along the rail, and then gets Orange for herself. "Hot work, steering that Chevy. Give me my VW any day."

She watches me take another drink. "You're feeling better already."

And I am, standing in front of the station, watching the car on the lift, and drinking a soda with Alice. "So, they call you Ally?"

"Well, some do. Mom doesn't approve. Mr. Smith, in third grade, started it. Mom says, 'If I wanted you to be called Ally, I'd've named you Ally. You're not a back street.'"

"So, what should I call you?"

"Ally is fine—just not in front of my mom." She takes a drink, inspects the level, and says, "I'm not going to be able to finish this!" She holds it out. "You want to finish it?"

I haven't drunk that much and shake my head.

"Hey, I don't slobber. I'll have you know I have a very clean mouth. I haven't missed a day of school my whole life!"

Ally puts the half-full bottles in the rack. "I'm heading to the bathroom—that stuff is going right through me. They're really clean here. That's why Mom trades with Chet. 'A clean bathroom is the sign of a well-run business!' is her motto." She hands me her purse.

I feel silly holding a little leather purse with a strap. Ally doesn't seem embarrassed by anything. She's refreshing. Open. Very much alive.

When Ally returns, she digs in the purse and hands me a piece of folded paper. "My number. You can call me and tell me when you are coming to get me."

Ally is the exact opposite of Whitney. She's a constantly moving force, and I'm fascinated.

I go to the car, tear a sheet out of my notebook, and write our number. When I turn, she has followed me, and is peering at my dashboard. "Nice old car, Freddy. Classic. Plymouth?"

I nod like a dopey bird and step out of her way.

She leans in, one hand on the seat, stretching forward. "Wow, very art deco."

Her waist is tiny. Whitney's waist is small, too.

Ally pops out and turns toward me. "If you have to go, Freddy, it's OK. Chet will take care of the car."

I hand her my phone number. She opens the paper and holds it to her heart. "Thanks."

The impact wrench is whirring, and with a hiss, the lift starts bringing the car down.

"They're almost done. I'll wait."

This gets me a sweet smile and dancing eyes that move quickly, scanning my face. I like this girl. The South Pacific music in my head sings, "I'm gonna wash *this woman*—right outta my hair."

Ally says thanks again and gets in the Chevy. She bounces a couple of times, getting her pillows situated, her hair enjoying the activity. Sitting as high as possible, she guides the car toward the exit. She turns her head toward me, wiggling her fingers in a "toodle-oo." It's only for an instant, and then she's back to the job of getting her mom's Chevy home.

Whitney- A Job

I've walked back and forth in front of Daisy's Diner. "Help Wanted, Weekends." I hurried here after school, and now I'm stuck outside. I want to help Mama. We still have most of the life insurance money, but Mama wants to keep that as a cushion. I know it's for college for Joey and me. I take a breath and pull open the door.

Inside, I go to the counter. A woman, about forty-five, looks over her shoulder. "I'll be with you in a sec, Hon." She's fiddling with the coffee maker. She puts the lid on and comes to the counter. "Sorry about that. What can I get for you?" She has Viv pinned on a white pinafore apron over her blouse and skirt.

"I'm interested in the job."

"Have you ever waited tables?"

"No, but I can carry plates and am good at math. Very good."

She stands on her tiptoes and looks me up and down. "You won't be bad for business—sorry, but facts are facts. Good looks don't hurt tips."

"Yes, Ma'am."

"Tell you what. Fill this out—you can sit at one of the tables over there. I'll have Eddie talk to you. He's probably out smoking."

She pushes a single sheet over the counter, plops a pen down on it, and gives me a smile. "With your looks, you'll get the job."

She leans forward, giving me a no-nonsense stare. "And don't take any foolishness from Eddie. He can get a little handsy, but swat him away, look him straight in the eye—" She leans across the counter to demonstrate and says, "Say, 'NO, Eddie,' like you're talking to a little kid." She checks over her shoulder. "He's harmless." She whispers the last word and winks.

I fill out the application and take it up when Viv isn't busy.

"Wait here. Eddie'll be right out."

It's not long until a guy with a terrible comb-over comes to the counter. He sticks out his hand, eyes doing a crawl. "I'm Eddie, the assistant manager." He gestures to his name tag, cigarette smell enveloping me.

I take his hand and tell him my name. He's still fixated, and I have to pull a bit to get my hand back.

"So," he looks at my application, "Whit-ley, I understand you want to work for me."

It seems pretty obvious, but I smile and say, "Yes, Sir."

"Saturday mornings are busy here. You'd have to start early. Everyone is here by four-forty-five. Will that be a problem?"

"No, I can be here."

"Minimum wage, buck 'n a quarter, but—the girls do well in tips. Some do *real* well." His eyes are traveling again, with the usual pause. I could probably stick my tongue out at him and he wouldn't notice.

Eddie takes out a package of gum, pulls out a piece, and turns the pack toward me. "Want a stick of gum?"

"No, thank you." I endure another eye scan before I say, "So, can I have the job?"

"Job? Sure. In fact, you can practice helping out by taking the Help Wanted sign out of the window."

I make the trip as dignified as possible, lean out to get the sign, and bring it back. He doesn't reach for it because he has probably forgotten why he sent me to the window, so I lay the sign on the counter.

Viv comes over, gives an eye-roll toward Eddie, and says, "The delivery truck is here."

Eddie pushes off the counter with one last look and shuffles toward the back.

When he's out of earshot, Viv says, "I don't think he can help it, but he's honest and comes to work every day."

I smile.

"OK, you can wear any dark colored blouse, but will need to buy a couple of these white pinafores. We have them in the back."

In a small room, she looks me over. "I think we can make this one work. It's a little big, but you can cinch it around your waist."

Viv wiggles the ties. "The material's not too bad, but try not to stain them." She gestures to her own apron. "We used to wear blue, but white is easier to bleach out spots."

I make sure Eddie is still in the back. "He wasn't real clear—should I come Saturday morning?"

"Yes. It'll be all morning—some Sundays. I'll be here. Another girl, Francie, will be here too. You'll like her. Has a kid and a husband who is 'too sick' to go to work a lot. 'Bad back.' Of course, he and Jack Daniels carried a buck out of Arrowhead a few weeks ago." She shakes her head in disgust.

Viv taps a chalkboard on the wall. "Sundays are lighter, so you and Francie will rotate. The schedule will be posted here ahead of time."

Viv irons one of the aprons with her hands. "Francie is always willing to take Sundays—she needs the money."

"Thank you, Viv."

Freddy- Research

I dig last year's Annual out and open it to the sophomore's pictures. Alice Thomas looks young. She hasn't grown much, but her face has matured.

I search in the flag girl section but don't find her.

I wish Whitney had been here last year. I would love to have a picture of her. School pictures were last week. Would I ever get the nerve to ask her for a picture?

Alice Thomas.

I look in the T's in junior and seniors.

Carolyn Thomas. Senior. I remember her. She was a cheerleader and a prom princess. Alice is right. She's tall and has an athletic glow.

Whitney could be a cheerleader if she wanted. And she's athletic —at least in track.

Alice Thomas.

I find Alice with the sophomore class officers. She was a representative last year. I recognize the dress she's wearing. She still wears it sometimes.

It would never occur to me to run for a class office. What does the student council do? I guess I don't have much school spirit.

Will Whitney run for a class office? I would vote for her. In my mind, I see her neatly placing her notebook, pencil, and pen on a desk. She has beautiful handwriting. Maybe she could be the secretary. Or treasurer—she's really good at math.

Alice Thomas, **Freddy**, *Alice Thomas.*

Whitney- Gina's Things

A note tells me Mama had a chance for some extra hours. She'll be exhausted, but she missed two days with Joey.

I walk down to Mrs. Fillmore's to get Joey. They are on the living room floor with little farm animals in a corral.

Mrs. Fillmore looks up. "OK, Joey, let's get this all back in the box."

"Can't we leave them until tomorrow?"

"You know the rules. If you don't put them back, they won't come out when you want them."

Joey takes this in stride and puts each animal back after a kiss. Sweet kid.

"Whitney, I have something for you." She hustles down the hall.

I resist the urge to help Joey, and Mrs. Fillmore returns with a cardboard box of clothes.

"These were my daughter's. She was slender but...." She waves her hand at her chest, "put together like you. Several of these blouses and dresses we made together. She got tired of things not fitting—you know—right. I taught her to sew, and some of these she sewed herself."

"She doesn't wear them?"

"Oh, Honey, my Gina was killed last year. Car accident. She was only twenty-two." The tears in Mrs. Fillmore's eyes are catching, and I make a swipe at mine and wait.

"The first time I saw you, it took my breath away. Oh, Gina had red hair..." She sets the box on the coffee table and brings a picture. "I have other boxes, but we'll see how these fit."

Gina is wearing the blue plaid dress on top. It fits her like a glove, the darts hugging her shape but not tight—just right. The tears are unrelenting. "She's lovely. You must miss her so much."

Mrs. Fillmore pats my arm. "You have no idea, Honey."

I put my arm around her, and she turns quickly and hugs me, holding me tight. I haven't been hugged like this since—for a long time. Her tears dissolve any fears of being hugged.

After a few moments, she holds me at arm's length. "Oh, hugging you is like hugging my Gina. These things are going to fit perfectly, I know." She catches herself. "If you want them. They're all laundered."

"Yes, I want them. I'd be honored to wear Gina's things."

"It took me a while to decide to part with them, but they are just sitting in boxes."

"You're sure?"

Mrs. Fillmore straightens her shoulders. "Absolutely." She gives me a shy smile. "I have a few things I held back—that I didn't launder."

I think of Daddy's long-sleeved shirts. We still have three in Mama's closet, and sometimes, I hold one to my nose and remember. Joey has fallen asleep on the couch.

I change in the bathroom, and I've never had a dress fit like this. I turn from side to side. As in the picture, the bodice is like it is made for me. I spend twenty minutes trying on the clothes. Gina had good taste. Not overly sexy, but not trying to hide things in loose tops. Everything in the box fits beautifully.

When Mama gets home, I have supper for her. I fed Joey early and put him down. She sinks into a kitchen chair.

"Sorry I'm late. I couldn't get the cash register to tally. Whitey came and asked what was wrong. I told him I was short twenty-five cents somehow. Whitey took a quarter out of his pocket, tossed it in the bag, and said, 'You're one of my best checkers. Go home, Martha.'"

She leans back in the chair. "He's the best boss."

I put on the blue plaid for Mama, and she says, "Oh, isn't that lovely?" She fingers a seam. "This is so well made!" When I tell her about Gina, she nods. She knows and shares my tears.

My voice isn't much better by the time I get to practice at seven. I'm not sick. I just had this guck running down my throat all night. The rain must have settled the dust because my throat hasn't felt yucky since English. But, as Jeremy would say, I could be a "Zoom Bass."

When it comes time for "Homesick," my voice breaks on the high A, and I cough.

"Let's take a rest," Mrs. A says, and I get a drink in the hall.

When I get back, Freddy is watching for me and beckons me to the piano. His eyes are earnest. "I can set 'Homesick' down. What do you think? A full step. You were singing Gs fine."

"You can do that?" It's a silly thing to say because he just offered, and then he plays my intro in E♭. I sit beside him.

He has to look down a couple of times, makes a misstep once, but falls into the piece as if it was written in E♭. I notice there is no music on the rack.

"Try it from the bridge."

He sings with the piano for a moment until I get my bearings. I get to the trouble spot and sail through it. "Oh, you're really good."

Mrs. A has come near. "E♭, Freddy? Just like that? I'm impressed."

Freddy gives her a shy look. "Well, I worked on the show in different keys. Jim's struggling with the D, and Whitney is a little gravelly today." He glances at me. "Can't have you splatting that A in front of everyone."

Splatting makes me laugh, and my laugh is so low I sound evil.

"Do you want to stop for the day, Whitney?" Mrs. A asks.

"I'm fine. I don't feel bad. I'm allergic to Bermuda."

Mrs. A starts getting the quartet on stage when Freddy says, "Did you fly down?"

I start to get up but stop. "I don't get it."

"Fly to Bermuda? Sorry. Corny joke."

Bermuda. Even corny charms me.

Freddy- The Dance

Ally and I decide her mom will take her to the band room, so I go to the game alone. I don't have a herd of friends, so I look for someone I know—maybe hoping Whitney goes to games. That seems a bit wrong, and I wouldn't sit with her anyway, so I sit with Schmitty. We aren't exactly friends, but he's in Trig and a decent guy.

The JV game is just finishing up, and I make a note to come later if they go on to the playoffs.

I'm not the only one. The stands are filling up. Loretta Stevens is sitting behind us with a girlfriend.

After an endless break, the cheerleaders come out and hold a paper banner between them. It's says, "Blackwater Bears" in big blue letters. The team runs onto the field, ripping through the banner, and making a mess of it. Loretta yells, "Yay, Ronny," and I figure Ron Packard.

Some cheerleaders jump and wave pom-poms, but three dutifully pick up the shreds, wad them into bundles, and lug them to a trash can.

I don't see Ally, but the band isn't there yet.

The game is more boring than I could have imagined, but the halftime show perks me up. The band is pretty good, and they march well.

It isn't hard to spot Ally—her flag is almost as tall as she is. But she's a trooper and twirls and waves with the best of them. There is a music break, with only the snares clicking their sticks, and I can hear the flags popping in the air. We all stand up and clap at the end.

After the Alma Mater, I'm not sure where to go. Loretta ends up beside me on the steps and says, "Hi, Freddy," and we walk down together.

When we're on the ground, she pauses. "Ally will be over there," pointing to an area next to the bleachers.

Loretta doesn't miss much. We know each other, but I was only in the cafeteria with Ally for ten minutes. Did Whitney, Minnie, and Loretta discuss me coming in with Ally?

Wash that woman…

I find Ally, and after the flags are rolled up and slipped into a big tube, she hurries over.

"Do you want me to change? I brought a dress and can

change!" She has her tiny duffle bag, but I suppose one of her dresses doesn't take up much room. Her uniform is white with blue trim around the hem and sleeves. It fits her perfectly, and she's cute.

"You look great."

She holds out the duffle. "Can you put this in your car? I have to go in with the band for a minute for the post-game talk. I'll meet you in the cafeteria."

Glad for something to do, I take the bag and make the quick walk to the student parking lot. A couple are necking in the car beside mine, and I toss the bag in the back seat. I miss, and it rolls onto the floor, but I leave it and get out of there. I pass Mr. Tyler on the way. He doesn't miss much.

In the cafeteria, I stand around, not knowing what to do. "Baby Love" is playing and I think about the chord structure. A few kids are dancing, and they don't look particularly good at it, which makes me feel better. Then Ally comes in, almost floating across the room with tiny steps. "Hi," she says.

The song is "Crazy." We dance close, and Ally seems taller until I realize she's dancing on her tiptoes, and I pull her closer. There's not much to her, but it's good to hold someone. Her hair smells terrific.

The words are bothering me. Is Ally falling for me, and does that make her crazy for falling...? I push the idea aside, and the song ends. She smiles. "You're a pretty good dancer."

The Bristol Stomp comes on and Ally begins the cutest set of moves, forward and back, and I just stand there.

"Come on, try once, and I won't bug you again!"

She does it half-time, and I stumble along. I'm not bad on my feet because of the sparring, and I sort of get it—good enough to make Ally smile.

Loretta and Ronny come and talk. Well, Loretta and Ally talk, and Ronny says, "Hey," and I nod.

"So, you guys are dating?" I hear Loretta ask.

I strain to catch Ally saying, "We're having fun. Freddy helped me change a flat tire, and we sorta got to know each other better."

Another slow song comes on, and Loretta drags Ronny away. Ally dangles her hand and pulls me closer. "You slow dance OK." And once again I am dazzled by her ease to compliment.

When the song ends, Ally says, "I'm pretty thirsty. Want to go get a Coke or something?"

"Sure, wherever you want to go."

Another slow record begins on and she says, "One more, I love

103

this old song."

"Put Your Head on My Shoulder" plays, and we dance. She sort of wiggles and says, "I'm so short, I will never get to put my head on anyone's shoulder."

Without thinking, I bend, put my arms around her waist, and lift her so her head is level with mine. She makes a little sigh, and her hair tickles my ear. It's as close as I have ever been to a girl.

Mr. Tyler cruises by and gives us an aside, "I think Miss Thomas can stand on her own two feet." He's nice about it.

I let her down, and we dance a little further apart. She wrinkles her eyes, grinning. "You 'bout got me in trouble!"

"Me? I was just correcting your height!" and we laugh.

She grabs my hand, "Come on, let's get out of here!"

We hold hands and walk toward the door. Loretta gives me a flicker of a wink over Ronny's shoulder.

When we get to the car, I open her door, and Ally doesn't hesitate to slide across to sit by me. I hand her the bag with her dress.

When I'm in, she says, "Now listen, you don't have to buy me a bunch of food. We can go Dutch."

I don't have much money, but Ally turns toward me, our faces about five inches apart.

"So, how much do you have?"

I'm surprised. "Four dollars and almost thirty cents," I admit. "I should have stopped at the bank. It was after hours, but my mom said they called earlier this afternoon begging me to bring a wheelbarrow because they were having trouble getting the vault closed."

Ally doesn't miss a beat. "I hate it when that happens! We had to take my dad's pickup down the other day." Ally unzips the duffel. "OK, confession. I have three dollars and," she digs around, "and two quarters. Know what that means?"

I start the car. "Well, we're not having steaks."

"Let's go to In-N-Out. Pepsi is only a dime, and we can each get fries. All that flag-twirling makes me hungry." She bumps my arm, and I ease out of the student parking lot.

Ally peers at the controls. She gets the heater going, but the engine is cold, and it's blowing cold air. "Like the Chevy. My VW puts out heat almost instantly!" She turns the fan off and leans forward, sticking her hand under the dash. "Come on, we're cold here!"

I have to laugh. "A watched heater never heats." I shift into third, and the temperature gauge lifts off the mark. "Try it now."

"That's better. Oh, it's going to be cozy in here."

And it is.

I take Ally home. We are full of fries, having circled around for another batch. I walk her to her door, and we kiss. She leans in, head back, and my first kiss is wonderful. Her lips are soft but not plappy. I smile at my word. Plappy: sort of floppy soft like a dead fish.

She leans away and looks up at me. "You're a nice guy, Freddy." I take it as an invitation and lean toward her, but she puts a finger to my lips.

"That's probably enough." She throws her arms around my neck, pulls me down, and kisses my cheek. "This was fun. We should do it again sometime." And she's gone.

I am confused. Does this mean I am supposed to call her? Tomorrow? Am I supposed to walk her to classes? Are we going out again?

Girls are hard to understand. Ally knows her own mind, that's for sure. Too bad *I* can't figure out what's on her mind. She's so different from Whitney but equally confusing. If Ally had said that's enough for tonight, it could mean that there is going to be another night—more kissing.

Whitney- My Fishermen

I'm so nervous. I go to the back door, and Viv lets me in. She hands me an apron. "This one is new. Don't tell Eddie." I slip it on, and Viv fiddles with the back. She comes around. "Let me get some safety pins. We're going to show them that slim waist."

I start to protest, but Viv says, "No. You listen to me. I'm just going to pull it in, not tight, so it's not a tent."

I go into the bathroom and look at myself from all sides. It's OK. It gives me a V shape, but nothing is tight.

Viv hands me a name tag with Whitney in bright letters. "How did they get this so fast?"

"The owner loves gizmos. He has a little machine that stamps the names on." She pins it on me. "OK. You work with me today. We don't buss the tables—unless we have to. Keep the dirty hands separate from the clean. Hal will clear tables and wipe them down. Then we go into action."

She leads me to an empty booth. "Alright, you know where the silver goes, right?" I nod, and she has me set the table for four.

"Looks real nice." She touches a corner of one of the napkins but doesn't move it. "You pour water, coffee—orange juice. I'll keep track of the food they order, but you pay attention and keep the drinks right."

At the first booth, there are four fishermen. One even wears one of those hats with furry little hooks in it. I have to lean over to pour, but they are all gentlemen.

"Miss, can I trouble you for a cup of tea?" the man in the hat asks. He has a sweet smile.

"Of course."

Viv is behind the counter and is quick to show me the hot water and the little chrome pitchers. There are nicer cups and saucers, and I put it all on a small tray. When I get to the table, the fellow on the end makes room for the tray. When I have the tea settled, I hear myself saying, "Would you like some honey?"

The fellow is surprised, and I blush.

"My mama likes honey in her tea. She says it's better for you than sugar." I am red-faced and flustered.

The fellow starts to say no but catches himself and says, "You know, maybe I'll try it. Your mama raised a nice girl."

I hurry to bring the honey. When the men leave, Viv says the tip is bigger than she usually gets. "They are regulars."

The morning flies by, but by eleven, I am feeling the lack of sleep. Two guys who look like they've been up all night come in for breakfast. Viv lets me handle the table. I write the orders—bacon, toast, and coffee, not complicated.

When I bring coffee around, I come from the side, and the one with his back to me says, "You think those are double Ds?"

Those were the days, I think, but for some reason, it doesn't bother me as much as usual.

His friend is fluttering a hand to the guy to try to shut him up. The first guy is so distracted, he doesn't even seem embarrassed.

Back behind the counter, there is a lull and I think about what just happened, wondering why I wasn't as embarrassed? Or ashamed?

Viv sidles up. "The guy at table two bothering you? He's a punk. Lives down the street. That coal car's got a half load." She takes a sip of coffee and sets it down. "I'll go tell the little twerp off."

I put my hand out. "Let it go. His friend is so embarrassed, I think I'll get a quarter out of him."

Viv raises one eyebrow. "There you go, Hon. Learning fast. Be so nice he tips until he bleeds."

And he does. He leaves thirty-five cents!

Freddy- The Chickering

I don't call Ally. After church, I spend the afternoon working on the musical without my earphones until Dad comes to my door. "Freddy, your mom wasn't kidding when she said you play well. I've been listening in the hall."

"You could've come in."

"Didn't want to disturb you."

I'm flattered and puzzled—glad that Dad isn't spending the afternoon—day—at the bar and grill.

"Let's go for a drive. I want to show you something."

He drives with his elbow out the window of his old pickup, and we navigate to G Street. We stop at a house that is a cousin to ours. "Come on."

An elderly woman answers the door, and we go inside. Dad introduces her as Mrs. Wilson. The house smells like old carpet and chocolate chip cookies. She leads us to an upright piano.

"It was my husband's. He took excellent care of it." She pats the top. "Joe was a piano tuner. He tuned for your teacher, Mr. Blackwater, until he got sick last summer. Try it."

I look at Dad, wondering how we can afford a piano, but he nods toward the bench. I play, getting lost in the rich sound. It's a Chickering.

I realize I've probably been playing too long, and look up. Dad is sitting with his eyes closed, and Mrs. Wilson has her head back in her chair. "Lovely, Fredrick," she says. "Mr. Blackwater said you were very good."

Mrs. Wilson insists we sit and have tea and cookies. Dad seems to be in no hurry, and Mrs. Wilson and I chat about the Christmas musical.

After two cups of tea and lots of cookies, Dad gives Mrs. Wilson two hundred fifty dollars.

The big surprise is Mrs. Wilson gives me her husband's piano tuning tools. "We married late and have no children. You will make a good home for them."

I look in the black case with lots of shiny doodads for working on pianos. She insists I take the books and a big box of piano wire, all marked as to size.

We carry the tools to Dad's pickup, and two buddies from work

108

arrive.

Mrs. Wilson produces a piano dolly. "May as well take this, too, Freddy. I won't be needing it."

Pianos are heavy, but the four of us get it loaded, covered with blankets, and tied down.

At the house, Dad asks, "You want it in your room or the living room?"

"I think my room would be better. That way, if you want to watch TV, I won't bother you."

We get it down the hall, but it won't make the turn into my room. Dad says, "Watch this. I'll show you how to cheat fair and square."

We tip the piano on end and slide it on cardboard down the hall and into my room. We tuck the Wurlitzer in the garage and rearrange my bed so the piano is on an inside wall. I know a kid who will give me forty for the Wurlitzer.

When the men are gone, Mom and Dad bring kitchen chairs into my room for a "concert." I play the whole Christmas musical, mostly from memory. I add the melody to Whitney's accompaniment. I finish with a tasty version of "Fly Me to the Moon."

When I look, Mom and Dad are dancing in the hall. I can't remember the last time I've seen them touch in a loving way.

Whitney- Can't Stop Crying

Freddy isn't waiting for me before English. I'm not surprised, but I can't say I wasn't hoping. He's not in his seat when I go in. *Is he with Alice?* It's none of my business, but it takes all my willpower not to go back outside.

He arrives a minute before class starts and leans forward. "I was waiting for the doughnut delivery, but apparently, there's a problem with the school board. I think you should go to the next meeting and protest."

I turn my head partway. "I've been thinking we should try peanut butter cookies. Peanut butter has protein, and glazed doughnuts can be messy."

"Whitney, if you and Freddy are done, perhaps you can pass out this extra poem?" I feel my face radiating enough heat to warm the room. I take the papers and fumble, trying to separate the sheets.

"Let me help her, Sir," Freddy says. Without waiting for an OK, Freddy comes to my side and takes the stack. "Watch this. I got a paper passing award—well, Honorable Mention—in the third grade."

"Class," he says, "when passing out papers, hold the pile flat in one hand and rub a circle in the middle with your index finger joint." He starts going around, and the sheets begin to fan out. He holds the papers up for everyone to see.

He hands me the papers, gives the class a little bow, and takes his seat. I wonder if Mr. Sanchez is upset by this outburst, but he's rubbing a stack of paper.

My face cools as I pass the poems to the first person in each row. Of course, I miscount and have to take a paper to the back of the third row. I put the rest on Mr. Sanchez's desk and practically fall into my chair.

"I hate it when I skip six," Freddy whispers. "I've had several complaints from the Numbers Union."

I give my head a slow shake.

A Cappella put me in such a good mood this morning. The arrangement of "It's Beginning to Look a Lot Like Christmas" is so cute. The basses haven't grown into Zoom Basses, but they lend a counterpoint to the other parts. I love this time of year. Thinking of snow, and thick sweaters, and Joanie.

And Daddy. I don't enjoy thinking about that part. *Oh, Daddy,*

I'm so mixed up. I miss you so much.

"You OK?" Freddy has a hand on my left shoulder, just lightly.

I must have made a sound in my throat and swipe at a tear with my right hand. "Yes," but I cross the hand over and put it on Freddy's hand. I'm crying pretty hard now.

"Whitney, are you all right?" Mr. Sanchez has stopped the class.

"Uh—yeah—can—get——water?" I can't even talk. I let Freddy take back his hand.

"Yes."

In my hurry, I catch my leg on the desktop, and my books flop on the floor. I stand, tears rolling, watching Philip gather my things and set them on my desk in a neat pile. I'm bawling so hard I sound like a dog barking and cover my mouth.

"Freddy, go with her—make sure she gets to the fountain. Mary, you go too."

I start for the door and Freddy is behind me, but giving me space. Around the corner, I stop at the fountain between the bathrooms. I don't want a drink, and I take a shaky breath. *Why are these things so low?*

Cool water is better than I imagined, and I take four big swallows. *I'll need the Girls' before lunch.*

Mary doesn't seem to know what to do and walks back to the corner.

I turn to Freddy. "You—can go—" I take a deep breath to stop the shaking. "I'm—OK, I just want to rinse my face." My voice has gone all squeaky.

He doesn't move, and when I look up, his head is cocked, brow furrowed. "I can wait."

Mary is looking toward the student parking lot.

It's not just Daddy. It's everything. Time of year. Wishing I could talk to Freddy. Wishing I wasn't such a chicken and would let Freddy put his arms around me. Hold me.

I splash water on my face, and there are no towels. When I come out, still wet, Freddy says, "Wait," and runs in the Boy's.

"No luck." He hands me his handkerchief. "It's clean."

He carries a handkerchief? "Thanks. I wipe my face, and my stupid nose is running. I blow it, look up horrified, and say, "Sorry. I'll launder it."

"I'm not worried. Keep it until you are not so upset."

I give him my genuine smile. "Thanks. You're always such a gentleman, and I'm—"

He leans down, hands on his knees, looking up into my eyes. "I just figure you're having a hard time."

Mary hasn't moved.

I put my hand on his upper arm and stand him up. "Don't be too nice—I'll start crying again."

We walk back. Freddy opens the door, and Mary goes in first. Mr. Sanchez looks at me and then at Freddy. He gives a kind smile and a head nod.

I mouth thank you to Mary. I breathe in and feel like a thousand pounds have been lifted off me.

Mr. Sanchez is saying, "Look down at the line, 'If gold ruste, what shall iren doo?'" How does this line speak to you?"

I find the line on the handout, and Freddy and I start talking at once. Freddy touches my shoulder. "Go ahead."

"The Parson is saying those in authority must hold themselves to a higher standard—because their charges—those under them—I'm not saying this right, but those who look up to them are watching—following."

"I think you put it pretty well." Mr. Sanchez closes his well-worn copy of *Canterbury Tales*. He moves in front of his desk, throwing one leg over the corner, and perches.

"I know this isn't a philosophy class, but in literature, we find great meaning——philosophy, if you will. And this passage contains a lesson for all who would listen."

I'm not sure how many are listening, but I am. I could use a little greatness today.

"As your teacher, I must hold myself to a higher standard. Gold doesn't rust or tarnish. I shouldn't rust or tarnish. If I were to cheat or am cruel—" He laughs. "I know some of you think I'm cruel," and the class laughs.

"Let's try it another way. If I spent time between classes throwing paper towels on the ceiling of the boy's bathroom, this would make it OK. 'Even Mr. Sanchez does it.'"

He adjusts himself on the desk. "But you kids also have folks who look up to you. Peers. Little brothers or sisters." He takes time to run his eyes up and down the rows. "The little ones are watching."

Philip clears his throat. He's listening.

The bell rings, breaking the magic. I realize I have hardly been breathing. I look down at my paper. *If gold ruste, what shal iren doo?*

Freddy- Ally

I don't know why I am making jokes with Whitney—flirting with Whitney. I have a chance to have a girlfriend. I had my first real kiss.

Actually, I know why. Before school, I tell myself I will ignore Whitney—not ignore her like being mean, but not go overboard.

Then I see her, and I'm drawn to her—her shiny black hair, which isn't perfect this morning, her shoulders—and I want her to notice me, spend time with me, and talk to me. So, I weaken, and she responds.

When we get caught talking, I rescue her and take over the class. I've never done anything like that before, but in her presence, I seem to think I'm clever. I'm not showing off—well, a little.

I'm lucky Mr. Sanchez doesn't send me back to my seat.

Later, I hear a muffled sob. I see it shake her shoulders and put my hand on her left shoulder. I haven't been touching her. She doesn't seem to want to be touched—by me. Does she want to be touched by someone else? Or is it just me?

Then she puts her hand on my hand. She doesn't pat. She just holds it there like she doesn't want my hand to go away.

Mr. Sanchez looks at me. I'm not sure what he's thinking, but when Whitney goes to pieces, he gets it, and I'm glad. Even Philip seems to understand something big is going on.

In the hallway, Whitney is a mess, and I feel helpless. Mary is with us, but I can tell she has no idea what to do, so she moves back to the corner of the building. Is she giving us privacy? I take the lesson I learned from Ally and try to get Whitney paper towels.

I see Ally on the way to lunch with a gaggle of girlfriends. She calls, "Hi, Freddy," but moves on with them.

Did I have bad breath when I kissed her? Was it too soon to kiss her? She made it clear one was enough.

I eat at my usual table and leave early.

Ally catches me outside. "Sorry about that. Donna had a crisis. Not sure we helped, but at least we showed we cared."

I smile.

"So, I brought my car today, and I was wondering if you could listen to it." She puts both palms toward me. "Don't need to change a flat tire, I promise!"

"I have rehearsal for the Christmas musical, but after. Say five? I could come by."

"I've been wanting to hear the musical. Paula said it's going to be great. I need to look up some history stuff in the library—then I'll swing by," and she's gone.

Whitney's class is still doing the track unit. I try not to stare, but she's a pretty good runner. Working with the bag or playing hard at PE helps me feel better about things. I hope she's feeling better.

At rehearsal, the quartet is coming along beautifully. Whitney's voice is almost back to normal. During the water break, I have her come to the piano.

"Shall we try 'Homesick' in the original key?" I ask.

She doesn't sit on the bench. "Freddy, Alice is here. You should go back and talk to her."

I turn and wave and hold up one finger. Ally smiles.

"This is important. I know I play as if everything is easy, but I need to settle on a key for 'Homesick.' You may not notice, but I'm faking some parts, and this needs to be right."

"I've been thinking about it. I know my voice has been off, but I'm more comfortable in E ♭. Does that cause problems getting to E ♭ and back to the interlude?"

I play the end of her solo, and do a little modulation and start the interlude.

She half turns and gazes at the stage, seeing nothing in particular. "Freddy, you are so talented."

"Mr. Blackwater, my piano teacher, helped me work it out."

Her head snaps around. "Blackwater? Like the school?!"

"Well, yes—an uncle gave the land to the district years ago." I play an ending to "Can't Help Lovin' That Man of Mine" as Mr. Blackwater taught me, note for note, pausing before the last chord. "He does things like this—effortlessly. You should hear it on his grand."

Whitney sighs. "Beautiful. Then she turns right toward me, leans a bit, and says, "Go talk to Alice."

When I get to the back row, Ally is holding the seat down with her right hand. "Freddy, I had no idea. I mean, Paula said you're good, but you are really good."

I wonder if I should try to hold hands, but when I look she has

114

laced her fingers around one knee.

"I have a great teacher. So you're not too bored? We have another half hour."

"You worry too much. I'm reading my notes for my paper—cogitating! But I need to get home. Can we look at the car tomorrow?"

A pang of guilt stabs at my insides, and Ally slips out.

Mrs. A calls for a run from the top, and I move to the piano.

Whitney- Kindred Spirit

Miss Gill, my counselor, is wearing a sweater that reminds me of fall. Winter is probably coming on in Ohio.

"Whitney, Mr. Sanchez tells me you were crying in English."

My eyes swell.

"I'm sorry I couldn't get you in yesterday." She gives me a half smile. "I want to be sure you're OK."

There is a long pause, and I squeeze my eyes shut, but tears force their way out. Miss Gill slides a box of Kleenex toward me.

"I think I'm OK—I...."

"You don't have to talk about it if you don't want to."

I want to. It would help to hear Joanie's voice. I wish it were easier to talk to Mama. I really want to talk to Freddy. Have him comfort me. "It's a lot of things."

I'm not sure I want to talk about Freddy.

When I manage to look up, Miss Gill has the sweetest smile.

"My dad died—three years ago. Sometimes I miss him so much. It comes on me when I least expect it."

"I *am* sorry."

"I called him Daddy, still do. Sounds so—like a little girl, but...."

"He was your daddy."

I stall, and Miss Gill says, "You said there were many things."

"I think it just piled up. I miss Ohio. I have a really good friend, Joanie. We've been friends forever. We write, but it's not the same."

"What would you tell Joanie if she were here?"

That opens the floodgates, and I am sobbing again. I sit up and take a deep breath, demanding my tears and gulping stop. Miss Gill is leaning on her elbows, chin in her hand. She waits.

"I would tell her I'm—so—tired of—being—"

Now I have the hiccups. "I'm sick of being the object of—remarks—hic—I guess they think they are—hic—jokes?"

"Students are bothering you?"

"Yes. No. Yes. Not by any one boy. Person. It just...."

Miss Gill waits for me to wipe my eyes again. Thankfully, my nose is behaving. She seems safe, and there is no doubt she cares.

"I'm—big..." I gesture. "I can live with that. But I hadn't been at Blackwater an hour until some guy said something—hic—to his buddies. They were laughing—horsing around." I study my knees.

"Mr. Sanchez said Fredrick Sanders had his hand on your shoulder. Is he bothering you?"

My head comes up fast, eyes wide. "No! Not at all." *Oh, Freddy, I've made a mess of things.*

"I don't want to get anyone in trouble! That won't hel—" I wish my voice would quit squeaking. "I'm probably making a bigger *deal* out of it than it *is*."

Miss Gill sits back. "Our feelings are ours to have. If this bothers you, that's OK."

We sit in silence, and Miss Gill says, "Excuse me for a second."

She's quick on her feet, and the picture of a lighthouse on her wall is peaceful.

She hands me a cup of water. "This might help."

I drink the whole cup, and my throat feels cooler.

"So, the tears the other morning. What else would you tell Joanie?"

"I think that morning I was crying because of Freddy. I push boys away. I pushed Freddy away. I can't seem to trust boys' motives."

The hiccups have stopped. "But Freddy has been nothing but kind. Polite. He's playing for the musical. He's been seeing Alice Thomas. I told him I just wanted to be friends. So—I guess I deserve that."

I hate how small all this sounds. I think of Minnie's Howard drama and am embarrassed. "It's silly to take up your time with boy troubles."

"Things that bother us keep us from doing our best. We want you to do well in your classes, the musical, and at home. This is what I'm here for."

"It's just that I am lonely. I'm making friends, but I'm lonely for the way it used to be." My breath catches.

"Whitney, a move across the country is a big deal, and losing a parent is huge. Life-changing events can throw us off balance." Miss Gill holds my gaze. "It's all very normal. Not easy, by any means, but absolutely normal."

"I'm just so emotional, and—I'll never see my old room again."

"Whitney, there is nothing wrong with tears. I have a whole cabinet of tissues. You aren't the only student who's cried in this office —and not just girls." She waits a long time.

"Is there anything else you want to tell me?"

I meet her eyes. "No." I'm not tearing up this time. "Thank you for listening. I think this helped."

Miss Gill considers this. "See how things go, but anytime you want to talk, leave a folded note with my name on it at the front desk. There is a stapler there. Staple it closed and slip it into the box with my name on it. I check it every day."

Ralph walks me toward Typing. He's a senior and plays basketball. He works that into every conversation. And he seems to always be around, between classes, to mention that he is captain, or high-point-something-or-other. I don't try to get rid of him for three reasons:

1. With Freddy out of the picture, I need to try to get along with boys. Get used to the idea of me and a boy.

2. He's polite. He isn't making any comments about my figure, although it seems he's more interested in talking about himself.

3. Other than Minnie, Loretta, and Laura, I'm not exactly making friends.

Before the turn to Typing, Taylor calls, "Hey, Babe, haven't seen you around."

Ralph slows. "Leave her alone, Taylor," and Taylor sort of shrinks. Maybe it's just my imagination, but he seems to lose two inches.

"Hey, it's a free country. I can talk to her if I want to."

"I don't think she wants to talk to you." Ralph bends a bit to look at my face. "You want Taylor to give you his song and dance?"

For the first time in a while, I'm comforted by a boy other than Freddy. "No," I whisper.

"There you have it. She says no, so leave her *alone!*" And Taylor does. He disappears into the crowd.

I lift my eyes to Ralph. "Thanks."

"He's a jerk. He was a jerk in grammar school." Ralph stays close but strikes up a basketball conversation with Jeff from History.

My mind is still buzzing with thoughts coming from all

directions.

I'm trying extra hard not to be too friendly with Freddy. He's doing such a great job for the musical. Mrs. A doesn't have to wear the sling all the time, but her hand still looks like a club. She compliments Freddy. Why don't I compliment him more?

I know why. Because I hate just being friends because being friends means keeping a wall between us. A wall I built. A wall I thought I wanted. A wall named Ally.

Freddy- Good Kisser

After school, we move fast, Ally punctuating our walk with chatter. "It's a 1959, and was my grandfather's. He gave it to me when he got his Buick."

The air is Santa Ana fresh, and Ally makes the late afternoon seem crystal clear. I've seen her bug lots of times. "So what sounds funny?"

She gets in and puts her head out the window. "It's shaky, and it sounds—uneven. It didn't used to do that. It purred. Now it putts. And it lost its pep."

I go to the front and tug on the handle.

"Freddy! I thought you would know about cars! The engine is in back!"

I go to the window, grinning. "Just checking."

She laughs, and I go to the rear. "Start it."

The second it starts, I call, "Shut it off," and she's by my side in seconds.

"Is it dying? Dead?"

"No, but let's have a look."

I open the engine lid.

"There it is. Look. This wire lying here is supposed to be connected to something. See anything?"

"What am I looking for?"

"Keep looking. Look for other wires like it."

She points. "It goes in that hole next to the others!"

I examine the end of the plug wire. "It's OK; someone just didn't get it pushed in all the way."

"My cousin. He thinks he's sooo funny! He made it so it wouldn't start. After everyone had a laugh, I told him to put it back the way it was!"

"And I bet he didn't get the wire in all the way. You put it in. Push 'till it pops in place."

Ally gives the wire a firm push.

"Try it now."

She cranks the engine and hangs her head out the window, hair flying. "Oh, it's perfect. Now it's purring."

I lean on the window frame. "Hey, you want to see a movie Friday?"

"Oh, Freddy—" She turns off the engine and gets out.

I step back.

"Freddy, I like you. You're fun. I like to have fun with you, but...."

I'm getting a bad feeling.

"When Whitney was at the piano or singing, your concentration was on nothing but her. In the cafeteria, you've moved to the other side of the table so you can watch her."

"How—?"

"Freddy, I'm not spying on you. But when we were eating the day of the flat tire, you glanced over—a lot."

"I'm sorry. I didn't mean—hey, I *do* like you."

"I know you do. But you are crazy about Whitney Tate. *And,*" she pauses, taking a deep breath, "I like you, too—but—I have a crush on Bill Fagan."

"Ally, I wasn't trying to make Whitney—I wasn't using you. I..."

Ally puts her hand on my forearm. "I know. I wasn't trying to make Bill jealous, either." She gives a long sigh. "I wish he was. He's been trying to date Barb Lewis."

She gets in the car, turning her head to me, hair dancing. "Don't fuss! We'll be great friends." She starts the car. "Hey, you *are* a good kisser! Thought you might like to know."

She backs out, gives me a toodle-oo, and away she goes.

Whitney- Alterations

I walk down the sidewalk to Mrs. Fillmore's, beyond heartsick. Ally's cute and comfortable with herself. I'm jealous that she likes Freddy. I'm jealous that she has a darling proportional figure.

Proportional. That's what I want to be.

When he was talking to her in the theater, she was leaning back as relaxed as if she were at home watching TV. Why can't I be natural? Comfortable with myself. Why do I second, third, fourth guess everything I do, everything anyone says?

And what's to be done about Freddy anyway? There is no Freddy if he likes Ally. I would never try to take away another girl's guy. He's gone.

Guys are pretty much leaving me alone. Well, yesterday, one dope said too loudly, "No need for a life jacket there." For once, I had the gumption to stand up for myself.

"Wow, Carl. You think that up all by yourself?" One guy shoved Carl's shoulder, and his buddies laughed at him.

Pete, from typing, seems OK. He doesn't leer or make comments. Maybe I could be a little more friendly.

I show Mrs. Fillmore two pinafores. "Could you help with these? I got a job at Daisy's Diner." I slip one over my head. "Viv at the café pinned it on me Saturday. It's OK on top, but the ties won't pull it closed enough without pins." I flap the material around my middle.

"I got pretty good at altering Gina's clothes. We don't want this fitting like socks on a rooster."

I laugh at the thought.

"Come with me." We go into a bedroom that is dedicated to sewing. "Let's see." With pins in her mouth, she wraps the tape around my ribs. "Like my Gina, not really a big person." She continues measuring, and I don't look to see what she's writing.

She talks like Eddie when he has a cigarette in his mouth. She pulls the material on my left and puts in a pin. She turns me back and forth, working the sides down to the hem. "OK, we're not going overboard, but I want you looking good coming and going." She winks. "The bow in the back needs to be cute, not trying to gather five or six inches of material."

I'm embarrassed, and Mrs. Fillmore senses it. "Honey, don't

fuss. This is the way you came—you have a lovely shape."

"*Too* lovely, sometimes."

She touches my elbow. "Oh, I know. But it can come in handy —Gina waited tables for a while. She made excellent tips." Mrs. Fillmore winks. "I'm guessing you're not working for the exercise?"

"No." I'm feeling better. "The last two hours, Viv let me do four tables by myself, and I made almost as much on tips as the hourly."

Mrs. Fillmore lays one apron on top of the other. "Just as I thought—not quite the same. Listen, let me work on these, then we'll make a pattern." She holds up the material. "I can make this for pennies—we'll use something that irons up a little crisper. This stuff is pretty limp."

"Thank you!"

"I like a good project," she says.

On the way home, I feel some of my problems have evaporated in the presence of Mrs. Fillmore.

Dear Whitney,

Carl Smith took me to the football game and dance. I am happy to report a first kiss! On my porch. It was nice. Veeeery nice.

Of course, I did most of the talking, but what's new? We are going to the movies this Friday.

I wish I had better advice for the Freddy problem. All I can say is you are so attractive. I know you don't like part of that, but remember- Be your funny cute self and out shine the bustline. (Look, I made a rhyme. Ooo, another one!) You're so good at clever banter. You have the best personality. Be the Whitney I know. Please? For me?

Love,

Joanie

123

Freddy- Distant

I can hardly wait for Science Club, but Tim and I are the only ones there.

Mr. Coulter has a tube with a downy feather and dime inside. With natural air, the dime falls while the feather flutters down. When we pump the air out of the tube, they fall together.

I watch the door constantly, hoping to see Whitney.

Suzie and the Thunderbird cut the session short, and I help Mr. Coulter put things away.

"Where are the others?" he wonders.

"Not sure. I hear Minnie and Howard are on the outs. Not sure about Whitney."

"Are you and Whitney 'on the outs' as well?" Mr. Coulter catches himself and holds up one hand. "None of my business. But the staff is worried about her. She was quite upset the other day."

"I think she's better."

"Good."

I've always been impressed with the teachers at Blackwater. Last year, Mrs. Keller asked me if I was OK when I was having a hard time with Dad. I couldn't tell her about things, but I appreciated her concern more than I let on. I should thank her some time.

On the drive home, I think about what might cause Whitney to cry when nothing was happening. Not that I hadn't thought about it all day Monday and today. She seemed OK in English but kept her reaction to my attempted humor—distant.

I do a light workout. Dad isn't on my case these days, but I find the exercise helps clear my Whitney head.

She wore a dress and cardigan today, and when she stood up to go to the next class, she took my breath away. The color made her big eyes seem larger. Sadder?

Ally wants to be friends. Whitney wants to be friends. Maybe I'm the guy girls feel safe being with as long as they don't have to be more than friends.

And yet Whitney seems to like me. I punch the bag harder. This conversation with myself is senseless. Concentrate on the musical, shine in English, and keep my head down.

No sooner do I tell myself to stop thinking about Whitney than I see her in my mind.

I noticed a senior walking with her earlier, and she didn't seem to mind. He's a basketball player and OK from what I can tell. OK, if I don't mind him making me ache with jealousy.

Whitney- Sashay

Minnie is in a full-tilt rant about Howard. "Cindy Caruthers asked for a ride home! And *then* she asked if they could stop at the In-N-Out for a Pepsi because she's *thirsty. Then* she decides she needs fries."

Minnie stops for a breath and takes a small bite of lasagna. "Loretta saw them, and Cindy had scooched over in the seat!"

Loretta has a tangerine slice halfway to her mouth. "I only asked Minnie if she and Howard had broken up, and I got the full interrogation." She pops the slice in her mouth, a clear indication she's done with the topic.

"Interrogation? What am I supposed to do? I have to have the facts if I am going to make the proper choices!"

"Minnie, I told you: Ronny and I were behind them at In-N-Out. I thought you were with him. Then Cindy jumps out and runs to the other line to talk to Alma Alvarado. She runs back, gets in, and they drive out. Ronny and I got Pepsi. That's all I know."

I decide to try. "What does Howard have to say about it?"

Loretta loses interest in her tangerine and waits.

Minnie humphs and slides lasagna onto her fork, lifts it, and lays it back on her tray. "Yes. He admitted the whole thing." She gives Loretta a look.

"But did you ask if he likes Cindy?" I wonder.

"I—I was pretty upset with him." Minnie thinks, pauses, is pleased with herself, and says, "Miffed. Oh yes, I'm miffed."

Loretta's eyelid flicks, and she begins stacking her peelings.

Minnie pushes her tray back. "How can I eat when I may have fallen victim to some craft?"

Loretta gives me an aside. "Was in the last novel I loaned her."

"I'm sure it's going to be OK," I say. "I have Cindy in History. She may be more interested in a boy with a car than science."

Loretta pokes the stack of peelings, making them fall. "See, Minnie. I told you. Cindy flits from guy to guy like flies at a pig farm."

I snicker, and Loretta gives me an appreciative smile.

Minnie pulls the tray forward, only to slide it away. "I am bereft!"

Loretta sighs. "Minnie, it is amazing how quickly you have given up your scientific pursuits when love is in the air."

"That's just it! I sit by Howard in Chemistry, and would you

126

believe I messed up one of the bonus questions!" She looks back and forth between us. "I got one hundred and seven point five instead of one hundred ten!"

"I'm sure your grade is not ruined," Loretta tries, but Minnie hisses, "Howard got a hundred ten. Apparently, he isn't bothered by this!"

Loretta glances across the room. "Howard is over at his usual table. Go talk to him."

"*Me!*" Minnie glances over her shoulder. "If he thinks I'm going to *sashay* over there and talk to him, he has another think coming."

Loretta was close to getting the last tangerine peel in her sack, but waves it to punctuate her words. "In my experience, boys are clueless. I doubt he's thinking you might *sashay* anywhere. He's probably thinking about gravity or something."

"Well, we do find it fascinating that lunar gravity can reach some three hundred thousand miles and affect the tides."

With that, Loretta wads her lunch bag. "I have to go."

Minnie pouts, and I look at Freddy. He isn't sitting with Ally, and he gives me a smile.

Dear Joanie,

A kiss! You win! At least one of us has been "romanced." Don't fret, I'm not even slightly jealous. I think you and Carl are perfect.

I got a job! I am gainfully employed. I walked into a diner that had a Help Wanted sign and applied. The manager is pretty awful. Being within ten feet of him is like smoking a pack of cigarettes. Viv, the head waitress, has been very helpful.

There is no news from the Freddy Front (notice the alliteration there?), but I'm trying to take your advice and be more outgoing. I just don't want to attract any of the leering guys in the halls.

By the way, the halls are <u>outside</u> here and the school is a single story sprawling sort of thing. It is still light sweater weather!

I don't want to tell you bad stuff, but the other day,

I had a crying fit in English. Freddy put his hand on my shoulder, and it made me cry harder. I couldn't stop, and the teacher finally sent me outside. He had Freddy go with me and a girl as a chaperone! Freddy tried to comfort me—not the fake hug comfort, but genuine caring.

Did you know that words that start with "ch" like chaperone but are pronounced "sh" are borrowed from the French? Our English teacher tells us the most interesting things. Sometimes I think Freddy and I are the only ones listening.

Keep sending me the news.

Love,

Whitney

Freddy- Openings

I get a whiff of bubble bath and press back in my seat. Mr. Sanchez has a tall pile of books on his desk.

"When you write your story, I want you to spend two, three times as long on the first sentences. We call it the hook."

He picks up a book. "It was the best of times and the worst of times." He lays the book down. "Famous. Raises questions." He chuckles, "Not my favorite—apologies to Dickens."

Whitney is nodding, and I lean back until my chair creaks.

"'Call me Ishmael.' Melville. *Moby Dick.* It does make us wonder if that's his real name."

Whitney is like a magnet. I squirm in my seat and turn sideways.

"*To Kill a Mockingbird.* Raise your hand when I reach the line that grabs your attention."

The class shifts—watching Whitney for a cue.

Whitney's hand goes up when "Dill came" and so does almost every other hand. I wait for Boo Radley.

"Everyone waited until the second paragraph, which is fine." Mr. Sanchez sits on the corner of his desk.

"You are to write a catchy opening—great from the first sentence. Within the confines of a thousand-word story, you won't have the luxury of waiting a hundred thirty-five words to get your story off the ground."

He stands. "Yes, I counted. Dill is the hundred and thirty-fifth word." He smiles, and so do I.

Whitney writes something in her notebook. She's using her pen. She's sure about what she's writing.

I prefer to think. I'm dreaming of a small town—maybe in the southwest.

"This is an important assignment. You should begin working on your story, but we will each read our first three sentences out loud Monday the twenty-second—you know, to see how soon hands go up."

As I write the date in my notebook, Philip is also writing the assignment. Monday is misspelled, but I'm impressed.

Whitney's shoulders have me entranced. Mr. Sanchez is reading other openings and asking for our opinion. I have to quit thinking about Whitney Tate all the time. The irony isn't lost on me. Thinking about not thinking about—

"Freddy, are you with me?"

I'm caught off guard and decide to be honest. "I may have drifted, Sir. Sorry."

Mr. Sanchez picks up another book and begins to read. Whitney says to her shoulder, "Better you than me. I was gone, too."

Too bad she wasn't daydreaming about me. The thought launches me into another round of pleasant Whitney dreams.

Whitney- Sleepover

At lunch, Loretta takes the stage, and Minnie doesn't seem to mind.

"Whitney, Minnie and I are having a sleepover at my house Friday night. Do you want to join us?"

I'm so flattered I can hardly stand it. "I'd love to, but I have to be at the diner at four forty-five every Saturday."

Loretta doesn't miss a beat, glancing at Minnie. "Well then, we could do it Saturday night. Is that OK?"

"Yes!" A sleepover with friends!

Mama drops me off with my bag. I don't know what to expect, but I have a couple of blankets, some fuzzy jammies, and toiletries. Loretta and Minnie are watching for me.

Loretta is already in PJs and reaches for my bag. "You are just in time for the fun. Mom is making peanut butter cookies. I know you are not a chocolate person."

Loretta is so thoughtful.

Mrs. Stevens looks over her shoulder from the stove. "Whitney, Loretta has told me so much about you."

Being a topic of "Loretta conversation" makes me warm inside. "Nice to meet you, Mrs. Stevens. Thank you for having me."

"Let's get you moved in," Loretta says, and I follow her down the hall to a large bedroom. There is a double bed and a single! "Put your stuff down anywhere."

We eat spaghetti and stuff ourselves with peanut butter cookies. Loretta's dad is a pleasant man who collects our plates when we are done.

In Loretta's room, we get pillows off the beds and wrap in blankets on the floor.

I go to the bathroom to change and have the debate I knew I would have. Bra or no bra. I pull out my PJs and decide this night feels as safe as a sleepover at Joanie's. I ditch the bra and join my friends.

"Whitney, cute jammies!" Minnie says.

She changes into pajamas with a bunny print, and we lounge around, nibbling popcorn. Minnie takes control of the conversation.

"What am I going to do about Howard?"

I can tell Loretta isn't keen on more Howard drama. "Minnie, there is nothing you can do if Howard isn't interested in dating."

"Retta!"

"It's true," Loretta insists. "You can't force someone to like you."

Minnie pretends to pout and takes another piece of popcorn.

"Whitney, what about Freddy?" Loretta asks. "He likes you."

My head comes up quickly. "You think so?"

Minnie nibbles. "He's always looking at lunch."

"And you're looking," Loretta adds.

I roll onto my back and stare at the ceiling. "I guess."

Minnie wiggles my toe through my sock. "You guess!?"

I sigh. "It's complicated." I turn my head and Loretta has her elbows on the carpet, hand under her chin.

"Don't waste your opportunity for romance," Minnie says. "Love is fleeting." She hugs her pillow.

Loretta gives a low chuckle. "Minnie, Howard isn't your last chance for love."

"Well, I don't want Whitney to fritter away her chances."

Loretta plays with a quilt tie. "Whitney may like someone else."

I sigh again. "No, for some reason, I've liked Freddy from that night when we looked through Howard's telescope."

"So, what's wrong?!" Minnie exclaims. "You're cute together!"

"Let her tell it," Loretta whispers.

"I told you. Boys like me—because of the way I'm built." I feel my face heat. "I'm not sure it's enough."

"I wish I had more of your—*attributes*," Minnie says. "Boys like that sort of thing."

"But, what if that's all they like? How do I know if a boy likes me for the right reasons?"

Loretta pushes up. "This floor is hard. Let's get up on the beds."

"Who's sleeping where?" Minnie wonders.

"Minnie, you're a squirmer. You can have the fold-out bed Dad brought in."

I look around, imagining the room without the extra bed.

Minnie flops around. "This isn't so bad, Retta."

I wonder if I should call Loretta Retta?

Minnie yawns. "It seems unfair that I'm lying here dreaming of Howard, and he's probably thinking of Cindy Caruthers."

Or he's at the movies with her, but I keep the thought to myself.

Minnie squirms again, and then we hear a little purr. Loretta smiles. "She's like one of those dolls. Lay her down and her eyes close."

I want to talk to Loretta. Of course, I wish I was with Joanie, but Loretta seems wise beyond her years.

As if sensing my thoughts, she says. "I heard you were crying pretty hard in English. I guess it's hard moving across the country?"

I begin to ramble about Joanie and bog down when I get to Daddy. But for some reason, with Loretta cozied up on her pillow watching me, I don't cry.

"My dad died three years ago—December second." I turn and face her. "My world went upside down. Still is sometimes. I—I'm out of balance. Mama is so sad. I miss Daddy and the way things were."

Loretta reaches for my arm. "I'm so sorry, Whitney. Really."

"Thanks."

"I've never even lost a grandparent."

I raise myself onto my pillow, getting it wadded up under my side. "But like I said the other day, I'm so sick of guys making remarks. At my old school, I sorta got used to it, or maybe they let up because—you know—Daddy died—that was really hard at first."

I squeeze the corner of the pillowcase. "But here, it started, and I…" I suck in a long breath. "I guess I hoped—you know, new school, new start."

I give a resigned laugh. "Not like I can announce, 'Hey, my dad died, and I feel like garbage, so don't make jokes about me.'" The second it is out of my mouth, it feels stupid. I don't want pity kindness.

Loretta waits, and the way she waits, I feel I can tell her. "I've never even been kissed." I put my face down and talk to the bed. "It's so stupid to be seventeen and never been kissed."

"And you think Freddy is the guy you may want to kiss?"

"Am I that obvious?"

"Well, let's just say I'm not shocked."

"How do I know he likes me for the right reasons?"

"I'm not sure we can tell. We are all a mix of features, talents, and personalities. I'm not sure your *attributes*," she smiles toward Minnie, "can be separated out. Could you separate Freddy from his piano playing?"

She's so right, and I'm happier than I've been in a long time. Safe.

"At least you're crazy about Freddy. Ronny is OK, but…" She flops onto her back. "Don't tell anyone, but he's kinda boring."

"I'm not a gossip."

"I know you're not. You're a good friend."

133

Loretta talks about wanting to be a reporter, capturing the news with her camera.

"So, journalism. It suits you."

"I started young. My uncle gave me his Rolleiflex and taught me darkroom work."

Minnie makes a little snock noise, and we smile.

We're quiet for a beat. Four o'clock was a long time ago, and I find myself drifting. I may have dozed, and Loretta reaches for the light. "Sleep well, Whitney."

And I do.

Freddy- aaand?

Whitney isn't at lunch, and I have no interest in the cafeteria when Whitney isn't there.

I'm surprised when Loretta brings her lunch bag near. She sorta tips her head toward a table that's just been left vacant. I tell Sam, "I'm going to talk to Loretta," and he goes back to his *Hot Rod* magazine.

Loretta makes a quick job of wiping her place at the table with a damp napkin and dries it with another. She spreads a third napkin on the table and fishes out a small bag of chips. She doesn't say anything and doesn't look like she's gearing up to say anything.

A little uncomfortable, I take a bite of ham and rice. Just a nibble because it doesn't want to stay on the fork. I look up.

"So, how are you doing these days?" she asks, like I'm recovering from an injury or something.

"Fine. I got a new piano." I instantly regret saying that. I doubt Loretta wants to talk about pianos.

"'Nice." She takes out a half-peeled tangerine and lays it on the napkin. About when I think we are just going to sit, she says, "I hear Whitney is knocking out the solos in the Christmas Musical." She puts her hand on the tangerine but doesn't pick it up.

"She's really good." I lean forward. "Her voice is—lovely, and it's a pleasure to play for her—for the musical."

Loretta considers this information, and picks up the tangerine and peels back a strip. "She said you are really good." She breaks the tangerine in half and wipes her fingers.

It seems like it's my turn, and I don't have anything to say, but questions are rattling in my head. *Why are we talking? Did Whitney ask Loretta to talk to me?*

Loretta touches the tangerine with both hands and peers at me through squinted eyes. "It seems like you may have a bit of a crush on Whitney." She puts a slice in her mouth.

I wonder if Loretta and Ally are cousins. Loretta is the opposite of Ally—tall, big-boned. But she, like Ally, doesn't have a hint of shyness.

I shrug, not sure how much I should say.

Loretta, head leaning down toward the tangerine, looks up as if she's peering over her glasses. She isn't wearing glasses. "How *do* you feel about Whitney?"

135

"I don't want her to be unhappy."

I'm pretty sure Loretta has swallowed the tangerine slice, but she pulls in her cheeks as if she's sucking on something. "I didn't ask what you wanted *for* Whitney. I asked how you feel *about* her?" She continues to look at me over the missing glasses, eyes wide.

I sit up, lean my elbows on the table, and then pull back, putting my hands on my thighs. She hasn't moved, but has half closed one eye. It says, 'aaand.'

"Are you going to talk to her? Tell her what I'm thinking. Spread it around?"

Loretta sits up, arms folded. "Freddy, I'm not a gossip. I just don't think you—or Whitney—know what you're doing." Loretta's undecided about what to do with the tangerine.

"The other day, she started crying in English. There was nothing going on, but I heard her make the start of a sob and put my hand on her shoulder."

Loretta's eyes give me the idea this is not a news flash.

"I don't think she likes being touched. At least by me," I say weakly.

Loretta picks white strings from the next slice. "I don't think it's you."

"Whitney put her hand on my hand—like she didn't want me to take it away or appreciated me trying to comfort her." The rice is cold, and I slide the tray to my right. "But then she really started crying. I mean, she couldn't help herself."

Loretta gives a tiny nod, and she's just looking. Her brow wrinkles as if she's undecided. "Freddy—" She leans forward, one hand on the other, almost to the middle of the table.

"Part of it is that she misses her friends. One girl in particular. From what I gather, they share a brain—someone she could tell anything to."

Share a brain makes me chuckle. I imagine Whitney with her friend. It's cute. "Whitney said she just wants to be friends."

Loretta eats the last bite and begins to clean up her place. "So, be her friend. The rest will come later. Just let her be herself. Comfortable with you."

"I don't know if I can make her comfortable."

Loretta reaches out and taps the back of my hand with one finger. Her smile shows white teeth. "Freddy, you've made *me* comfortable." She pulls back and laughs to herself. "I didn't know if I should talk to you, and you've made it OK."

136

Loretta wads her bag tight. "Be yourself. Whitney'll be OK, too."

Whitney- Letters

Dear Whitney,

Sorry to hear about your crying jag. It made me cry- I hate it when you are unhappy.

I had a term paper for History. I did the Teapot Dome Scandal, but you know me. I went to the library early with 3 X 5 cards and then wrote most of the paper. Mom wanted to see it, and of course that brought about a rewrite—3 to be exact. She had me busy every night for a week!

Carl and I have gone out three times, resulting in eleven kisses, but who's counting? I think I'm a good kisser, but what do I know?

Write soon. I enjoy knowing what my wonderful Whitney is up to.

Love,

Joanie

I try three responses. I am so afraid Joanie will feel left out, which is odd, because I'm the one left out of the life we've always had. It doesn't make sense, but I'm afraid I will hurt her feelings. If I could only see her face to face, I would know how my letters "land." After a lonesome cry, I settle on this:

Dear Joanie,

Good luck with the History paper. We know how much you love history. Grrr. Ha.

I went to Loretta's house for a sleepover- Loretta,

138

Minnie, and me. It was really fun. Nothing like all the times we spent together. The only way it could have been better would be for you to have been there. I would love to introduce you to them- to have them know you in person. Loretta and I had a lovely talk after Minnie fell asleep. (She corked out right away.)

I told Loretta about you- she understood.

I'm trying to figure out the Freddy thing. I said he was interested in Ally, the elf girl, but I don't think they are dating. They don't hold hands, and I rarely see them together. It's all so confusing, especially when I have no boy skills.

Love,

Whitney

Freddy- Reduced

On Wednesday evening, we have our first dress rehearsal. Mrs. A says we shouldn't leave too much to the last minute.

Whitney is gorgeous! She's wearing a sweater, matching scarf, and knee socks. I'm inspired and even change the harmony for the last line of her first solo. On the last note, her voice fades with the piano's ring. I watch and let the pedal up at the exact moment she stops. She catches my eye and smiles, and I feel like I could float up beside her.

At the break, Mrs. A comes over. "Show me what you did at the end of 'Christmas Is In the Air.'"

"My piano teacher says to make them wait for the five-seven chord. We all know it is coming, so make them wait." I show her the progression.

"I have to meet this piano teacher of yours in person! I've taught for years, studied music my whole life, but the things you do are so natural and so right. Tasty."

"I'm sure he'd be happy to meet you. I've invited him for opening night."

"That's wonderful, Freddy. Be sure to introduce us."

Whitney is standing near. Mrs. A has a quick word, and then Whitney moves to the bend of the piano. "You inspired me, Freddy. I felt like I was able to float the notes as if they were weightless crystal."

"Your solo inspired me." I stand quickly. "Whitney, can I take you home tonight? I know Laura usually gives you a ride, but—"

She holds my gaze. "Yes."

She said yes! So simple a question, and a simple answer. But it's the best answer I can imagine.

I let Whitney in on the passenger side, and she doesn't slide over, like Ally, but I didn't expect her to. Ally is quick and eager for life. Whitney is cautious, and as I get behind the wheel, I choose cautious.

There's so much I want to say. Want to ask her. Talk to her about—well, I'm not sure what, but I know I want to talk. I get the car started and back out of the parking slot.

Whitney's quiet until we get out of the student lot. "I like the dashboard—so much chrome."

"Yeah. They went all out after the war."

We drive to the first turn. "Can I stop for a moment?" I panic. "Not to neck or anything. I just want to talk without being interrupted."

"Yes."

There it is again—that simple yet complete sentence.

I pull over in front of a vacant lot. "Are you cold? I can leave the engine running so the heater warms up."

"Actually, I'm dying." She unwinds the scarf and lays it between us. She fans her face with both hands.

I turn off the engine and headlights, leaving the parking lights on. "Roll the window down."

"Thank you." She cranks it all the way down and leans her head out. "I may live."

"I hope so," I say quietly and open my window.

Whitney turns back and sits up. The cool air feels good, although the evening is unseasonably warm.

"Whitney, I really like you. I want to take you to a movie or to eat. But if you don't want to, I won't ask again."

"Yes."

"Yes, you want to go somewhere together, or yes, you want me to never ask again?"

She turns toward me and scoots a little closer, her face honest and open—so pretty in the glow of the dash lights. I want to lean over and kiss her so badly I push back against the door, holding myself away.

"I want to try, Freddy." She turns forward. She has a lovely profile. Yes, I notice her whole profile, but I could look at her nose, with just a tiny upturn, forever.

She's struggling to get her words right. "I like you, I do, but I'm afraid. Of—" She turns away.

I wait. Then I lightly touch her left shoulder, and she puts her hand on my hand like she did in English. "It's stupid," she almost whines.

"Not to me. I know you're having trouble, and I'm glad I'm not the cause. If I were a magician, I would fix whatever it is."

Her hand is still on my hand. "You almost *are* a magician—I'm just scared."

"Of what? I'm not going to hurt you. I would do anything to keep you from being hurt."

141

"I know." She turns a bit, staring, seeing nothing. "I think I finally know."

"So, should we go to a movie one of these times?"

"No. Yes. Yes, but first...." Her grip on my hand tightens.

I wait.

"Can we start slow? I don't want to walk around the school holding hands, having to be with each other every second...."

I feel a flash of hurt. "You don't want to be seen with me?"

Her head comes around fast. "No! It's not that at all—but—I told you it's so stupid—could we just really go slow?"

The corners of her eyes are glistening, and I don't want her to cry.

"We can do whatever you want. I mean, can I talk to you at school?"

"Yes, of course!" She's fixated on the dash again, reaching her other hand forward, running a finger up and down the chrome ridges on the radio speaker.

"Oh!" she exclaims, thumping her hand on her lap. "I'm not saying this right." She turns, leaning close. "It's the—touching..."

I start to pull my hand back, but she holds tight, keeping it there.

When I relax, she pats my hand, tears running down her cheeks, and I resist the temptation to brush them away.

She sits for a long moment, struggling. "OK, I'm gonna tell you something that—that casts a shadow on my life—not all the time—but is never gone. For three years, I feel like I'm a curiosity. An object."

I give her shoulder a tiny squeeze—of encouragement, I hope, and her hand tightens on mine. And then she's crying again.

"Whitney! Don't cry! Do you want to go home? I can take you home." I take my hand off her shoulder and dig in my pocket for a clean handkerchief. I carry two these days, just for these moments. I hold it where she can see it.

She takes it and cries harder, and it makes me ache inside. "I don't want to go home yet. I think I have to say this."

But she doesn't. She stares at the dashboard.

"I've been reduced," she sniffs.

I don't understand. "Reduced? You've been on a diet?"

She turns back toward me. "No," she laugh-cries, "I haven't been on a diet."

We sit in silence, and I realize this may take a while.

"Oh!" She says it so loud, I almost startle. "Oh!" Now she's

142

turned toward me. "This is not something I can talk about. At all. Ever."

She takes a shaky breath. "Well, with my friend Joanie, in Ohio. and Loretta is a kind soul. But even with my mom, we—avoid the subject. And yet, for some, it seems to be the *only* subject!"

She's crying again and waves her hands at her front. "I'm more than this!" she squeaks. "Please, Freddy—tell me you are interested in me for more than one small part of me." She choke laughs, "Big part of me? Oh!" And now she's laugh-crying.

"Whitney! No. I mean, yes, I notice your—figure. I won't—can't say I don't. You're—very attractive. But you have big eyes. Cute mouth. Great legs. Delicate hands. You sing like an angel."

She stares at nothing out the windshield.

I try a bit of humor. "You think we should have peanut butter cookies delivered every morning at first period." I grin at her. "I'm thinking of adding milk to the delivery. Cold, not that cafeteria-been-on-ice-for-twenty-minutes stuff."

She leans forward, head almost against the dash.

"Just tell me what to do—what not to do. It's OK. Really. I just want to spend time with you."

Loretta said to be friends, and the rest would come.

She sits back. "Let me lead for a while? If I take your hand, hold my hand? If I were to—" her voice catches, "hug, then hug the way I'm hugging. Only as hard as I hug?"

I'm happy but confused. "Oh, does..." I gesture, pretty sure I shouldn't have. "Does it hurt to... ?"

She's confused for a second and then laughs. "No. Oh! This is such a mess."

She's shaking her head. "Tonight, I will be so embarrassed that we even talked about this. No, it doesn't hurt to hug." She pauses for a split second. "Well, don't crush me *too* hard." She uses both hands to fan herself. "Freddy, I have to get out of this sweater."

"I'll get out, give you some privacy."

"Thank you, you splendid gentleman!" She's looking at me with those big eyes—eyes I could drown in. Then she gently gathers my shirt just below the collar and pulls me ever so slowly until our lips meet. And lavender, and tears, and joy mix and swirl in my heart.

After ten seconds or two years, it doesn't matter, she lets me go and we pull back so our lips are inches apart.

"Freddy, I'm dying in this sweater." She shoos me.

Whitney- Daddy's Car

In all the first kiss scenarios I've played in my mind, I never thought I would grab a guy's shirt and kiss *him!* I must be crazy!

Freddy dutifully gets out of the car, and I start pulling my sweater up. There's room to lean forward, and I'm trying not to stretch the bottom hem. I reach over my shoulders and get it going. Of course, my blouse tries to ride up with it, only stopping at my bra. Freddy's back is still to the window when I finally emerge.

I run my fingers through my hair and tell him I'm ready. While he's getting in, I pull my blouse down for the third time. I'm a mess, but there's no sense in trying to tuck in my blouse until I can stand.

We start for home, and I watch him drive, long piano fingers lightly holding the wheel. He looks over and says, "Better?"

"Better," I breathe. I love his profile.

At home, the garage is open—I suppose Mama is wondering where I am.

Freddy sets the brake, and I slide out, but I don't see Mama. I tuck my blouse in and slide my hand around the inside of my skirt to smooth the tail.

We step into the garage, and Freddy asks, "What's under the cover?"

I don't know if I'm ready for this, but I say, "My dad's car." He doesn't say anything, so I add, "He died December second, three years ago. Sudden cardiac arrest, SCA—a failure in the heart's electrical system."

I have no idea why I am talking like a doctor other than it was this "doctor talk" that took Daddy away from us. "His heart stopped."

"Oh. I am so sorry." He doesn't use it as an excuse to hug me. At the memorial, I wasn't—quite like I am, but I got too many hugs—some that lasted too long.

I stand by Daddy's car. "It's silly because we had it shipped out here, and for what?"

"I didn't know your dad, but I bet he'd be glad you have it here."

"Mama says I should learn to drive it."

"Do you want to?"

"I don't know." I can't stop sighing. I wish I had the sweater on. Not because I'm cold. Just another layer between us. "Neither

Mama nor I can drive a stick." I turn to Freddy with a smile. "Hey, it's a four-speed. I know that much!"

"I could help you practice—in my car. I can help you get your dad's car going—if you—when you're ready."

Mama comes into the garage as I am pulling the cover back. She doesn't say anything.

"Mama, this is Freddy Sanders. Freddy, this is my mom, Mrs. Tate."

"Martha," Mama says.

"Pleased to meet you, Mrs. Tate."

"You're the pianist who's playing for the Christmas musical. Whitney says you play beautifully."

Freddy offers a shy smile. "Mrs. A wrote a beautiful score and lyrics. Whitney—" He pauses to glance at me. "Whitney has a beautiful voice."

Mama gives the moment our secret "I Approve" eyebrow treatment. "Would you like to come in, Freddy? I was just making some cocoa."

I know Mama is a little nervous because she knows I don't drink cocoa with her.

Freddy's eyes flick to me for a split second. "It must be getting late. Maybe another time?"

"You are always welcome." Mama turns on the steps. "I'll let you say good night."

When she's gone, I move close to Freddy. "Thank you. I'll see you in English. We can discuss the milk delivery." I put my hand against his chest so our bodies don't quite touch. But I want to hug. I want to hug him to death.

Freddy doesn't seem to mind, and puts his hand on my left cheek rubbing it softly with his thumb. "I better go." His lips wrinkle into a half smile. "I look forward to important discussions about peanut butter as part of student diet."

I watch as he backs down the drive and listen to the burble of his car as he drives away, thinking, this is too good to be true, while the back of my brain is screaming, *I can't believe I discussed my bustline with a boy!*

> Dear Joanie,
>   Well, I'm in the "Been Kissed" club! "Have
> Kissed" club to be more accurate.

Freddy drove me home after Musical practice and we stopped to talk. You're going to be proud of me, because, if you can believe it, I told him about my— whatever this hangup is, and he was nothing but a gentleman.

But then!! For unknown reasons, I got ahold of a wad of his shirt, up by the top button, pulled him toward me, and kissed him!

To be fair, he was kissing too. I guess your advice paid off, but dragging him in for a kiss? Me?

He was so funny when I said I wanted to take things slow. I told him if I hug (a little bit) he should hug a little- copy what I do.

He got all confused because I'd been talking about my bustline, and he asked if it hurt to hug? Ha!

I was pretty mortified by the time I got home- but not after the kiss- because he's so sweet to me.

I just read through this, and it's a jumble, but my mind is a jumble.

So kisses are 11 to 1, although I imagine you have added a kiss or two?

Love,

Whitney, the Boy Kisser

Freddy- 100%

Dad's been drinking. I can smell it. He's sitting on the couch with Mom, watching TV. "Practice go long?" he asks.

He's not in a mood, but this could be the touch point that blows up the whole evening. "I gave one of the cast members a ride home." I wait, almost holding my breath. Mom smiles.

"A *girl* cast member?" Dad asks.

"Yes. Whitney Tate. She has the lead. You'll really like her voice."

Dad seems stuck for a moment, staring at the TV. "Sounds like a nice girl." He looks up again. "Be careful."

"I am."

And he seems to be satisfied. "I see you did your bag work. Good job."

"Thanks. I have some History to do."

It's only nine-thirty, but it seems like a month since rehearsal was over.

Whitney kissed me.

I force myself to open my binder and review my notes. I'm glad I spent some library time this afternoon because my mind replays Whitney's revelations over and over. She lost her dad! Saying I'm sorry seemed inadequate.

Mom is eating breakfast with Dad. He isn't hung over; I know the signs. I haven't seen her sit at the breakfast table for years.

"I have another rehearsal tonight. We're having extras."

My folks take this in stride. I almost wish they would ask more about Whitney. I want to talk about Whitney.

I take my time eating, and give my teeth an extra good scrubbing before going to my car. The weather has changed; the morning is cold, and the starter is sluggish. It does this sometimes in the winter when I've been driving at night. I let it roll back and pop the clutch.

I've been putting off getting a new battery, so I watch the amps and drive in second gear to keep the generator spinning.

Whitney is at the corner of the building wearing the black sweater with a white blouse. She's like a model or something. "Hi?" she says.

"Hey." I try to sound casual. "You OK?" *Why did I ask that?*

"If you are?"

I want to touch her, but I rock on my heels. "I am more than OK. I had a good time last night."

"Thanks. I was a pretty big mess."

"Maybe I like messes."

She rolls her eyes, and I follow her into the room. At her desk, she goes through her routine of laying out her pencil and pen, notepad and book. Then she turns.

"I was thinking about the end of "Home." Could we pick up the pace in the last verse? I'm holding that G for a long time." She turns further and leans toward me, reducing my brain to mush. "I don't want to run out of air," she whispers.

"Sure. Push the beat, and I'm there with you."

"Thank you." She faces the front.

"When you turned around, I thought you would want to discuss peanut butter. Protein is supposed to be good for brain development."

"Then my brother, Joey, should be a genius." I love the way she talks to her left shoulder. "He went through a whole year of peanut butter and jelly sandwiches."

"I'll have to start bringing you peanuts in the mornings—until our plan is in place. Your brain is going to need it because I'm going to bump you out of top student in here."

Whitney half turns and rolls her eyes. "Talk's big, Mister."

Mr. Sanchez calls roll. Whitney has a beautiful, slender neck.

When our tests are passed back, she gives me an over-the-shoulder look when I whisper, "One hundred, here. How about you?"

She hangs her paper over her back. 100%.

Whitney- The Substitute

After English, Freddy sorta hangs back, and I motion for him to join me. "You don't have to walk ten feet behind me like a servant."

"I like walking with *you.*" He emphasizes the 'you' as if I don't enjoy walking with him, and I smirk.

"So, today, I need to sit with Loretta and Minnie at lunch—I think."

"OK."

"You still hanging around with that guy?" Mike-the-Senior grumbles.

I'm feeling happy and in control. I want to walk over and say, "Yes, because he's a gentleman, Mike. Do you want me to ask him to give you some pointers?" I settle for, "Yup."

Mike sorta drifts away, and I edge closer to Freddy. "You should start a gentleman's comportment class for guys like Mike."

"I could get a big bulletin board and give gold stars."

I nudge his shoulder. "See ya."

I meet Laura outside the room. "You OK?"

"Yes, just waiting for you." She studies my face. "Did I see you walking with Freddy?"

My heart flutters. "Yes."

"'bout time." She turns, and I follow her into the room.

Mr. Tompkins has a substitute who looks like he has been out of high school for twelve minutes.

"OK, sit down and do this worksheet your teacher left for you. No talking."

Laura and I exchange glances; four easy questions won't take long—poor substitute may have to actually teach. Some kids are sniffing the dittos.

Jerry Jackson raises his hand. "I have to use the restroom."

The substitute, who has yet to tell us his name, checks the clock and says, "Hurry back." Hands fly into the air.

Poor substitute—the first sign of weakness, and the sharks are circling.

"I forgot my book—can I go to my locker?" Kandi asks.

"Don't be long. Alright, class. Get to work." Two more kids try the bathroom ploy, but the sub is getting smarter.

I take my time with the worksheet, figuring Mr. Tompkins

might get around to grading it. I secretly suspect he tosses the assignments we don't get back.

Mr. Tyler appears in the doorway with Kandi and Jerry in tow. There is a low "Ooo," which Mr. Tyler silences with a glance. "Mr. Martinson, I found these two necking behind one of the baseball backstops. Is there a reason they are not in class?"

Mr. Martinson makes a weak gesture. "He asked to go to the restroom, and she needed to get her book."

"Miss Price, which desk is yours?"

Kandi points to the first desk in the fourth row.

In two steps, Mr. Tyler is at her desk and holds up Kandi's textbook. "What is this, Miss Price?"

Kandi searches the ceiling for an answer. "My History book?" She has enough sense to take her seat.

A glance sends Jerry to *his* place as well.

Mr. Martinson has shoved the comic book he was reading into his lap. Mr. Tyler sighs and says, "Mr. Martinson, stop by my office before you leave for the day."

At the end of the period, I raise my hand. "Mr. Martinson, what do you want us to do with the worksheet?"

The poor guy has clearly forgotten about the assignment. "Yes. Perhaps you can collect them."

This wasn't what I planned, but like Mr. Martinson, I've made a rookie mistake.

I start moving up and down the rows. As I pass the kid with dirty hair, he pats my behind, and without thinking, I turn and pop the back of his head with the flat of my fingers.

He rubs his head. "What was that for?" he tries, but Mr. Martinson only smiles—at me.

I should wash my hands after that episode, but it was worth it.

I take the papers to Mr. Tompkins' desk. Mr. Martinson is giving me the once-over. I grab a slip of paper from the plastic holder, write Second Period on it, and put out my hand. "The stapler is in the top righthand drawer."

Mr. Martinson stops gawking long enough to fumble for the stapler and hands it to me. I put the note in the upper left corner of the papers and slam the stapler down. I'm immediately sorry because the effect transfixes Mr. Martinson.

I give him a withering look and return to my seat. I wish I had told Freddy I would meet him after this period.

Freddy- Finger Wiggle

"Hey, Freddy," Ally says. "I saw you walking with Whitney. So, you bucked up?"

"Yes, I told her I wanted to take her on a date."

"Good job. I'm proud of you!" She slides in beside me, lengthening her stride.

"How about you and Dean Fagan?"

Ally's face shows a split second of anguish before she recovers. "Too soon to tell." She gives me a crooked grin.

"Have you talked to him?"

"He's so spellbound by Barb Lewis it's hard to strike up a conversation."

"Well, he's driving his ducks to a poor market with Barb." I see Whitney across the quad. "I was in Spanish with her last year. When she's not gossiping, she's *talking* about people."

Whitney wiggles her fingers, waist high, and I give her a dopey wave.

"Well, Barb has Dean's attention. Hey, good to talk," and Ally turns off to Room 314.

At lunch, Sam doesn't have a Hot Rod magazine. "They're going to put me down to the C team, I just know it. They brought Hoffmann up, and he's shooting way better than me."

I consider this information. "Last year, you said you would never go out for a sport."

"Yeah, well, I wanted to be cooler. One of the 'guys'. You know, somebody."

I don't need to ask how that's going because Sam still eats with me. In PE last year, I was better than Sam in basketball, so I was surprised he made the team.

"Have you been practicing—outside of practice?"

"Not really. I want to get the Ford going."

Finally, I say, "You can stay on the Bs—just keep your head in the game." I don't have the same tenor as Coach.

"Yeah. It won't make any difference if I don't get my Algebra grade up. If I get the Ford going, I won't be driving it because I'll be grounded for life."

"You want help? I may have a half hour after school."

Sam brightens. "That would be cool."

151

"Library? Right after school?" *Would Whitney like to come?*

Whitney- Tutor

Minnie is beside herself. "He says he wants to 'take a break' from our relationship!"

Loretta hasn't started peeling her tangerine.

"We have everything in common, and Cindy Caruthers, Cindy Caruthers is…."

I pat her arm.

"I gave him my first *kiss*. I was *his* first kiss. What was I, just a Sierra Stan-ette?"

Loretta leans forward for a stage whisper. "Sierra Stanette? Minnie, what are you even talking about?"

"Sierra Stan is the test dummy they use for crashes. They put one in a car and crash it. Then, they see how the dummy fared in the test. Expendable! Apparently, I'm expendable."

I put my straw in my milk, and Loretta wipes her tangerine fingers.

"Cindy Caruthers doesn't even know which way **north** is! Retta! Tell Whitney!"

Loretta gives me a sheepish look. "I didn't mean to gossip—I thought I was helping."

"Tell her, Retta!"

Loretta is concentrating on the first peel, so Minnie charges on.

"Oh, what's the use—they were beginning a map unit, and Mr. Branson asked if anyone knew which way north is. Cindy raised her hand, and he called on her, and you know what she did?"

There's a pause, and Minnie gestures to Loretta.

Loretta puts down a peel and points toward the ceiling. It takes me a second, and then I almost snort my milk.

"She thinks north is up," Minnie wails. "Oh, Howard."

Freddy sorta cruises by me after lunch. "Hey, I'm going to help Sam with algebra in the library—after school. You want to come?"

I perk up at the idea. "Sure!"

"Excellent!"

We are walking about three feet apart.

A girl walks between us, so I move closer. Out of the corner of my mouth, I say, "You can walk beside me."

"Good to know. By the way—the little hand ripple across the quad this morning—very cute."

"Oh, yes, it's the 'Hi, I'm happy to see you' without letting everyone know I'm happy to see you. I call it a tickle wave." I put my hand out as if I'm going to tickle his side, and he jumps away.

"Oh, are we a little ticklish, Freddy Sanders?"

He straightens his jacket. "Nah, you just startled me." He slows. "How would it be if I gave you a ride home today?"

"I'd like that." We walk in happy silence toward the locker rooms. When the sidewalk splits, Freddy stops. "Hurdles today?"

I make a face. "Yeah, last day of the unit. I'll be glad when it's over."

"Yeah, last day for basketball. See you out there. Maybe I can figure out an understated guy wave."

"I can't promise I can watch all the time, but any effort will be appreciated."

We separate, and I get into the two bras and pin the gap closed.

The boys are on the courts when we start for the field. The coach tells us to jog, which I don't like doing this close to the boys. Too many are watching, but only one gives me a waist-high palm with fingers up. I don't know how it is possible to blush when jogging, but I manage.

I come in fourth in the low hurdles. I'm glad the coach set them up on the far side of the track.

Freddy and Sam are in the library when I get there, and I approach cautiously, but Freddy pats the tabletop next to him, and I slip into a chair.

"Sam, you know Whitney, right? There's a rumor she's an algebra ace." He gestures to himself. "I am an ace as well, but Whitney is lightning fast."

Apparently, Freddy's of the opinion that I'm good at everything, and even though I'm not, I appreciate the compliment. I brush his hand, which is further away than I thought, so it's almost like I batted him. He locks our pinkies together for just a second, and my pinky gives his pinky a squeeze.

Sam's problems require building a formula, and I can see he has trouble with abstracts. The first is the old handshake question with sixty people in the room.

Freddy tries, and poor Sam is floundering. I go around and lean over Sam's paper, asking questions like Mr. Hodges did in Ohio.

Sam is staring, and I tap his paper. "Eyes down here."

When Sam is able to write the formula, Freddy winks, I blush, and Sam says, "You should be a teacher, Whitney."

I lead Sam through the rest of his problems. He's not there yet, but the light is coming on.

Freddy- Group One Battery

"Hey, I have a thrilling excursion for you. This could be a banner experience."

Whitney's intrigued.

"OK, first, do you need to get home right away?"

"No. Mama had the day off."

"OK, my car's battery is on its last legs."

Whitney says, "I liked the pinky hold in the library," and holds out her pinky. I loop my little finger in hers, and we walk toward the student parking lot.

"So, are we going to a battery store?"

"Well, I'm not exactly a rich man, but here is the exciting part. Ted Crawford told me about a place that sells rebuilt batteries for five bucks."

"I'm guessing this is a good price?"

"Yes." We get to the car, and I open Whitney's door. When I get in, she says, "I like this going slow—but I feel close to you—so," and Whitney slides across. It's Santa Anna weather, and there is a pop when our arms get close. We both jump.

"You are electric." I hit the starter, and the engine makes two weak turns followed by clicking. "Oops."

Whitney wrinkles her lips. "Apparently, the battery isn't as electric as we are. Now what? The jumper thingy?"

"You claim to be a good runner, right?"

"Freddy, I am not running to the battery store."

"No, just questioning your physical conditioning."

She gives me an eye roll.

"All we have to do is get the car rolling, I jump in, pop the clutch, and away we go. You'll notice I backed in this morning in anticipation of this situation."

"Ah, tricky guy. You invite me to the library, woo me with compliments, and then offer an exciting excursion, so I'll push you to the battery store."

"Clever, don't you think?"

"So what do I do?"

"Go to the back, and when I say push, push. Watch where your feet are going so you don't slip."

She follows me out on my side and we walk to the back. "Aw, I

156

love the little Mayflower cut into the glass." She traces the center tail light. "I hate to get hand prints on your shiny paint."

"Don't worry." I take the car out of gear and turn on the ignition. "Ready?"

"I'm already pushing! Are you?"

I let off the brake and push hard on the door frame. The car begins to roll, and I wait until it is going faster. I jump in, jam it in low, let out the clutch, and the engine sputters to life.

Whitney comes around, gets in on her side, touches the dash, and slides over. "So, how was my pushing?"

"You are the best girl pusher I have ever had help get the car going."

"Whoa. How many times have you had girls push your car?"

"Just one, but you set the bar very high."

"Compliments, compliments."

When I pull into Baker's Batteries, Whitney says, "Should I come in?"

"We're getting to the fun part!"

Whitney steps carefully around some unidentified goo in the parking place next to us. The shop smells like grease, rubber, and chemicals. She wrinkles her nose, and I nudge her shoulder lightly.

A man comes to the counter, wiping his hands. "What can I do for you?" He's looking at Whitney.

"I need a battery," she says and gives him a big smile.

"You came to the right place." The guy is thirty, but he's enjoying Whitney.

"We need a battery for the Plymouth." Whitney jerks her thumb toward the door.

"Forty-seven," I say.

The fellow puts the rag on the counter. "Six volt, Group One."

"Yes," Whitney says. While the guy is gone, she mutters under her breath, "I wouldn't have stood for a Group Two. A Group Two would never do."

"Agreed. Group Twos are over-rated, although I do appreciate Group Threes with red lettering," and this gets me a smile. I love her smile.

The fellow hefts a battery onto the counter. "Five bucks, one year guarantee." He's still talking to Whitney.

"Do you have any two-year warranties?"

"Sure. For ten dollars, I'll guarantee this battery for two years." He smiles.

Whitney gives him the head-tipped-to-one-side treatment.

"Tell you what, you want two years, you can have two years. Want me to put it in?"

I'm not sure I want this guy touching my car, so I say, "I'll take care of it. Let me get the old one out." I get my wrench and make quick work of bringing the old battery inside.

"Yes, there are still tickets available for both Friday and Saturday." Whitney glances at the man's wedding ring. "Your wife would love it." She plops two tickets on the counter. "So what'cha say? Friday?"

I stand enchanted as Whitney collects two dollars.

"I hope to see you there, Cliff."

Cliff smiles. "You're OK, kid, you're OK." He gives me a sideways glance. "Stick with this one. Ten more minutes, and she would have me giving you the battery."

Whitney feigns surprise. "Whatever do you mean?"

The car starts right up, and she hands me the two-year warranty.

"You made quite the impression on Cliff—and me. I've never seen you work your wily ways."

A tiny bit of pink shows on Whitney's cheeks. "Listen, if I have to put up with comments about how I look, I might as well get a few perks." She's quiet for a while. "Besides, you can tell."

I'm unsure what she means. "Tell what?"

"Cliff's a good guy—enjoying the scenery and having fun with the banter." She turns on the radio. "Besides, I don't want to be pushing this car every time we go somewhere."

Whitney- Fun Effect

Dear Whitney,

Kissed Freddy! Wow. I am so proud of you.

Between the lines of your letters, I knew Freddy was more than one of our childhood crushes. I would love to meet him. Do you have a picture? Of you two together? I long to see my friend's California face.

I got a B+ on the History term paper- not too bad for me. Mom took it in stride, but we know she was hoping for an A.

It finally turned cold, and we are <u>not</u> in sweaters. I may be a little jealous of California weather, but can't imagine a winter without snow.

Carl and I are no longer dating. It's OK. I am a little sad, but we just didn't have that much fun together. Between you and me, he's kinda boring. Nice, but he hardly talks and then only about science fiction.

I read your letters to the gang. Well, not the parts that I know you want to keep between us. They say hi.

Write me when you get time.

Love,

Joanie

I fold the letter and stick it in my purse because Freddy is here.

Mama is happy to see Freddy again. Joey is ecstatic to have another male person around. He tows Freddy away to his room, and Freddy doesn't seem to mind. *This guy is growing on me!*

"Freddy seems like a very nice boy."

"He really is."

"And he's a gentleman when you're alone?"

"Very much so."

"Help me with the salad." She points to the lettuce.

Freddy sits by Joey at the table and listens to endless chatter about army tanks, Joey's latest thing. Mama and I watch, loving the moment.

When we're done eating, Freddy takes his and Joey's plate to the sink and starts to run the water.

"You don't have to do dishes, Freddy," Mama says, but Freddy says, "You cooked, Mrs. Tate. Put your feet up."

Freddy washes, and I dry. I can't believe I am so at ease with a boy.

Mrs. A is pleased with the dress rehearsal and stops after one run-through. She has cupcakes and punch for us, and we sit in groups, chatting.

Freddy moves to the piano and plays "Up On the House Top," and we sing. Laura and I put our heads close and harmonize. Mrs. A takes small books of carols from a box and gives us each a copy.

For the next twenty minutes, I enjoy the glowing eyes of everyone in the cast.

Tucker, from Theater, turns out to have quite a bass voice. Mrs. A says, "Tucker, I think you should consider joining Choir! Organizing backstage and opening the curtain may be a waste of your talent."

Tucker manages to say, "I sing with my family. Bluegrass."

"Do you play an instrument?"

He takes a sip of punch. "Guitar, banjo—a little fiddle."

"You must come by after Christmas and play for A Capella. I'm sure we would enjoy it."

"Yes, Ma'am."

Freddy does 'Rudolph' and teaches us a jazzy variation of the bridge. Singers jump to parts in their range, and harmony fills the room.

"Kids, we're going to have a short sing-along at the end of our performances. On 'Rudolph,' I'll turn at the end, lead you in Freddy's bridge variation, and then lead the audience in singing the last verse again."

Mrs. A and Freddy exchange a conspiratorial look, and it dawns on me they've planned this.

We clean up, and Freddy and I walk out together. At the car, I say, "Wasn't that fun!"

"Well, we don't know if the car will start. The fun effect of the evening may be downgraded if you have to push again." He hits the starter, and the car comes to life. He turns his head toward me. "Yes, I am having a great time."

"We got out early, so can we stop somewhere for a few minutes?" I say. "Not to neck Just to—be."

He pulls over at the vacant lot and shuts off the engine. He clicks on the radio, adjusting the volume low, and we listen to "Mr. Sandman."

I sit back, not caring how things look. I don't even feel the need to cross my arms. I reach for Freddy's hand.

"Is this OK?" I ask. "I'm getting there. My—reluctance—has nothing to do with you. I—it's just so hard." The words seem inadequate.

"I guess I've been lonesome. I mentioned Joanie the other night. We've known each other since grammar school. I would give anything to hear her voice. To have a chance to talk to her."

Without thinking, I take the letter out and hold it to my breast, think better of it, and lay it in my lap.

Freddy reaches for the letter, and I let him take it. "Richardson?" he asks.

"Yes. Joanie Richardson."

"I wish I could meet her. I can tell she's special."

"She is. Tall, long red hair." Joanie's smile flickers in my memory. "But I'm making a new life here. I mean, we aren't ever moving back." *Ohio would not have Freddy Sanders.*

Freddy brushes my hand with the envelope, and I take it. It's nice to be sharing Joanie with him.

"Anyway, we're doing OK, aren't we? I don't want you to think I'm a bigger mess than I am."

Freddy clicks on the parking lights, the dash glowing. He twists the knob so it is only a hint of light. "My dad is an alcoholic. He's not drinking right now." There's a long pause. "This is new, so I'm not sure how long it will last."

I squeeze his hand.

"Sometimes, he knocks my mom around."

I try to suppress a gasp and fake a cough, but I know I gave myself away. Freddy tenses for a second, and I put my right hand on

161

our hands.

We sit, Freddy restless.

"He's had me boxing since I was eight. He has a routine I do every day except Sunday. Punching bag, situps, pushups—you know."

I rub our two hands slowly, letting him know I'm on his side.

"My hand. You were so great. The ice didn't take the pain away, but the fact that you got it for me…" He turns part way toward me.

I've slouched down, but I don't even care.

"He was in one of his moods. When it started, I could tell he had a bee in his bonnet over something and wouldn't let go until he hurt someone." Freddy reaches around with his left hand and moves my face so I'm looking at him, at those dark—sad right now—eyes in the dim light.

"You get so you can tell. It's not something you can describe. You just know about a person. Maybe like when you told me you knew Cliff was OK."

I want to say, "Go on," but I wait.

"So he was in that mood and started in on Mom, complaining that the pork chops were dry." He winces. "It was ten-thirty. We ate at five-thirty." His voice catches.

I don't stop looking at him. I hardly blink.

"He tried to hit Mom, and—well, I decked him. He had a bruise on his cheek, and I had—the knuckle."

He's peering at me so intently I want to kiss him, but can tell he's not done.

"You have to know, I hated it." He breaks our gaze and stares beyond me. "I'm not bragging, but I didn't hit him as hard as I could." He still has his hand on my cheek, and I wait for him to look back.

And, after a sigh, he does. He comes so close I can feel his breath on my face. "I hate it, Whitney. I'm not a mean guy. I'm not a fighter—but if this upsets you—scares you, I will leave you alone."

"I'm not scared of you." I sit up, and as I did on our first kiss, I gently pull him until our lips touch. The kiss is soft—comforting.

"Whitney, when we were—trying to figure out being friends, all I wanted was to spend time with you. I'm happy being here with you."

"Me, too." I squeeze his hand. "But, I better get home."

At the door, I want to swoop Freddy into my arms, but I settle for a light kiss. He looks straight into my eyes and says, "You are absolutely lovely, Whitney."

162

Freddy- Punching Bag

Dad's pickup isn't in the driveway. Mom's on the couch, and her eyes and nose are red.

"Dad out?" I don't say at the bar.

She nods. "He thinks he can handle it."

"Do you think he can handle it?"

"He's trying, Freddy. He's had a hard week at work."

I've read about this enough to know about enablers. "Mom, you can't defend him. Making excuses doesn't help."

She dabs her eyes. "I know. I wonder if it's something I've done? Am I too plain? Not interesting?"

"Mom, you're the best looking of all the moms, and you're fun. It's not you."

We sit in silence.

I catch her eye. "I thought it was *me*. I thought if I boxed good enough, got better grades, he would quit drinking." I lean my elbows on my knees. "It's not me either, Mom. Dad drinks. Period."

"I know, but he doesn't mean anything by it."

I feel the old frustration building up. "No, Mom. I cannot let him knock you around just because he's having a tantrum."

"Freddy! Your father doesn't have tantrums—he gets—"

"Oh, he doesn't lay on the floor and pound his fists, but when he gets mad, and yells, and hits things—people—that's a tantrum."

She sighs.

"He's made me spar with him since I was eight. A little kid. And for a long time, I couldn't handle him. But this year." I pick my words carefully. "I've been pulling punches."

"I don't like the boxing."

"Well, I don't like it much either, but he trained me, and if he tries to hit you, he's gonna have to get through me."

"I don't want you to get hurt."

"Rather you get hurt?" I struggle with the next part. "When I knocked him on his k'up'a the other night, I hardly punched him. If I would have hit him hard, I would have broken his cheekbone."

"I don't like this kind of talk."

"I'm sorry. I can't watch him hitting you. He can punch the lath and plaster. Or go punch the bag in the garage. But *you* are *not* his punching bag. You have to get over that idea." I stand. "And so will he

163

if he hits you again." I start toward the hall but look back. "The whole problem with being a tough guy is there is always someone who is tougher."

I hear his truck door shut. "I'll be in my room." But I leave the door ajar.

At first it's quiet, and then I hear, "Why's the clothes basket in the living room?"

I move up the hall.

"I was folding clothes. I just put them away."

"Well, put the basket in—" He notices me leaning on the wall at the end of the hall. "Go back to bed, Freddy!"

I fold my arms.

"You hear me? Go back to bed."

I don't look away.

"This is my house! I won't have your mouth!"

"Haven't said a word, Dad." It's odd—I'm not afraid.

He comes toward me, a little off-kilter, but I don't move, and he stops. "Did you hear me?!"

"Yes."

Mom's watching but not moving.

"Then get out of this room!"

"No. Not until you calm down."

"Why, you little..." He can't find the word he wants, and I stand up straight.

"Don't make me *put* you in your room."

"No, Dad. Not until I know Mom's safe."

He seems to weigh his options. "You leave your mother out of it!"

"No. Mom is the whole point here. You can't come home drunk and take it out on her."

"I'll take it out on whoever I want! This is my house!"

I move a half step toward him. "Dad, I don't think you want to try."

"Oh, we're gonna try. Come on, get in the garage! Get the gloves on." He's doing that gravelly yell.

"No, Dad, you're drunk."

"I can whip you drunk!" He catches his leg on the corner of the coffee table, and a flower vase falls over. "Get out there."

I make a quick decision—get him out of the house. "OK."

He storms through the door to the garage, and I follow. We slip on the gloves, and he takes a swing at me before I can even pull my

164

right glove on. I duck easily and half catch him, and this inflames him.

"Put 'em up." He squares off, and I catch the cuff in my teeth and work the glove on, never taking my eyes off him. He takes a wild swing, and I lean back. "Fight, you little chicken." He gets his feet under him and lands a jab that snaps my head a little. "Come on!"

I give him a quick left and he staggers back three steps before he catches himself. I let my hands drop to my sides.

"Fight! Come on. One lucky hit, and you think I am done?" He dances toward me and tries three jabs. One catches my shoulder, and another is coming hard.

From instinct, I fake a left, blocking, and the right sends him into the cabinets. "Come on, Dad. You can't beat me anymore."

He growls and dances close. He tries a punch to my gut, but I block it, and he hugs me, pounding my side, trying to knock the wind out of me. After three hard punches, I realize he may be drunk but still has his strength, so I bring my arms up and push him back. "Let it go, Dad!"

He comes up from below with an uppercut that is going to do damage. I dodge to the left, he misses, and I put him on the floor with a right followed by a left. He lands hard, starts to push up, and then stays down.

"You had enough?"

He squints at me from one eye. He puts out his hand, we lock wrists, and I pull him up. Before I know it, he pops me in the solar plexus. I gasp and return one to his gut, one to his sternum, and one square in the face. His head whips back, and I follow, gloves up. "Stop it, Dad, or you are going to spend all night on the floor."

For a minute, I think he's going to try again, but he walks over to the box and struggles to get his gloves off. I put mine in the box, and we start for the door to the house.

At the steps, he spins and tries to punch my face. He almost catches my ear and before I know it, I hit his right shoulder hard enough to spin him, and he stumbles against the steps. He manages to slide into a sitting position, breathing hard.

He holds the shoulder and slurs, "Now that wussa punch. I didn't think you had it in you."

"Well, I do. I'm not even out of breath. I can punch harder than that for twenty minutes and still do my sits and pushups."

The air seems to go out of him. He gets to his feet and turns toward the door, but not before I say, "I'm serious, Dad. No more punching anything unless you want one that will make that last one feel

165

like a feather hit you. I wasn't even trying." And it's the truth.

Whitney- Order Up!

Three of my fishermen are back, and I pour coffee and bring tea for the guy in the fisherman's hat. "So what kind of fish do you fellows catch?"

Heads come up, smiling that I am striking up a conversation. These guys are OK. The man with the fish hooks on his hat takes it off, revealing a thick crop of gray hair. "We're gonna try our luck up at Deep Creek."

I shake my head in a question.

"'bout two hours or so, up by Lake Arrowhead."

"Pretty fancy hooks in your hat."

He removes a fuzzy one. "I tie these flies."

"Aww, that's cute."

He holds it out, and I take it gingerly. "Am I holding a hook that's been in some fish's mouth?"

"Never been in the water. Made that one last night..." When I hand it back, he says, "I'm Jim." He gestures with his head. "Pete and Duke—Steve isn't here yet."

Jim concentrates on hooking the fly back on his hat, and Pete says, "Jim's flies are first class. First-class lawyer—catching fish—hmm." He gives Jim a playful fist on the shoulder, and Jim gives me a sheepish grin.

"So, you ready to order, or are you waiting for Steve?"

"We'll wait a bit if it's OK?"

I look around and say, "First ones here, but once there are a hundred waiting outside, I'll have to toss you guys out."

Jim has his hat back on and chuckles. Steve arrives, and I take their orders.

My section begins to fill, and I hurry, pouring coffee and taking orders. We have a substitute cook, and he's slow.

My fishermen are getting antsy, and I reach up and spin the order wheel. "What's going on? This order has been here for twenty minutes. They were the first ones here."

There's no answer, so I pull the order and go around to the kitchen half door and almost run into Eddie. "What's going on? My Table Four were first here, and the order was still on the wheel."

Eddie's drinking coffee. "Substitute cook—just slow this morning."

He starts pushing the gate toward me, and I put up my hand.

167

"Eddie! I have three tables waiting!"

He takes another sip of coffee. "Don't know what we can do about it." He starts to push through, but I have my leg against the gate. "Excuse me! I'm going for a smoke."

I lean closer than I like. "Eddie, you need to set that coffee down and start the second grill."

Eddie blinks as if this has never occurred to him. "Listen Sweet Cheeks, let's not forget who's boss here."

The *Sweet Cheeks* thing sets me off, plus the father from Table Twelve has gotten up and is talking to Francie.

"Eddie, go cook. And start with this order." I wave it in front of his face. "Don't make me come in there and do it for you." I can't believe I just said that.

Eddie considers the situation, notices I have squared off in front of the door, and grabs an apron off the hook.

I check my tables, apologizing for the delay.

At the coffee, Viv sidles up to me. "Good job," she whispers. "Like I told you, you have to treat him like a little kid."

"Order UP!" Eddie calls and slaps a plate of biscuits and gravy up on the counter. The order wheel is empty.

Pleasant surprise—Eddie can cook.

When I take the orders to my fishermen, Jim's tea is empty. "Sorry it's so slow today."

Steve says, "I love the way you got after Eddie. He's an OK guy but not exactly a self-starter."

I'm embarrassed that they heard me and worried that my voice carried to the floor.

I fumble with Jim's water pitcher, and Steve says, "Hey, Kiddo. Don't worry. I was over getting more cream."

"Oh, I am so sorry. I'll pay more attention."

Jim looks up from his egg. "Steve went over to honey up to Viv. She's his wife."

"Good to know!" and I make a beeline for the hot water and a teabag.

"Order up," Eddie calls.

"I'm sailing across the floor when I see Freddy come in. He gives me a waist-high finger wiggle. I pause, and my cheeks warm.

"Friend of yours?" Jim asks when I put the hot water down.

"Yeah—Freddy Sanders. He's really nice." I'm glowing all sorts of red.

"Good for you, Kiddo," Steve says. "I know him from the

hardware store. Good kid."

Freddy sits at the counter. Viv starts to ask him what he wants when I gently put my shoulder against hers. "OK if I wait on this guy?"

Viv sings a drawn-out "Aaaa-ha." She smiles at Freddy. "I like you already, fella. You have good taste in women."

I give him a napkin, silver, and a menu. "I'll be right back. We're swamped."

I'm moving to pick up the order for Table Three when I hear him say, "I hope this place has peanut butter cookies."

Man, I like this guy.

My fishermen leave such a big tip, I'm embarrassed, and it's already six-thirty. They won't get to the creek until after eight. I hurry back to Freddy.

"OK," I gasp. "Sorry to make you wait."

"I don't mind waiting on you, but do you have a complaint box?"

I half-close one eye like Loretta. "No peanut butter cookies?"

"Exactly." He points to the bottom of the menu. "Just tea. I ate breakfast at home."

Freddy came to see me!

Freddy- A Wingnut

Whitney looks so cute in the apron—breathtaking. And she turns a bit pink when I give her the wave she taught me.

She's busy, and I go to the counter. A woman with Viv on her name tag says, "What can I get you, Hon?" I'm about to answer when Whitney hurries over. She has a terrific smile.

We do the peanut butter cookie thing, and I could talk to her for the next fifty years. I take a couple of swallows of tea, and when she's back, I get a dollar bill out of my pocket.

She starts to reach for it. "Let me get you change."

I keep my hand on the bill. "Nope. I'm good."

"Freddy, the tea is thirty cents!"

"The dollar's for you. If you decide you want to give thirty cents to the diner, it comes out of *your* pocket." I pat her fingers as she reaches for the bill.

I hustle down the street to the hardware. As I slide back the accordion gates around the cement, I hope the guy with the station wagon hasn't decided to pour a new slab for a shed. The morning is brisk, and I help Saturday Fixers get what they need.

At noon, Whitney walks in, still in her apron, and my heart goes into overdrive. Chuck goes to help her, but she points at me. She stands back as I ring up the molly bolts and one of the dime screwdrivers in the number ten coffee can by the cash register.

Whitney approaches, a wry grin on her face. "Mr. Hardware Man, I heard you helping that nice lady find molly bolts for her husband, but I'm wondering—do you name all your bolts after women? I mean, do you have any Whitney bolts?"

I think fast. "Alas, our bolts only go through the letter T. We have some first-rate toggle bolts."

"Oh, whatever am I to do? Here I am, a damsel in distress with a handsome Mr. Hardware Man, only to learn that he can't help me."

"Well, if you are looking for something with a W, can I show you some wingnuts?"

Whitney stops the game for a moment. "Wait, there are *wingnuts?*"

"Yes."

"What, like little bolt tighteners with *wings?*"

"Exactly. Can I show you a few?"

"Lead the way, Mr. Hardware Man. This I have to see!"

I add, "We also have a great selection of washers."

"For clothes?"

"No, only for bolts—especially the kind with wingnuts."

"So, no laundry detergent?"

"No, Ma'am."

The ma'am gets me a playful push. "Hey, Mr. Hardware Man, I'm not thirty!"

"No, Ma'am." I hand her a five-sixteenth wingnut. "These are of the highest quality."

"I think it's cute. It's all shiny, and you don't even need to wrench it."

Wrench it makes me smile. I fish a two-inch bolt from the bin and hold it up for her to try. "Like clock hands go," I tease.

"I know which way to twist a bolt!"

"Wingnut."

Whitney lifts her chin, and I'm glad she's not that short—it would be easy to tilt my head slightly and kiss her.

"I have to say, I thought you were putting me on." She bats an ear of the wingnut, and it twirls down the threads. "Very smooth. I'll take it."

"Really?" I didn't think she'd go this far. "Then you're gonna need a washer!" I scoop a flat washer from the bin.

I reach for the bolt and remove the wingnut, my hand brushing hers. I slip on the washer and give the wingnut a twist.

She leans close, giving me a whiff of bubble bath. "I like the service I'm getting, Mr. Hardware Man."

We go to the register, and I ring up eight cents.

She hands me a dime. "I had a big tip this morning. I should have gotten a matched brace of wingnuts!"

"Would you like a sack?"

"I like it just the way it is," and out she goes.

Whitney- The Gown

Mrs. Fillmore is surrounded by material and boxes.

I stand in front of the full-length mirror. "The aprons you altered are perfect—thank you."

"Just you wait until you see these." She takes down a hanger from a hook on the inside of the closet door. "Feel this material. It has a little body but isn't stiff. Try it on."

I slip it on and tie it behind me.

"Oh my, oh my." Mrs. Fillmore has her cheeks between her hands, leaning back. "Look in the mirror. What do you think?"

The material breaks over my top parts. The taper increases the effect of my waist. I turn sideways.

I catch her eye in the mirror. "Do I look like I am trying to look sexy?" I turn sideways again.

Mrs. Fillmore slips up behind me and puts a hand on each upper arm. "You look lovely, Whitney."

"But not too sexy?"

"Well, you have a lovely figure. The apron is just a cover."

I am undecided, and Mrs. Fillmore says, "I know, Dear. It took my Gina a while to get—used to herself, but…."

She turns me and looks me in the eye. "You have nothing to be ashamed of. This is the way God made you. Do you remember raising your hand and asking God to give you big bosoms?"

I laugh a weak, "No."

"Put your arms over your head. We don't want it tugging at your waist."

When I put my hands up, she inspects the result. "Almost perfect." She walks round me, hand on her chin. "The ties are staying parallel to the floor."

"OK, here you are." She hands me two more hangers.

"Mrs. Fillmore, you have to let me pay you."

A horrified look comes to her face. "Absolutely *not!* I love to sew! It's more fun sewing for someone. I make aprons for the church bazaar, but I don't get to think how to make them fit best because I don't know who will buy them."

I start for the bedroom door when Mrs. Fillmore says, "Wait a moment. I have some other things here."

I lay the pinafores over the back of a chair and turn.

She's holding up a beautiful red gown. "Do you like it?"

"Oh, Mrs. Fillmore!" I've never seen anything like it. It's plain yet elegant.

"Try it on. I think it will fit like a glove."

I've been shy about dressing in front of anyone, but Mrs. Fillmore is so natural that I slip out of my jeans and blouse.

"I see you have a well-fitting bra. Very important. You don't want anything squishing out in front of your armpits. Still, I would stay away from sleeveless."

"I had a wonderful friend, Joanie, in Ohio who helped me figure out bras. She had me on a bus to downtown Columbus at eight in the morning, and we didn't get home until after seven that evening. She made me try endless bras before she was satisfied."

Mrs. Fillmore gives me a sad smile. "You miss Joanie, don't you?"

"You have no idea."

When the dress is zipped, I'm alarmed. "Oh, I don't know!" I look at myself sideways in the mirror. "I'm huge," the last word trailing off.

Mrs. Fillmore comes to stand beside me. "I know, Honey, but if we make it looser, you're still there."

My voice has gone to a whisper. "I know. I just wish...." She's patting my arm, and I admit, "It is so pretty. I've never had anything so beautiful. How do you do it?"

"Well, remember, I did measure you. But there are some tricks. This is a square neckline, but I kept it about an inch higher than the pattern. It still draws the eye to your neck but stops before there is too much going on below." Her eyes meet mine in the mirror. "Give yourself time to get used to it."

"OK."

Mrs. Fillmore is looking at the hem above my ankle. "Hold still. This is about an inch too short."

I stand while she pinches here and measures there. She spends a lot of time with the back. "You always stand nice and straight—we don't want enough space here for some boy to put a frog down your back."

This gives me the shivers, and I giggle.

After trying on two more dresses, one that was Gina's, we go to Mrs. Fillmore's kitchen, and have cookies and tea on delicate china.

We sit in pleasant silence, and I think about Freddy. I want to see him. I'm the one who asked Freddy to let me lead—decide how things go. Should I call? Is it improper to call? If his mom answers, will she think I'm too forward? What if his dad answers?

When I get ready to leave, I hug Mrs. Fillmore for a long time. "You don't know how much this means to me."

Whitney- I Was Thirteen...

Loretta and Minnie put their bags on the floor of my room.

"Sorry I don't have as much room as we had at Loretta's."

"We didn't come to sleep that much anyway," Minnie says.

Loretta gives Minnie an eye-roll. "Joey is cute," she says to me.

"He can be a pest, and I told him to stay out while we are in here." Loretta listened to endless submarine talk at supper.

"Tonight, I am not going to mention Howard," Minnie declares, and Loretta gives me a wink. "I wouldn't waste my time even giving him the time of day. He's already moved on to Patti something."

There is a long pause and I say, "I know two Patti's."

Minnie puts her glasses aside. "She's the tall one who rats her hair to the size of a space helmet."

I have Patti in typing. "Isn't she the Junior Class President?"

"I suppose." Minnie digs in her bag and drags out her blue bear. "I even voted for her!"

"Well, now you know better," Loretta jokes.

Minnie puts a pillow between her back and my desk. "Howard is fickle."

I decide to help Minnie not talk about Howard. "Our neighbor —I wear her daughter's clothes—made me a dress."

Minnie hugs the bear. "Show us."

I blush, but Loretta's kind smile gives me courage.

"OK, but please don't say anything to anybody. I'm not sure about this."

I slip off my jeans and sweater by the closet door.

"Whitney, you really have a figure!" Minnie exclaims.

"*Minnie*," Loretta warns.

I'm bright red and hesitate.

"Only if you want to," Loretta says quietly, giving Minnie a severe look.

I step into the dress behind the cover of the partially opened closet door. I hear Loretta whisper, "Minnie, you really need to think before you open your mouth."

I pull the side zipper up and step out.

"Oh, Whitney," Loretta says. "Wow."

I want to bring my arms up to cover myself. "Too wow?"

Loretta is on her feet. "Gorgeous."

"But?"

Loretta chooses her words carefully. "It is stunning."

I'm not convinced and hang the dress back in my closet.

Not taking any more chances with Minnie's comments, I pull my PJs top over my head, slip out of my bra and wrap in my blanket.

"I'm sorry," Minnie says. "I meant it as a compliment. I know you are sensitive…."

"It's OK." I sigh. "It's just such a pain, being this way. *This* being the first thing people seem to notice."

"Well, I really am sorry."

I wish I would get over being teary. "When this first started to happen…." I pause and then rush ahead, "Really happening—it was after Daddy died, and I thought if I lost weight, 'they' would stop growing."

Neither of my friends say anything.

"I mean, I was thirteen." I turn toward them. "I didn't feel like eating, anyway—but I thought…." I put my head down. "I was so stupid."

"It's OK," Loretta whispers.

"So, I lost about six pounds. I was skinny as a rail, except…."

"My mom is always on my case about eating right," Minnie says. "I always have to eat a hot lunch."

Loretta shushes her. "Let her tell her story."

"Mama didn't say anything. I don't think she noticed. She was in horrible shape—especially at first, after Daddy. But then she couldn't ignore it because I hadn't been eating breakfast—and not much the rest of the time—and I keeled over in history class."

"Oh, Whitney." Minnie crawls toward me and puts her arm around my shoulder. Loretta reaches for my hand.

"The nurse got to the bottom of it pretty fast, Mama was *informed*, and off to the doctor I went."

Loretta is rubbing the back of my hand.

"Thanks." In sudden anger, I thump the other hand on the floor. "My bra had to go to the first hooks and…" Suddenly tired, I ball up on the floor. "And it was getting too small for what I was trying to get rid of."

They are rubbing and patting, and I lie curled on my side. After a while Loretta gets me a tissue.

Disgusted, I say, "Sorry. I don't know why I even told that story. We're supposed to have fun tonight."

"My big mouth started it," Minnie whines. "But, Whitney, you are really…" She fights for the right word, "pretty."

Loretta starts to say something, but I squeeze her arm. "It's OK, Retta."

Minnie and Loretta tell about silly things they did when they were thirteen, and I feel better. We make popcorn and play Clue.

Dear Joanie,

Would you believe I sorta back-talked my boss? Well, I told him what to do. We had a substitute cook who was probably rubbing sticks together to make a fire. Eddie was drinking coffee, and we had a "discussion." He called me Sweet Cheeks! And that fired me up. I told him to put his coffee down and start the second grill! And he did!

I have four fishermen who come in very early. They are so cute. They kid around with each other and are great tippers.

By the way, Freddy works in a hardware store. I went in, and we had some clever banter about wingnuts. Never heard of the things, but we had fun and I now own a wingnut, bolt, and matching washer. Thanks for encouraging me to let myself have fun.

A neighbor is helping me with clothes. Her daughter was built like me, and she can make blouses and dresses fit perfectly! It's been so long since I could wear a dress that wasn't flopping around my middle. I will try to send a picture. I still cover up with sweaters, but these clothes don't need constant adjustment.

Sorry this is so long, but I am leaving half of it out! We need a sleepover to get everything said.

Love,
Whitney

Freddy- Leading in Dance

After my piano lesson, I say, "I want to take Whitney to the Christmas Formal at school. The trouble is, I'm not much of a dancer."

Mr. Blackwater's playing "I Remember Clifford" and doesn't miss a beat. "I have a young friend, Alan, who teaches at a dance studio. I imagine he could give you some pointers." He pauses to let the beginning of the second verse ring. "Would you like me to give him a call?"

"That would be great."

Mr. Blackwater ripples effortless notes down two octaves and goes to the phone.

I go to the piano and silently recreate the scale.

Alan must have picked up because they have a quick conversation. Mr. Blackwater puts his hand over the receiver. "Friday, after Thanksgiving, at four, here?"

I'm nervous because I haven't even mentioned this to Whitney. "Yes. Tell him thank you."

I am pleased with myself. I want to make the evening of the formal perfect. At home, I shower and start for her house.

We park by our vacant lot. I'm having trouble bringing up the Christmas Formal and a dance lesson.

Whitney hums to "I'll be Home for Christmas" playing on the radio, and she breaks into a second part. It's beautiful.

I let the song finish and squirm in my seat.

"What's up?"

"I know I'm supposed to let you lead, but the Christmas Formal is coming. I'd like to take you."

"Yes."

"I love your one-word answers. I'll get tickets."

"I was on the fence, but this is perfect—but—we are still in the Dutch mode. I'm paying half."

"Tell you what—I'll pay for yours; you pay for mine."

"Deal."

"There's more." I sigh, and she reaches for my hand. "My piano teacher knows a guy who's a few years older than us who can really dance. His aunt has a dance studio. Anyway, he will give us a few pointers."

"Would we go to the studio?"

"Mr. Blackwater's house. You'll love it. It's really something."

Whitney is quiet, and I'm not sure what that means.

"We don't have to. If you're uncomfortable, I can go by myself. You said you had dance class—maybe I could catch up."

"Freddy, you are *not* going by yourself. It's fine. Really. I think I'm just surprised." She turns quickly. "Nice surprised. It's very thoughtful."

"I want you to have a wonderful Christmas Formal—well, I want one, too. I don't want to be stepping on your feet all evening."

She slides away and swings her knee up on the seat. "Look at you, Freddy Sanders. All Mr. Planner Man. I have to say, I'm impressed." She leans in and kisses me, and I melt.

Whitney- Fading

Dear Whitney,

I had started this letter when yours came. It made my day, so I started over. I think you are doing _so_ well.

I am- sorta doing well. The Winter Wonderland Dance is coming up, and I don't have a date. There are still two weeks, so one of these guys at this school better get with it.

Do you remember Doug Patterson? He was in seventh but moved away. Well, he's back. He has gotten tall! Anyway, he remembered me, and we talked after school the other day. His parents got a divorce and so he's back here with his mom. I felt pretty bad for him, but he seemed to want to tell me. I get the idea he's been pretty lonely.

Mom had a little fender-bender and you know her! It was her fault, she got a ticket, and that's hard for the perfectionist in her. Dad was very laid back about the whole thing and took the car to his friend Ernie who has that paint shop. I'm just glad I didn't do it!

So glad you and Freddy are having fun. If I wasn't so happy for you, I would be jealous.

Love,

Joanie

Oh, Joanie.

When I read Joanie's letters, I am right there with her, but our letters are sometimes days and days apart. We'll never sit in my room finishing each other's sentences because my room isn't there like it was

180

all my life. I feel like I'm fading. Or maybe Joanie is fading. I still love and miss her.

Maybe it's like losing Daddy? I'm not over it, but getting used to it?

That sounds like I don't care, and I do. But our relationship is changing. Joanie is changing. I'm changing. I hope the new parts of Joanie's life, the parts that don't include me, are as wonderful as the new things in my life.

I'm overwhelmed with a nostalgic sadness that makes my breath catch.

Oh, Joanie.

Freddy- In-N-Out

I have Whitney brain. We come home after church, and Dad is there. He hasn't been drinking and doesn't act like he's working up to an excuse to go to Stucky's. I read about tuning pianos and turn the tuning hammer over and over in my hand. There is a high E that has a bit of wobble.

By seven-thirty, Mom and Dad are playing cribbage, and the E is clean. I've heard fifteen-two, fifteen-four more than I want to. I have Whitney's number memorized and stand in the kitchen, trying to decide if I should call. When the phone rings, I jump and say, "Sander's residence."

"Freddy?"

Her voice sounds tiny and unsure.

"Are you alright?"

There's a long pause involving some breathing. "Just nervous."

"What's wrong?"

She sighs. "Don't fuss, I'm fine. I just—wasn't sure if I should call."

"Of course you should call." I stretch the cord around the corner to the living room and mouth "Whitney" to my parents.

I switch to the other ear. "I was standing by the phone, trying to decide if I should call you."

"Really? I feel better," is followed by a long silence.

"Freddy, I don't know what I'm doing. I told you to let me lead. So? Maybe we could go for a drive—or?" She catches herself. "If you want to—if it's alright."

"Sounds fun."

"I want to see you."

"Be there in ten minutes."

I tell my folks I am going out for a while, and they don't seem surprised. "Be a gentleman," Mom says, and I smile.

I give my teeth an extra brushing, put on my Pendleton, and am out the door.

When I get to the Tate porch, Whitney opens the door with her finger to her lips. "Shhh. Mama is reading Joey to sleep."

I've never seen her in jeans and limit myself to a momentary glance at her slender legs.

"I told Mama we'd be back before nine-thirty." She eases the

182

door closed behind her, and I follow her to my side of the car. I let her in, and she sits pretty close. "Thanks, Mr. Hardware Man."

"Coffee Shop?"

"Would In-N-Out be OK? I've heard so much about it."

"Wait. You've never had In-N-Out?"

"Freddy, I've been here six weeks!"

It seems like I can't remember a time when Whitney wasn't dazzling my days.

At the hamburger stand, Whitney says, "Now, listen, we're going Dutch."

"I got paid at the hardware yesterday." I get in line behind a cherry '57 Chevy.

"I got big tips yesterday. Mama and I have a deal. I contribute my hourly and keep my tips."

"I didn't get any tips, but a cute girl came in, and we had a clever moment."

"I'm not experienced, but I think if she didn't buy a wingnut, she's probably a nobody."

"Oh, she got a wingnut, bolt, *and* a washer."

Whitney is distracted. "Is that Howard's car in the other line?"

I look over. "Yup. Howard and..." It's hard to see in the shadows. "A blonde."

Whitney uses my arm to raise herself a bit. "Minnie is 'bereft,' to use her word. Howard has been 'playing the field.'"

"Not really our business."

"I know, but I wish the girl with Howard was Minnie."

The Chevy pulls forward, and Whitney sits back. "I'm not spying, but poor Minnie is miserable."

We get hamburgers, fries, and Pepsi and back into a space. Apparently, backing in is the cool thing.

She leans over and takes a big bite, eyes wide. "Oh, that's good!"

"Everything is fresh, daily."

Whitney points to our right. "That car doesn't have door handles!"

Sure enough, the beautiful yellow paint goes right past where the door handles would be.

"How does he get in? Climb in the window?" Whitney is sitting up straight, peering out.

"We may never know. I've never seen that car before."

Whitney leans over and takes another bite. "How will I ever

describe this to Joanie?" We nibble on fries and sip our drinks. I have to finish Whitney's burger for her.

"Freddy, can you teach me to drive a stick? I want to get my dad's car going. I want to know how to drive it."

"No time like the present!" I hand her the fries. "We'll go to the Safeway parking lot."

Whitney- Stick Shift

Freddy's steering wheel is larger than Mama's car. I'm not short, but we have to slide the seat up. It catches, and we both try to bounce it together.

"Pull on the steering wheel," Freddy says. He grabs under the glovebox.

I lean to reach the release lever. The seat suddenly flies forward, and the horn starts honking. I push back, and it stops.

"Oh, Freddy!" I gasp. "This is so embarrassing—I'll never reach the lever without the horn honking."

I brace my right forearm against the wheel and reach down. The horn makes another little toot, and I force myself back until the seat creaks. "Oh, for dumb!"

Freddy hustles around, opens my door, and releases the lever. The seat flies back a few inches, and I breathe a sigh of relief. "I'm so mortified. You cannot tell a soul!"

Freddy makes a fist as if he's holding a microphone, and in a reporter's voice, says, "Teen pinned behind steering wheel. Quick-thinking boyfriend comes to the rescue."

I have to smile. "Oh—that was so ridiculous, and I haven't even tried to drive."

With his help, we get the seat forward enough so that the pedals are comfortable.

Freddy gets back in on the passenger side. "OK, first, before you start a car with stick shift, you have to make sure it's in neutral and the clutch is all the way down."

I check my feet, glad he's moving beyond the horn episode. "Got it."

He shows me first gear, and I'm ready for my first takeoff.

"A little gas and let the clutch out a tiny bit at a time."

"Nothing is happening!"

"It's OK. Let the clutch out a *little* faster."

"The car lurches forward, and I squeal, "Oh, it's going too fast!"

"Ease off the gas; it will be OK. Don't forget to steer. Make a big circle."

I can't hold the gas pedal even, and we go faster and slower, bouncing me in the seat.

"I want to stop a second." I forget to press the clutch, and we come to a jerky halt. "I don't know if I can do this!"

Freddy scoots closer. "Sure you can. You didn't stall it on your first takeoff. That's good!"

Freddy is patient, and I get going several times. While I'm concentrating on driving in wide circles, I talk to Daddy in my head. *I'm learning to drive a stick shift, Daddy. This wonderful boy is so patient—like you were when you taught me to ride a bike and roller skate.* I get much better and even manage to shift into second gear, doing large figure eights.

"That's enough for tonight," I finally say.

"Yeah? We can keep working on it if you want."

"No, that's enough. Come around and drive," and he does.

"Can we go to my house and look at my dad's car?"

"Sure."

We park outside the garage, and Freddy pulls up the door. I slip inside the house to make sure Mama knows we are here.

Freddy helps uncover the car and my heart races. I walk around, running my finger over the little chrome strips on the fenders. I feel tears pressing the corners of my eyes. "Oh, Daddy," I whisper.

"You all right?"

When I look up, Freddy is watching from across the car, his brow knitted.

"Yeah. It was such fun being picked up at school." I steel myself. "But I want to drive his car."

"It's beautiful." He leans over to look at the gauges behind the steering wheel. "It only has a little over twelve thousand miles."

"He got it a year and a half before…."

Freddy is still watching me, concern in his eyes.

"I don't even know how to open the hood," I moan.

He points at a little chrome peak. "There's some kind of tool that goes in here."

Then I remember. "Wait." I reach into the side pocket of the driver's door and pull out a T-like tool. I hand it to Freddy and sob.

I know Freddy is coming back from the front of the car, and I start to hold him away. Instead, I put my palms on his chest between us and let him put his arms around me.

I get ahold of myself and take his handkerchief. "Getting to be a habit." I wipe my nose. "I'm usually not like this! Really." When I lift my eyes, he's watching.

"You can be any way you want." Freddy turns the tool in his hands. "What was his name?"

"Charlie—Charles, but everyone called him Charlie."

"Do you have a picture?"

I dig in my wallet and show him the picture I always carry, and Freddy studies it carefully. "You have his eyes."

Somehow, sharing Daddy with Freddy chases my tears away, and I put my hand on his shoulder. "I'm OK. Let's see about this motor."

Freddy lifts the hood, and I'm glad there is only dust and no grease.

Freddy fingers one of the loose battery cables. "We may have to go back to your friend, Cliff. You can talk him into giving you a three-year warranty."

"The battery is in the trunk. Mr. Paulson, our neighbor in Ohio, said we should take it out of the engine compartment."

When I open the trunk, the battery is in a wooden frame. "Look, he didn't want it to tip or slide." *I should write to the Paulsons.*

"It's probably dead. Batteries don't like sitting. I can bring my charger and see if it takes a charge."

"Mr. Hardware Man is a battery maven. So, what else do we have to do?"

"We'll check all the fluids. After I first saw the car, I was interested, so I checked out a manual telling me about the carburetors."

He checked out a book to help with Daddy's car. "Your car doesn't have the same carburetors?"

He laughs. "No, nothing so exotic."

I lean close and hold his cheeks in my hands. "You are officially a good guy, Freddy Sanders. I give you the Whitney Tate stamp of approval," and I kiss him.

Not sure I could ever get tired of kissing this guy.

Dear Joanie,

If I were there, I would give you a long hug. I hope one of those yahoos there asks you to the dance. You are one of the most statuesque girls I know. That probably eliminates some of the shorter guys from asking.

Yes, glad you weren't driving! Escaped that one and put points in the bank in case anything ever does happen. Between you and me, you are a better driver than your mom.

Speaking of driving, Freddy's teaching me to drive a stick shift. He's helping me get Daddy's car on the road.

We were practicing in a parking lot, and we were trying to get the seat to slide forward. He got the car from a really short woman who had the seat fixed to go further forward than normal. So we were rocking it, trying to get it to move and it flies forward and I was squished. And you know what was pressing the horn ring!

I was mortified but laughing. I was pressing back on the steering wheel to keep the stupid thing quiet but when I tried to reach the seat lever, it honked! Freddy had to come around to work the lever. He was so good about it, but I know he thought it was pretty funny. He pretended he was a reporter covering the incident.

Write when you get time. I know you so well and hate it when my wonderful friend is frustrated. Good Luck!

Love,

Whitney

Freddy- First Lines

I pick Whitney up for school and am rewarded with a morning fresh hint of lavender. She doesn't wear too much, which I appreciate. In Geometry last year, Janice Gregg wore something that made my nose burn.

"Did you finish your story opening?" she asks.

"Yup. You inspire me."

Her head comes around in horror. "Tell me you did **not** write about me?"

"No, but I want to get a better grade than you."

"Oh, good luck, Mr. English Man."

"No need for luck."

Whitney rolls her eyes, and we get out. "We shall see, Mr. English Man, we shall see."

Whitney goes to A Capella, and I go to the library. I enjoy the extra time to study without interruptions. When the ten-minute bell rings, I meet Whitney, and we stroll down to English.

Mr. Sanchez greets us with a half-smile, and we take our seats.

Whitney's hair is silky this morning, and I lean forward. "Did you hear that the freshman class is protesting peanut butter cookies? They are lobbying for Fig Newtons."

"That would never do," she says to her shoulder.

Mr. Sanchez prefaces roll call by saying we will read our opening lines out loud to the class, starting with Whitney. The complete stories are due next Monday.

When Whitney walks to the front, she pulls her sweater closed, catches my eye for a split second, and reads:

Lilly wasn't a liar. She just didn't tell the truth very often. She said embellished near-truths were much more interesting.

Hands go up, indicating that they would keep reading, and she gives me a "beat that" look.

I realize we are presenting in reverse alphabetical order of first names. When we get to Philip, we are pleasantly surprised by:

John's grandma knew things. He didn't want her to find out
anything that would disappoint her, so he decided to keep
this new piece of information to himself.

I'm impressed, and Whitney turns and says, "That was good,
Philip," and I tag on, "Lots of hands."

Philip mumbles, "Thanks," but his head stays down.

Seven students don't have the assignment. At this rate, Philip
will not be at the bottom of the class.

When it's my turn, I read:

I remember the day he drove into town in that old truck
with bad brakes. Everyone remembers because he knocked
over the US Letter box in front of the hardware. What we
didn't know was how that moment would change us.

I ignore the hands because Whitney is giving me a nod of
approval. As I go by, she whispers. "I'm impressed, Mr. English Man."

When class is over, Philip turns to Whitney. He has a clump of
not-so-neat papers half crumpled in his hand. "Could you—please—
take a look at this? You don't have to fix it—but maybe put some of
those edit marks?" He glances at me and back to Whitney. "It's about
the apple tree at the farm."

Whitney gives him the sweetest smile. "Of course. Can I take it
with me? I'll give it back to you tomorrow."

Philip seems shy, which is not my first impression. He hands
the papers to Whitney. "Freddy can read it. I know you two…."

Whitney puts the story carefully in her binder. "I'll take good
care of it."

Philip starts to get up and then leans across the aisle. "Sorry I
almost got you two in trouble. It wasn't cool."

Whitney is still smiling. "And now you're doing *so* much
better!"

"Yeah, well. I need to talk to Mr. Sanchez. Thanks."

I let Whitney lead but glance back. Mr. Sanchez and Philip are
in deep conversation. Philip has a nice smile when he uses it.

Whitney- Group 24

The TR3's battery still hasn't taken a charge, so we go to see Cliff after Science Club. Freddy tells me I can drive, and I have my forearm ready on the steering wheel, but the seat slides forward smoothly. I turn, giving him a questioning smile.

"I lubed it."

Freddy is beyond thoughtful.

I concentrate on my driving but feel Freddy watching. He's not being a Nervous Nelly.

At Cliff's, Freddy starts to get the battery out of the trunk, but I say, "Leave it for a minute. I'm going to have some fun with Cliff," and I march to the counter.

"Hey, Cliff. Good to see you. I return a happy customer." I jerk my thumb at Freddy. "I haven't had to push this guy's car once."

Cliff is already smiling.

"So here's the thing, Cliff. I find myself in the need of a battery for a 1960 Triumph TR3. I'm thinking a six-volt Group 1 battery is not going to work."

"TR3? Pretty fancy."

"It was my dad's," and I do pretty well bringing Daddy into the conversation. Maybe talking about him more helps control the tears.

Cliff's eyebrows show a quizzical crook at the word *was*. "I think you're going to need a Group 24, but let me check." He thumbs through a thick dog-eared binder on the counter. "Yup, Group 24 will work just fine."

I turn to Freddy. "A Group 24 is twenty-three better than a Group 1. I'm thinking the Group 24 is *the* battery for cool cars."

Cliff lets the pages flutter. "Whitney, you know that a rebuilt twelve-volt Group 24 battery is going to be eight dollars?"

I give him my best incredulous look. "Cliff, this hits me like a gob of mud in the face. I know the Group 24 is superior, but three dollars?"

Cliff is right there with me. "But remember, I'm giving you twice as many volts for less than twice the price."

He's gone for a while and brings the battery out. "You're getting a deal on this *Group 24*. However, I suggest you put on a new ground cable." He pulls a short braided cable from his coveralls pocket.

It's nice and shiny.

"The original cables can be a pain. It's two dollars, but the way to go." He glances at Freddy, and Freddy nods.

"A girl wants a battery, and now I need a cable?" I stand on my tiptoes, looking toward the back room. "Got any bumpers back there? I suppose you'll try to sell me a bumper next."

This gets a chuckle out of Cliff.

I hand him ten dollars and dig in my purse for the tax while Freddy fetches the battery.

Cliff gives me a sly glance when pushing the cash drawer closed. "You made me look it up, and you had the battery all the time?" he teases.

"I have to make sure my *Battery Man* knows his stuff. What if he tried to sell me a Group 25 battery?" I give him my best smile and say, "See you next Friday night?"

"We're going to see my sister the day after Thanksgiving." He's grinning.

"No, that's *this* Friday."

Cliff's eyes are dancing. "Whitney, there are no Fridays between now and the day after Thanksgiving." He points casually. "So, *this* Friday is the *next* Friday!"

Sharp cookie, this Cliff. I think quickly. "Will I see you Friday, December third?"

Cliff is very pleased with himself. "We'll be there."

I put both hands on the edge of the counter. "That's good because I told my teacher I have special friends coming. There will be two seats with your name on them. Center, ninth row."

Cliff may be blushing. He reaches for the receipt, scribbles, and hands the slip back. "Two-year warranty for my young friend."

I take the receipt and stick out my hand. Cliff hesitates, pulls off his glove, and shakes. "Jean's gonna like you."

At the house, Freddy lugs the battery to the car and puts it in place.

He puts in the new cable and fiddles with the other cable. "Can you hand me a screwdriver, please?"

I grab the first yellow handle I see and pass it over his shoulder. Freddy passes it back. "That's a Philips screwdriver."

"Philip from English? You stealing tools now?"

Freddy snorts. "There is a regular—flat blade—black handle."

192

I am more than tired by last period, Wednesday. Joey had a hard night with another earache. Mama and I took turns, but it was hard to sleep when a little boy was crying in the next room.

Mrs. A has a short Musical meeting in the auditorium. Her cast is off, and her wrist is wrapped in an ace bandage.

"You are ready. You've prepared for this, and we've sold lots of tickets." She encourages each of us by name, ending with, "So, put the musical aside for this beautiful time of year and have a wonderful Thanksgiving."

Freddy and I walk slowly to the student parking lot.

At the house, Freddy comes close but doesn't hug.

I lean my head against his shoulder, keeping my forearms between us. "Have a good day tomorrow," I whisper and give him a tender kiss. I miss him already.

"You too, sweet girl. Get some sleep," and he kisses me.

Joey's medicine is working, and he always gets a little pesky when he's starting to feel better.

In late morning, Auntie Barbara comes with mashed potatoes and a salad.

"So, your mother tells me you have a boyfriend. Tell me about him."

I gush about piano, fixing the car, and dance lessons.

Auntie leans forward, "And he's a good boy?" Her eyebrows are high.

"Yes, very good. An absolute gentleman."

"Good." Her eyes flick toward Mama. "I know you told me, but I wanted to see it in her eyes."

Whitney- Swing Dance

We start work on the car at seven a.m. on Friday. I started cleaning the wire wheels at six, too excited to sleep.

Freddy looks pretty official in coveralls.

"There's really not much to do," he says. "The car is like new, but the gas has probably gone bad."

We take turns with the bicycle pump, and I am determined to work every bit as hard as Freddy until all the tires are at the correct pressure. He spins each one, looking for cracks.

Joey is underfoot, asking a million questions, and I finally take him to Mama.

When Freddy is satisfied, we take the car off the wooden blocks and raise the rear. I help brace it, and Freddy squeezes underneath to drain the old gas.

By nine-thirty, Freddy washes his hands in the laundry tub with Tide. I have a spot of grease and try a little.

"That stuff gets hot!"

Don't use too much, or your hands will look like mine."

We roll the car out of the garage.

"OK," Freddy says. "Fresh gas. The SUs have oil. Are you ready to try it?"

"Me? Maybe you should."

"Whitney, it's your Daddy's car. You should start it."

I'm so glad Freddy lets girls do things. "Let me get Mama and Joey."

Joey is pretty excited, but Mama keeps a firm grip on his shoulders.

I climb in and turn the key. I've learned enough to wiggle the shifter twice to make sure it's in neutral. "Ready?"

Freddy has been looking at the carburetors and reminds me to pull the choke.

I press the button, and the little engine cranks. It doesn't start, but the sound of it turning over takes me back, but this time, I'm met with happiness.

"Start it, Whitney, start the car!"

Mama shushes Joey.

Freddy does something and says, "Try again."

The engine sputters but doesn't start.

"Again."

I press the starter, and the engine comes to life.

Mama is smiling, holding Joey against her legs.

Freddy leans over me to study the gauges. "Oil's good, battery is charging. You can start pushing the choke back in a little at a time as it warms up. It will buck to let you know."

I lean toward the middle, reading which little round gauge reports what. When I sit up, Joey is at the door and puts his hand on my shoulder.

"Can I have a ride? Can I have a ride?"

"Let Freddy and I make sure everything is working right first."

Mama pulls Joey back.

Freddy slips out of his coveralls. "Ready?"

"No! You do it. I want to make sure I don't run into something. Let me practice at Safeway."

Mama isn't crying, but her eyes haven't left me. She comes over and leans to hug my neck. "Your daddy would be so proud of you." She puts one hand over her heart. I know she means she's proud of me, too.

I switch places with Freddy and automatically reach into the side pocket in my door. My scarf is still there, and I pull it over my head and tie it under my chin. When I look up, Freddy has the sweetest smile.

"You know you are lovely, right?"

"Yes. You help me realize I—" I gesture to my face, "I have lots of nice features."

"Oh, wait." Freddy jumps out and runs to his car. When he comes back, he has on a button-billed cap, looking very sporty.

I pat his arm. "Thank you, Mr. Sports Car Mechanic."

Freddy backs down the drive.

Mama and Joey wave, and the car sounds like it always did as Freddy eases down the road.

"You don't have to baby it. Daddy always said these cars were made to be driven."

Freddy gives the engine some gas, and I'm pressed back in the seat with the wind around my face. I feel like I'm thirteen again.

At the almost empty Safeway, lessons in the Plymouth pay off, and although the pedals are practically straight out in front of me, I get the feel of the car. I stall it twice but learn the combination to take off with authority. The car's so low I could reach out and drag my hand on the ground.

We stop because I have so many questions. "What's this one again?"

"Tachometer. Don't take it above that red line."

I rev the engine several times. "I get it! A speedometer for the engine."

Freddy smiles, and I can tell he's happy, and that makes me happy.

We take the long way around. The clutch-gas-shifting thing clicks, and I drive without thinking about my feet.

There are four people at Mr. Blackwater's. His niece, Maggie, is darling. Willowy. Her boyfriend, Chris, is tall and handsome and can't keep his eyes off her.

The house is marvelous, with a living room big enough for two couches, chairs, and a large black grand piano.

Alan has a stack of records ready, and we begin with the waltz. "I know they may not do many waltzes, but the waltz teaches position."

The record plays, and Freddy and I certainly know what three-four time is. Alan dances with me, and Maggie dances with Freddy.

I remember the steps and Alan makes everything effortless. We dance to the record twice, and then Chris and Maggie demonstrate. They look so good together.

When it's Freddy and my turn, we do quite well. Alan watches, gives us pointers, and demonstrates again with me, and then with Freddy. Freddy seems embarrassed to dance with a guy, but Alan says, "It won't take a second." He enforces the importance of giving cues to his partner.

The foxtrot always gave me trouble, but Alan makes it easy. Freddy is light on his feet, and soon we are able to move around the room. Chris and Maggie stand in different places, and Freddy learns to guide me around them.

Uncle T, as they call Mr. Blackwater, brings us sodas, and while we are taking a break, I whisper, "You're pretty light on your feet, Mr. Hardware Man."

"Part of boxing. You learn balance and to be on your toes."

Alan and Maggie are dancing again, and Freddy points to their feet. Alan floats effortlessly in fluid motion.

The fun part is the Swing. Alan plays a couple of Beach Boys songs, and we catch on to this one quickly. Freddy learns to twirl me and pull me in backward to his chest. I totally forget myself.

Uncle T has Freddy play the piano, and Chris and Maggie glide around. Even Uncle T dances with Maggie and then me. He's like Alan, fluid and sure.

Chris plays for us, and then Freddy and I do "Homesick."

"Lovely," Maggie says.

Freddy doesn't seem to be in the slightest hurry, and we gather on the two couches.

Maggie turns to me. "So, Whitney, Uncle says you moved here from Ohio?"

"Yes." She's one of those young women who seems to know things and be at ease with the knowledge.

"I came from Wisconsin five years ago. I was your age. Blackwater High, Uncle, these guys, and some other friends changed my life."

"My life is already changing."

"I hear Freddy's lessons sometimes." Maggie's gaze drifts across the room. "I live here some weekends and summers. I'm a senior at La Verne College, a few miles from here."

Freddy turns to Alan. "So, are you going to school?"

"Film school at USC. I teach at my aunt's dance school on weekends and Tuesday nights. I can get you in for a free trial lesson next Tuesday?"

"Aw, it wouldn't be fair. I don't think we'll be signing up for regular lessons."

Alan hands him a card. "The studio is on Foothill. My treat." He looks around the room. "Uncle T, Chris, and Maggie have been very generous to me."

Freddy- Hanger Kiss

I spend Sunday afternoon at Whitney's house. Joey and I fiddle with a submarine from cereal boxes a few years back; baking powder makes it bubble up and down. I remember having one.

Whitney sits on the closed toilet seat, watching. A couple of times she rubs my shoulder, her hand thanking me for spending time with her little brother.

"Come to the table, you three!"

Joey is up and moving instantly. I clean the baking powder out of the sub and pull the plug. When I'm on my feet, Whitney is still sitting. It is odd to be in a bathroom with her, yet it is as natural as can be. She lets me pull her up.

"I think good boyfriends get rewards!" She gives me a brush of a kiss, whispering, "I smell cobbler!"

We sit, four of us, around the table. It dawns on me that I'm probably sitting where Charlie would sit, but it seems OK. The Tates are laughing and eating, and I am content.

"So, has Whitney shown you her dress?"

"Mama, I was going to surprise him."

"Too late, now," I tease.

"OK, but you only get to see the dress on the hanger. I'm not modeling it before the big night."

In her bedroom, Whitney pulls the most beautiful red gown from her closet. "Joey, sit at my desk. Your hands are a mess."

She makes a face. "What do you think?" She holds it against herself.

"I don't know who will be chosen Snow Queen, but you will be the prettiest one there."

"Too much?" She's alarmed and presses the dress against her middle, bending to look down.

"Nope. You could show up in a gunny sack and still be the prettiest one there."

"Let's not go overboard, Fella."

I lift the hanger, poke my lips through, and kiss her nose.

"Freddy kissed Whitney's nose! Eeew," Joey runs out. "Eeeeew, they're kissing. Freddy kissed Whitney on the nose," fades as he runs down the hall. "Mama...."

"You make quite the impression, Mr. Hardware Man."

198

We watch a movie on 5, *The Lost Continent*, because Joey loves the dinosaurs. During every commercial, he brings out more plastic dinosaurs until the coffee table is covered. I put a triceratops behind the vase, making it peek around.

"Joey, watch the movie, or I'm changing the channel." Whitney has the newspaper. "*Singing in the Rain* is on 11."

"No singing, no singing." Joey sits back, hugging a dinosaur.

"You don't have to stay here with us," Mrs. Tate says.

Whitney turns her eyes to me. It's a question.

"We could go to the hardware store and get a few stove bolts. Open until five," I tease.

"I sorta like the carriage bolts."

Mrs. Tate is amused. "What are you two talking about?"

"Whitney heard me selling molly bolts and wanted a Whitney bolt."

"You had to be there," Whitney offers.

"No, I get it. Your Daddy tried to wow me with fancy levitation talk."

Whitney has a faraway look in her eyes. "Daddy could be pretty silly. We used to try to end commercials on TV. You know, just thinking it to be over."

"You can end commercials?" Joey wonders. "Let's do it."

I know the current commercial. "OK, everyone, I'll count down, and everyone thinks END when I get to one."

The Stanley Chevrolet jingle has about ten seconds. "OK, I'm gonna count. Five—four—three—two—one—think—end!"

Joey scrunches up his face, eyes closed.

The movie starts, and Joey's little eyes pop open. "We did it! It's over. Freddy's magic."

Whitney's big eyes roll to mine, and she mouths, "Thank you," and blows a two-finger kiss.

We end up driving in the rain. I take her up San Gabriel Canyon, and we park on a vista of Morris Dam. Rain almost obscures the water, and it sounds great on the roof. Whitney sighs.

"Thanks for this afternoon. Joey adores you, and you're so good to him."

"He's a good little guy. I don't mind."

She leans her head on my shoulder, and we only kiss once or twice.

"Take me to your house sometime?"

I take in a huge breath. "I never know what it will be like."

"Freddy, I'm a big girl."

"I don't think I could stand to have you see it when it's bad."

She slides away and swings her knee up on the seat, facing me. "I think we should." She's pull-rubbing my arm. "It's part of the deal. I don't get Freddy without his dad."

"You'll love Mom."

"It's four. Let's stop by. If nothing else, I have to see the piano."

It takes me a while to agree. Maybe if Dad sees me with Whitney, he will understand that I am not his little boy to boss around. We start down the hill, and the clouds are clearing.

Dad is on his way to his pickup when we arrive. He waits with his hand on the door handle until we get out. He's looking for trouble.

"Where you been?" He's in the pre-Stumpy's attitude. Gripe about stuff until he "needs a drink."

"Dad, this is Whitney Tate. Whitney, this is—"

Whitney sails toward him. "Hi, Mr. Sanders. Good to meet you. We've been at my house, but my brother Joey is watching a dinosaur movie on TV."

Dad takes his hand off the handle and may be a bit surprised. "Good to meet you, Whitney."

"Freddy's going to show me the piano you got him. He says it's beautiful!" Whitney steps back. "If you have a few minutes, we could give you a preview of the musical."

She's really trying.

Dad's still not moving. He finally says, "We're outta milk." He climbs in and backs down the drive.

Inside, Mom jumps off the couch. "You must be Whitney. It's good to finally meet you." Mom's eyes are red. "Freddy, you didn't tell me how pretty Whitney is!"

It's one of those parent moments when they say things that embarrass their kids, and I can tell Whitney is, too.

"I'm gonna show Whitney the piano."

"Leave the door open, please."

I lead Whitney to the refrigerator, open the door, and take out a carton of milk. It's almost full.

I start to hand it to Whitney, but she puts her hand on mine to

200

stop me. "I see," is all she says.

Bad idea? Does she want to leave? Is this worse than she imagined? I whisper, "You OK?"

As she often does, she says, "We're OK."

Here I am, in my house, with my mother, who is upset, and Dad going out because he needs a drink. My nightmare, and this stunning, kind girl says it's OK.

In my room, I'm glad Dad has the make-your-bed rule.

Whitney gasps. "Beautiful." She slides onto the bench and plays Chopin's Prelude in A Major. Whitney has a nice touch.

I lean my chin on my hand on the lid. The music is beautiful, but I have a hard time listening. Her fingers, her profile, and her hair all give strong competition to one of the simplest yet beautiful compositions known to man.

She rolls her eyes up to me in a way that almost takes my breath away. "Not like Mr. Piano Man, but...?"

"Beautiful. I didn't know you played."

"Your turn."

We start to change places when the front door closes, and I freeze. He's back too soon. Mad?

Whitney seems to sense the gravity of the situation.

I can't let the moment be spoiled, so I play "Soon It's Gonna Rain" from *The Fantasticks*. It's Mr. Blackwater's tasty arrangement I learned early on, and I add my own ending. When I stop, the floor creaks.

"Hey, kids. I got some chips and soda."

Freddy- The Fight

Whitney doesn't have A Cappella and insists she drive me to school, so I'm ready at seven-thirty. I'm starting to worry at seven-forty, and then the phone rings.

Whitney is out of breath. "Freddy, you're going to have to come get me. The car won't start."

"Did you pull the choke?"

"Oh! I'm such a dodo," and the phone clatters in my ear until she finally gets it on the cradle.

I go back outside and hear the car coming. She wheels into the drive, and if I ever thought she was cute, today puts all former impressions to shame. She's wearing a different sweater and a matching scarf. But the best thing is how confident and happy she is.

"Wow," I say. "Good thing I'm not driving because I wouldn't be able to keep my eyes on the road."

"You say the nicest things, but you pay attention. There will be traffic near the school, and I don't want to do something stupid."

And I do, but I can't help but notice her changing gears. She's become quite smooth, and we ease into the student parking lot.

"I'm going to park over there where there are fewer cars." She guides the car between the parking lines. She leans out and exclaims, "I love this car. I can see where the front wheel is!"

We get our books, and she grabs my hand, fingers lacing together.

Carter Watkins says, "Hey Whitney, cool car." He looks her over. "What say you let me drive it this afternoon?" He gestures up and down. "Nice sweater."

Whitney holds my hand a little tighter.

Carter stops in front of us. "Whitney, you're hot! Why you even hang around with this guy? You look like you're ready for some fun. *Freddy* won't mind."

"Because *Freddy* doesn't say rude things like that, Carter."

Carter's lip twitches, but he recovers and bumps my shoulder as he walks past and turns. "I bet this guy doesn't say much of *anything*, huh, Sanders?"

"Freddy, don't let him bother you."

"Yeah, *Freddy*. Keep your mouth shut, cuz I'll squash you like a bug."

202

Whitney tugs my hand, and we start to walk around Carter, but he grabs my shoulder and spins me around. Our hands pull apart, and I keep my arms at my side. I can't take a chance of hurting a hand.

"I never liked you much, Sanders. What say we have a little fight for her?"

"Are you kidding, Carter?!" Whitney hisses. "Leave us alone."

Carter has always been a bully but he seems extra mad this morning. I know the look. Carter won't be happy until he has hit someone.

I put up my open palm. "Not looking for trouble here."

"What if I am?" Carter gives my left shoulder a little push. "Huh, punk?" He pushes again. "Huh?"

I start to turn, but he grabs my shoulder again, and I shake it loose. "Leave it, Carter."

"What say you try to make me leave you alone?"

Several have gathered, and the first bell rings.

One of the football players says, "Come on, Carter, let it go."

"No, this skinny punk needs to be taught a lesson." And then it comes. I'm just standing there, and the fool takes a swing. He's not a fighter and signals the punch. I dodge it easily, but that just makes him madder.

The football guy says, "Carter, come on." He grabs Carter's arm, but Carter jerks it free.

"This'll just take a second," and Carter swings wide and hard.

When you've trained, time slows down, and you can think and see things. In the back of my mind, I analyze the moment: *Let the books drop. Don't let him get a hold of me—I can't out-wrestle him.*

When I duck out of his swing, that's what he decides to do. He reaches for my shirt, and as I feel him begin to pull, I calmly think, *Go for the nose. Quick jab—the nose will give—I won't hurt my hand.* Only, I'm not thinking it. I just know it.

Then time speeds up, and I bring my left arm inside, loop over his arm, and push down. I hear a button pop, but the move draws his attention for the split second I need.

His nose folds a bit, and I'm sorry. I should have pulled the punch more, but my hand didn't feel much shock.

Carter's head flies back. He grabs his nose, sees red, and comes at me with both fists. "Oh, that's gonna cost you, punk. I'm gonna mess you up!"

He's big and awkward on his feet. I dance a bit, dodging two wild shots, but then he starts for the bear hug, so I pop the nose again, with a left this time.

Carter screams, blood hits the cement, and he staggers into the arms of his buddies. Two have enough sense to hold him back. I step back and have my hands at my side when Mr. Sanchez takes my arm.

"All right, you two, that's enough."

"He boke my nos," Carter wails.

Mr. Sanchez lets me go and pans his index finger to include everyone. "Don't go anywhere."

Tears and blood are running down Carter's face. "He boke my nos. He shou gu' spended!"

"You'll get your chance, Carter, but I saw Freddy try to walk away two times."

I'm worried about being in trouble, but I'm more worried by the look on Whitney's face. I can't read her. She's looking at me like I'm a stranger.

News travels fast because Mr. Tyler is between us. "Thank you for breaking this up, Mr. Sanchez. You can go on to your class."

Whitney comes forward. "Mr. Tyler, we were coming up the sidewalk, and Carter started bothering us. Freddy tried to walk away, but Carter wouldn't stop."

"I was near the English building and saw the last of this." Mr. Tyler has four inches on Carter, and he moves close and stares down. "Mr. Carter, get to the nurse. This is the second time this month. We'll talk later."

He pulls a small notepad and pen from his suit coat and hands it to one of the football players. "Write your names and wait for me on the benches in the hall outside my office."

He turns to me. "Mr. Sanders, wait in my office. I'll be there in a minute."

Whitney looks as if she's going to argue, but I give my head a tiny shake.

"Miss Tate, you better come as well, but I want you at least twenty feet from Mr. Sanders. No talking—anyone."

In the office, everyone gets a legal pad and a pen. "Write what you saw in less than fifty words. Mr. Castro, let's not chat about this." Mr. Tyler leans against his doorjamb.

Whitney- Can't Stop Shaking

I walk with my books held to my chest. I try to stay ahead of the football guys, but I don't like them behind me. No one is saying anything, and I don't know where Mr. Tyler is.

What just happened? Freddy isn't a big guy. Sorta tall. Carter must weigh eighty pounds more than Freddy.

I should have tried harder to lead Freddy away. But Carter grabbed his arm and turned him around.

I was scared to death. Freddy just stood there while Carter shoved his shoulder. If I had gotten between them, would Carter have stopped?

I glance back, and the football guys are all spread out, and Mr. Tyler is behind everyone.

Freddy boxed Carter on the nose, like lightning, and when Carter came at him again, 'pop!' and it was over. Carter was a mess.

I try to remember everything that happened in order. I have to explain this—I can't let Freddy get in trouble. My hands are shaking, and I hug my books tighter.

It dawns on me—I'm not even close to crying. I hate it when I cry when I'm frustrated. My shaking is anger! I would like to slap Carter into the middle of next week.

This isn't like me, but the jitters won't stop. I feel like I could run as fast as Laura right now.

We're going to be late for English. What will Minnie and Loretta think? Will Mr. Tyler call Mama? Will she have to take time off work to deal with her delinquent daughter?

I'm *not* a delinquent. Will she make me stop seeing Freddy? The thought brings a wave of panic. *This was **not** Freddy's fault.*

We turn toward the office, and kids are watching. I suppose everyone has heard about the fight. Letty Crocker rushes to Carter, taking his arm, trying to uncover his face, but he won't have it. He grumbles something at her, and she recoils and steps back with the other cheerleaders.

I've never been in trouble at school. I'm used to boys gawking at me, but having half the school watch us on our way to the office is much worse. Minnie is on the grass, halfway to the office, and gives me the questioning eye treatment.

I try for a smile, but my face is frozen.

Mr. Tyler makes everyone sit in the hallway to the offices, but he has me sit in the main office. I don't see Freddy.

When I'm handed a yellow pad and pen, my hand shakes so bad I can hardly write. I scribble two and a half pages. I know it's more than fifty words, but I can't stop.

Mr. Tyler comes and takes my pad. He scans it, flipping back and forth.

"Sorry my writing is so messy. I usually have good handwriting, but I can't stop shaking."

"Do you need to see the nurse?"

Go in there where Carter is? "No, I'll be OK. Can I go to class?"

"You write that you and Freddy tried to walk away twice?"

"Yes. He just wouldn't stop."

Mr. Tyler smiles. "Yes, Whitney. Get a late pass and go on to class. If I have any questions, I'll call you in, but you have written a— most comprehensive account here." He almost chuckles.

Mr. Sanchez raises his eyebrows when I come in. I can tell he's looking at Freddy's empty seat.

The clock says we still have twenty-two minutes until the bell. I just want to see Freddy.

Freddy- Advice

Mr. Tyler has me come into the hallway. I don't know where Whitney is. Mr. Tyler reads all the papers and shakes his head slowly. "Well, all of your accounts are quite similar. Mr. Sanders, better get that hand looked at."

I'm not going to see Miss Odegaard and chance running into Carter. "I just need to wash it. I didn't hit him that hard."

Castro snorts, "Hard enough," but he doesn't seem mad. If I didn't know any better, I'd say he's pleased.

Mr. Tyler gives Castro the obligatory scowl, but I may have caught a twinkle in his eye. "All right, use the bathroom down the hall. Then come back to my office."

I wash and look my hand over carefully. It's a little red but nothing like before. Back in the hall, everyone is gone. I rap on the jamb of Mr. Tyler's open door. *Don't get Dad involved.*

"Come in, Freddy. Take a seat."

Mr. Tyler sifts through the papers the kids wrote. "I'm not going to discipline you, but want to talk."

I nod.

"I saw the last punch, the one that probably broke Carter's nose. That was a clean, quick shot. Where did you learn to do that?"

I shift in my chair. "My dad has had me sparring—just in the garage, since I was eight."

Mr. Tyler considers this information. "Freddy, I'm a pretty big guy. I had to learn to control myself. I'm big enough to have handled most anyone when I was in high school—college, for that matter."

I don't doubt it.

"Well, maybe not you," he chuckles.

"I tried not to fight him."

"I know. But when you have your abilities, you have to be extra careful."

"Yes, Sir."

"I know—saw you defending yourself. We don't condone fighting, but these things happen."

I hold up my hands. "I pulled both punches, Sir. I can hit way harder than that."

Mr. Tyler gives me a sad smile. "I don't doubt it." He puts his fingertips together, resting his elbows on his desk. "Be careful."

He locks eyes with me. "If Carter says anything to you, anything at all, I want to know immediately. Clear? That's an order."

"Yes, Sir."

"OK—and good luck with the musical. I hear good things about you."

When I get outside, it's between classes, and Whitney's there.

"I'm so sorry," I start, but she touches my arm.

"I know. You gave him every chance." She's studying my face. "You weren't kidding when you said your dad made you learn to fight."

I give her a half smile.

"Are you suspended? Detention?"

"I have to stay away from Carter."

Whitney- Fisticuffs

When we get to the cafeteria, Freddy says he'll eat with Sam. We're OK, but there's lots of talk around school. Carter has been suspended.

Loretta stops peeling her tangerine when I get to the table. "So, I hear Freddy beat the snot—literally—out of Carter Watkins."

Minnie stiffens. "I detest fisticuffs—but Carter Watkins is a bully. He hassles Howard all the time."

Loretta waits for Minnie to finish and turns back to me. "So, the cute little car? Ronny says it's a TR3?"

I smile, glad Loretta is quick to move on.

"Wait, I want to know more about the fight," Minnie pouts.

Loretta has one strip almost pealed but stops. "I thought you despised fisticuffs."

"Well, it's important when it concerns our friend's honor. He was defending your honor, right, Whitney?"

I hadn't thought of it that way. "We tried to ignore him several times. Carter thinks girls should fall at his feet. When I said no, he didn't take it well."

Loretta gives Minnie a look. "Let's move on to the car. Ronny says it's a sports car."

I decide to let Loretta get on with her peeling and say, "It was my dad's. It's just been sitting, and Freddy helped us get it going."

Loretta reaches across with both hands and grabs my forearms. "Oh, Whitney, I'm glad you're driving your daddy's car."

"I am too." I grab her arms, locking us together. "Ronny's right —1960 TR3. Freddy says it's in perfect condition."

I realize Minnie is sort of left out, and I lean my shoulder against hers.

It's cloudy after practice, and Freddy says, "We better get the car in the garage. We can figure out how to put the top on one of these times."

I remember the choke, and we drive to Freddy's house.

"How's your hand?" I reach for it. "You played beautifully."

"Thanks." He flexes his fingers. "Not bad. I guess Carter has a soft nose."

Dear Whitney,

Disaster averted! Doug asked me to the dance. We've been hanging around, and he took me to a movie.

So you are up to date: This Guy Can Kiss! And I don't mean the slobbery tongue thing. His kisses are sweet, but—wow. I could kiss this guy forever.

I cracked up about the horn thing. I even read it to Mary Ann and Paula. I hope that's alright, but your description was so "Whitney" and they got a big kick out of it. Mary Ann said this gives new meaning to honkers. Grin.

Thank you for your kind thoughts. Just knowing you are on my side even at this great distance gives me confidence. Maybe we will end up at the same college someday.

Love,

Joanie

Freddy- Making Waves

As soon as Whitney leaves, I hurry to Martin's to see how much it costs to rent a tux. Dad suggested it. I guess when you aren't pouring money down your throat at the bar and betting on punch-drunk fighters, you have money to spare. One thing's for sure; I want to look perfect for Whitney in that red dress. I reserve the tux.

My second stop is Mrs. Fillmore's. I park around the block and walk.

"Freddy, come in." She lets me into a living room that smells like something good. She picks up a piece of red material. "This is it."

"So, I should try to get something to match this?"

"Take it to the florist. They'll know what to do. But come back here. I want you to try something on."

We go into Mrs. Fillmore's sewing room, and she holds up a tie and cummerbund that match the dress.

"I've never made a cummerbund before and certainly not a bow tie but you'd be surprised what you can learn from a little research. Let's see how I did."

She dangles the cummerbund. "I don't have one of the traditional clasps, so I put button holes on in the back. Button it in front and slide it around."

I start to wrap it when she says, "The pleats go up. They say 'to catch the crumbs,' but I think that's just a way to remember."

The middle buttonhole works perfectly.

"You're going to knock 'em dead."

There's only one person I want to impress.

Mrs. Fillmore ties my tie, and I look in the mirror. "I'll never be able to do that."

"Maybe your mom can help. If not, stop by here. After you pick up Whitney, you have to come by. I must see you two."

"We will, for sure."

My last stop is at Mrs. Wilson's. "I wanted to give you this ticket to our Christmas Musical, if you would like to come?"

Mrs. Wilson pushes the screen door open. "Come in, Freddy." The wall where the piano was sitting is still bare.

"I have tickets for all three nights." I catch myself. "I mean for the night that works best for you."

"This is so kind, but I'm going to my sister's that week. But,

211

thank you for thinking of me."

We sit in silence for a few minutes, and I sense she's not having a good day. "Well, I'll leave you. Have a good evening."

"Thank you, Freddy."

On Tuesday, Whitney drives us to school. Carter is out for the week, and Castro says, "Hey, Freddy. How's the hand?"

I hold it up and flex it. "I'll live."

"You get detention or anything?"

I'm a little nervous he will be unhappy with the answer, but say, "No. Mr. Tyler said I have to steer clear of Carter."

"Cool," and Castro trots to catch up with a group of guys.

Philip, in English, says, "'bout time that punk got taken down a notch."

The rest of the day, kids pretty much leave the subject alone. After classes, I walk to Science Club with Whitney and Minnie.

"Howard is already there, helping set up the wave experiment! His last class is next door."

Whitney offers me a sideways smile.

"Howard says most people don't understand wave cancellation and place their stereo speakers incorrectly."

I squeeze Whitney's hand. "I was going to get a stereo, but I may *cancel* the order."

My joke goes completely over Minnie's head. "All one has to do is think carefully where the chairs and couches are placed in relation to the speakers."

Minnie, unable to contain herself, runs toward the open room door, and Whitney stops me. "She doesn't mean anything by all the chatter."

"You forget, I was in the club with Minnie before you came. She means well."

"Why were you in the club? I mean, it's OK, but you don't talk about science much."

I tilt my head toward her and gently pull her chin until she is looking at me. "I was waiting for you."

She hugs my arm. "If I'd known, I would have come sooner."

Mr. Coulter has big square pans and little motors to tap the water in two places. We try different speeds and measure where the waves cross. It's interesting, but mostly I enjoy the scent of lavender that makes my head swim.

Whitney has a map, but I have an idea where the studio is. When we pull into the parking lot, she tries to fold the map. "These things never go back right." She shakes it open and starts again. "Mama and I have a whole set of Southern California from Triple-A, but this is never going to fit back in the glove compartment."

We laugh and manage to mash it into obedience.

The studio is large, with mirrors lining one wall. "Glad you came!" Alan exclaims. "We're about to begin."

Whitney and I dance together, and Alan mixes the dancers. It's interesting how fluid some dancers are and how awkward others can be.

One fellow is quite taken with Whitney and manages to partner with her several times. She's pretty miserable.

During the break, she says, "That poor guy has no sense of rhythm. I know he can hear because we chit-chatted a bit, but it's as if the music isn't even playing. I tried tapping on his shoulder a bit to give him the beat, but he kept saying, 'Yes?' as if he thought I was trying to get his attention."

"The tall brunette is a great dancer, and I felt like I had two left feet. Twice, she told me, 'Don't be afraid to lead with more presence', which made me even more nervous about leading."

As the evening draws to a close, Whitney and I are gliding around like pros. The true joy is watching Alan and the other instructor. Their steps in the Swing make me wonder if I could ever learn all those moves.

Whitney- I'm A Delinquent

Dear Joanie,

I knew you would not be sitting at home the night of the dance. I am so happy for you!

Would you believe, I'm a delinquent! Not really, but I drove Freddy to school in Daddy's car. I'm doing so well! We were just walking to class when a huge guy started in with how hot I looked, saying I should dump Freddy. I tried to tell him to get lost.

Then he started in on Freddy. Freddy tried to walk away twice, but the guy takes a swing! Freddy was suddenly on his toes, sort of dancing like a boxing fighter and made a quick duck. The guy took a couple more really hard wild swings, and Freddy popped him on the nose. It was like lightning. I hardly saw it happen!

I thought the bozo would have had enough cause it was bleeding and his buddies were pulling his arms, but he rushes Freddy like he was going to wrestle. I was scared to death because he probably could throw Freddy into the middle of next week.

So, Freddy bopped him on the nose again! Blood was running down his face, and he was almost crying. Slow learner.

A teacher came, and we all had to go to the office. We got separated, and I was worried they would expel Freddy or something. But the Vice Principal, who they call Superman because he wears horn-rim glasses like Clark Kent was pretty nice. The guy who attacked us got suspended for the week. Good riddance!

So, I've learned to kiss, to drive a stick shift, and got sent to the office. Don't think badly of Freddy.

The guy probably weighed 80 pounds more than Freddy. Freddy is a slim wiry guy and taller than me, but not a big guy. This lug was like 6'2". Joanie, Freddy stood up for me!

On a happier note, the Musical is coming soon, and it is going to be really good. It starts on the day Daddy died. I think about that December day, wondering if it hadn't been almost 60 and clear, Daddy wouldn't have gone out to have a last game before winter. Stupid weather. But I'm OK. Freddy knows how much I miss Daddy and has been sweet.

We are going to the Christmas dance here. I have a dress to die for. The neighbor who sews made it. I'm pretty nervous about wearing it. I mean, it covers me up but leaves no doubt what is underneath.

I love your letters, and feel like you are with me on this adventure. Have a great dance, and send a picture. I will send some as soon as they are back from the drugstore.

Love and Hugs,

Whitney

Freddy- Opening Night

Mom and Dad are dressed up, and we have a quick supper.

"Freddy, are you excited or worried?" Mom wonders.

"A little of both. I'm not worried about my part, but there's a lot going on."

"And Whitney?"

"She's ready, but I think she's nervous. She has the singing, the dialogue, and the acting."

"But you say she's good, right?"

"Very good. You'll love her part."

But I'm worried. It's December second.

Dad is quiet but sober. He's wearing a sports coat and tie. I hope they enjoy the evening as much as *I* plan to.

"I'm picking up Whitney and her mom in a few minutes. See you there? Go to the fifth row. Mrs. A reserved seats for you."

Dad says, "Break a leg, Son."

Whitney has her sweater and scarf over her arm, and I take a big chance. It's not like Whitney and Mrs. Tate aren't aware of the date.

"Let's come over here for a moment." I take Whitney's hand. "Maybe I shouldn't bring up things that will upset you, but why don't we take a minute by your Daddy's picture?"

The three of us stand in silence.

"You are a remarkable boy, Freddy." Mrs. Tate pulls me into a sideways hug. "Thank you."

Whitney is only sniffling a bit, and I hand her handkerchief number one. I'm rewarded with an arm tug. "You remembered, and that is so sweet."

I take a last look at Mr. Tate, with his arms around Whitney and Mrs. Tate with Joey on Mrs. Tate's hip.

We decide to all ride in the front seat, and I drive with extra care.

Mrs. Tate insists I call her Martha, but it's not how I was raised. I leave the radio off, and Whitney touches my arm in the silence.

When we get to the parking lot, she whispers, "Thanks for letting Mama ride with us, and...."

I lean into bubble bath heaven and whisper, "Of course," and I mean it. I would drive a load of pigs in my car if I got to spend one minute with Whitney Tate.

I go backstage, and the actors are getting ready. It turns out Miss Odegaard is something of a makeup artist. She works fast, her accent charming the cast. I notice a man standing apart and realize he's with her, and I am happy for her.

Ten minutes before opening, I go to the little grand and open the keyboard. I play soft, jazzy carols, nothing fancy. Just mood music until Mrs. A comes out.

She makes a short, lovely welcome and patters down the steps. She sits a few feet to my left.

I begin the overture, and the curtain whisks back. Whitney is there, looking pensive, gazing over the audience, and the cast is greeted with applause.

The cast holds the tableau until Whitney sings. I watch as she moves, her voice floating through the auditorium. She is exquisite. No other word can describe the moment.

As we move through the scenes, the quartet is inspired. Lois and Jim's duet has the perfect blend, and I provide a solid but quiet foundation.

The only glitch is when the telephone is missing from the end table when Whitney is supposed to make a call. Tucker strides onto the stage in his suit and tie. He presents her with the phone, his deep voice rumbling, "You may need this, Ma'am." He gives Whitney a quick bow, and the audience roars.

When Whitney sings "Homesick," her performance almost moves me to tears. She gives the composition a plaintive treatment that leads the audience to the heart of her character's longing. When the last note fades, there is a moment of complete silence, followed by enthusiastic applause, and I watch in wonder.

The full chorus reprise brings the performance to a close, followed by more applause. Mrs. A goes up, and we sing "Jingle Bells", "Rudolph" with the jazzy bridge, and end with "Silent Night". I feel like I'm in church as the notes fill the auditorium.

After the bows, I close the fallboard. Kids and adults surround Whitney and the cast, and folks pat my back and slather on praise.

My parents finally get to me, and Mom is beside herself. "Oh, Freddy, that was so good." Dad shakes my hand, and I introduce them

217

to Mrs. Tate.

And then Whitney is there. She's glowing, but I know she's hot in the sweater. Mom and Dad are definitely under the Whitney spell.

As the crowd begins to thin, Whitney excuses herself, and I turn to my folks. "Thanks for coming." It seems formal and inadequate but fitting.

"See you in the morning, Son," Dad says. "Don't stay out too late. It's a school night."

I nod and catch Whitney as she stops to greet every cast member and audience person. She's beautiful to watch, and it's fun to see the eyes of everyone she meets. How did I ever get so lucky to be "keeping company" with this marvelous creature?

Mrs. A finds me and puts her cheek on mine, enveloping me in subtle perfume. "Oh, Freddy, you saved our musical."

I don't know what to say, but settle on, "Your musical—it's beautiful, Mrs. A, just beautiful."

"Freddy, I want you to meet my husband, Martin. Marty, this is Freddy, who made my music come to life."

We shake hands, and Mr. Blackwater comes to my side, looking dapper in a three-piece suit.

"Mr. Blackwater, it is my pleasure to introduce you to, in person, Mrs. Albertson, the composer, and her husband, Mr. Albertson. Mrs. A, I am pleased for you to meet my piano teacher, Mr. Blackwater."

I leave them to their happy chatter. When I find Whitney, I slip up beside her and whisper, "How you doing in the sweater?"

She turns her big eyes on me and hands me the scarf. "Hold this, please," and away she goes. Mrs. Tate is talking with two women.

Mr. Blackwater moves away from Mrs. A, and he comes near. "Where is Whitney? I want to congratulate you both on a wonderful show."

"Whitney is changing. She's roasting in that sweater."

Across the room, Mrs. A pats Tucker's shoulder, laughing.

Whitney comes back, flustered. The thing is, Whitney looks great even when she isn't trying.

"Oh, Mr. Blackwater. Thank you again for arranging a dance lesson for us. We went to the studio and are getting the hang of things."

"It was my pleasure. Thank you for the reserved seat."

"I didn't get to say this at your home, but Freddy is a marvelous pianist and accompanist. You are a talented teacher."

"Freddy makes the lessons easy. I don't usually teach piano, but this young man," he jiggles my shoulder, "has a true talent. He's one of two students."

Mr. Blackwater pauses, gazing into Whitney's eyes. "And you, young lady, sing like you've been uptown all your life." He clasps his hands together, giving them a little shake. "Brava!"

Whitney holds his gaze. "Thank you."

Whitney- Alphabetical Fasteners

The Friday performance is better than Thursday, if possible. Cliff and his wife are there and we have a few minutes after the crowd thins.

Mrs. Baker is one of those women with a peaches and cream complexion, almost as tall as Cliff. She's lovely, with her arm in his.

"Cliffy has told me so much about you and Freddy. Where is he?"

I give Cliff a head tilt. "Cliffy, huh?" I turn to Mrs. Baker. "So glad you could come. Cliff has been very good to me at the store." I see Freddy talking with a couple and give him the "come here" eye treatment.

Freddy winds his way through the crowd and joins us. Mrs. Baker jiggles her husband's arm. "You're right. They are cute together."

I almost blush and say, "Visiting the store is so much fun, I can hardly wait for Mama's car to need a battery."

Cliff grins, looking at his wife. "Every sale," he gestures toward me, "this one seems to talk me into a better deal."

Mrs. Baker bends close, tugging Cliff with her. "He's a sucker for a pretty face!" Cliff blushes.

If there was ever a pretty face, Mrs. Baker has one.

I turn to Freddy. "We better go. Four o'clock comes pretty early."

Mrs. Baker gives me a questioning look.

"I work at Daisy's Diner, Saturday mornings."

She gives me a knowing nod. "Treat 'em nice, and get those tips," she says.

All four of my fishermen are on time.

"What I want to know, gentlemen, is why do I never see any fish? I hear you're great fishermen—well, maybe not Jim," I tease, and Jim gives me a wink. "But, I'm thinking, where's the proof? For all I know, you guys go back home and lay around all day."

"Next week, Kiddo," Steve says. "Next week, you're eating browns."

I give him a puzzled look, and he adds, "Trout, Kid, trout."

I finish topping off their coffee. "Seeing's believing. More hot water, Jim?"

"And the honey."

"Oh, how could I forget!" I dash across the floor and return with honey and water. "Honey, for the sweet guy," I say. I surprise myself with the comment, but it feels natural, and Jim *is* the sweetest man.

I breeze through the morning, not bothered by the leering looks from a portly fellow who calls me Baby Cakes. And he turns out to be a lousy tipper.

Baby Cakes! A real charmer.

When Freddy comes in, it makes my day, and I get him tea and toast. "So, what's the deal, fella? You coming in for tea or trying to impress the waitress?"

"Waitress? I hadn't noticed any special waitress. Besides, my girlfriend probably would be wildly jealous if I was making eyes at one of the waitresses."

Girlfriend! I tingle inside.

I put a butter packet on his small plate. "So, you have a girlfriend. That's too bad." I lean one hand on the counter and look toward the end. "Cause I was thinking I kinda like this guy," I say absently. "But, if he's taken—"

Freddy keeps the patter going. "I mean, you're cute and all, but I'm a one-girl sort of guy. Now, if you were a singer, I might reconsider."

"Listen, Pal, I'm a singer." I pat the counter and hurry to table six.

By the time I'm back, Freddy is gone, and a crisp dollar bill is lying on the counter.

When my shift is over, I hurry to the hardware store.

"So, Mr. Hardware Man, I have some fastener needs."

"Well, Ma'am, you have come to the right place."

I give my eyes an extra roll at the *ma'am*. "You seem to give your bolts names, but let's see if you know your stuff. I want to see a bolt that starts with A."

"Easy, anchor bolt." Freddy leads me to bins with all manner of shiny bolt things.

"How much?"

"I can make you a sweet deal on this quarter-inch job. Three cents."

"I'll take one. B."

"Blind bolts. But we seem to be out of them today."

I can't believe what I'm hearing. "What, they can't see?"

"Sorta. They're for when you can't get to the other side to put on a nut."

"Or a wingnut?"

"You're getting the hang of this."

"C?"

"Carriage bolts." He pulls a domed bolt from a bin.

"Mr. Hardware Man, are you making this stuff up?!"

"Nope!"

I look toward the back of the store, see a tall man, and hurry to him. "Quick question. Is this an anchor bolt?"

"That's an anchor bolt."

"Is there such a thing as a blind bolt, or is that hardware guy making it up?"

The fellow takes a drink of coffee. "No, there are blind bolts, but we seem to be out of them today."

"Carriage?"

He nods, a grin starting, and I can tell he's looking at Freddy.

"You're about to call me *ma'am*, aren't you?"

"No, Ma'am."

I look between him and Freddy. "You're Chuck. You guys are having a good time, aren't you?"

"We aim to please."

"I bet there isn't a bolt with a name that starts with D, is there?"

Freddy has arrived.

Chuck says, "This young lady seems to think she has stumped us with bolts that start with D."

"Alas, I can't think of one," Freddy says but then brightens "But, we make it up with elevator bolts and eye bolts."

I try to act indignant. "Oh sure, blind bolts and eye bolts. Does the eye bolt lead the blind bolt around?" I put the anchor bolt by Chuck's coffee cup. "I've changed my mind. I want a five-sixteenth eye bolt to go with my wingnut and washer."

"Freddy will be happy to help you, Ma'am."

I start toward the bolt department but turn back.

"Did you guys work this out ahead of time?"

"We may have thought of a few examples."

Then it comes to me. "Deadbolts! Ha! Technically not in the same bolt family, but a bolt is a bolt."

Mama had one installed after Daddy died. Her confidence had been shaken in so many ways.

I half turn, arms folded, and tilt my head expectantly.

Freddy and Chuck look at each other, eyebrows raised.

I pull out two tickets from my apron and go back. "You want to come to our Christmas musical? I have tickets—Freddy's playing."

"June and I were there Thursday night. We enjoyed you kids' performance very much."

"Freddy! Did you get them good seats?"

"They sat behind my parents."

I look at Chuck. "Well, I'm glad he didn't make you sit in the back." I stick out my hand. "I'm Whitney."

Chuck tilts his head back, so he can see me in his bifocals and takes my hand. "I know."

Freddy- Grrr

When Whitney leaves, Chuck says, "No wonder you're crazy about that girl. She could charm the stripes off a skunk."

The day goes quickly, with only three sacks of concrete to load. One is for Ally.

"It's for my dad. He's flushing the radiator on his pickup and wanted me to bring the Chevy, but I told him my trusty VW could haul eighty pounds."

Let me make sure it fits before you buy it." I lug the sack to her car and ask, "So, Dean?"

"You know, I've decided Dean is a lightweight! That guy has no loyalty whatsoever. After he gave up on Barb, he sidled up to me in the library, and asked me to the movies for last night. I say, sure. Then, the next day we're talking, and I ask what movie, and he says *Redline 7000!*"

I shut the front of the car and give her a questioning look.

"Freddy, it's a movie about stock car racing. Redline is the speed or something!"

"So, you backed out?"

"Oh, no, it gets worse. I'm thinking a movie date will give Dean time to know me better." Ally is fully animated now, skipping into the store with me. "Then, yesterday, he says his buddy Bill doesn't have to work at the hamburger joint, and the 'guys' are going to the drive-in!'"

"So, no date?"

"I went bowling with Nancy Caldwell." Ally beams. "I made a 100! My first time."

Thinking of Ally with a heavy bowling ball makes me smile inside.

"We're coming to the musical tonight."

I stop. "So, you're OK about Dean?"

"Oh, sure." She waves her hand dismissively. "His loss." She pays for the concrete. "So, see you tonight."

Whitney and I practice putting the top up on the TR3. When Whitney is satisfied, we fold it back down, and she dusts an imaginary spot on the trunk lid.

I brought my wax and Whitney is a fireball. She works fast and with vigor. When she wipes off the hood, she says, "Oh, Freddy. Come here!"

We stand in front of the car, with her hand on my lower back. I put my arm lightly on her shoulder.

Whitney leans forward and rubs an imaginary spot with her rag. "Isn't it beautiful?"

I turn her around. "So are you, Whitney, so are you."

"Thank you." She gives me a peck of a kiss. "How are you doing with the sides and trunk?"

"Trunk's great. I have to rub out the sides."

She bends over and attacks the driver's door with a vengeance. I admire her waist for a moment and then work on the other side.

When we finish, Whitney straightens her blouse, wiggling it into place, giving me a grrr face, and gives her shirttail one last twist. She laughs and tosses her rag on the trunk, and it keeps going, slipping off the other side. "Look, the rag just kept sliding!"

She shakes it out and tries it again. "So smooth. I bet the car will be faster now."

Mrs. Tate comes with her camera, and we pose for several pictures.

Joey comes out. "Freddy! Come look at what I made!"

"Joey, leave Freddy alone." Whitney's eyes are doing the "we talked about this" thing.

Joey is already tugging on my hand. "It's OK," I mouth.

Joey has set up an army battle scene in his room. His little soldiers are a mix of sizes and colors, but we make the tanks mow the enemy down with growly crash sounds. When I look up, Whitney is leaning against the doorway. Her eyes are misty, but I know the difference; these are happy eyes.

"Hey, Joey, want to go for a ride in the TR3 with Freddy and me?"

Joey is on his feet, army guys toppling.

Freddy- No Handles

The little bench in the back has no room, but Joey squeezes in.

"Seat belt, Joey." Whitney hands him one end. When she turns away, she mumbles, "Daddy put them back there for a reason."

She starts toward the passenger's side, but I say, "Nope. Your car, you're driving."

She fires it up, and turns to back out of the drive.

"Don't you want your scarf?" I ask.

"Going to wash and dry it before tonight."

"Go fast, Whitney, make it go fast!"

Whitney makes a quick shift to second and accelerates. It's a fun little car. Being so close to the ground gives the feeling of speed, but the speedometer only reads thirty.

"Go around a corner like a race car, Whitney!"

Joey makes a squealing sound even though the turn is tame. Suddenly, she pulls over and spins in her seat.

"Joey! Seatbelt back on! If I ever catch you on your knees in this car I will swat your bottom and not let you ride again!"

I've never seen Whitney in big sister mode, but Joey plops down and snaps the belt.

"Pull it tight, or we're not going."

Satisfied, we drive to In-N-Out and order fries and Pepsi.

Whitney pokes my elbow. "Freddy. No Handles."

Sure enough, the yellow Olds is backing in one car over.

Whitney is sitting up, squinting. "He's tall. No way is he going to shinny in over that nice paint. Should I ask?"

"I'm not sure about that." I turn and pick up the fries Joey spilled.

"What if all three of us went?"

Whitney's newfound bravery is making me nervous, but she's unbuckled and climbing out.

"Joey, we're going to ask a man a question. You are going to hold my hand the whole time and you are *not*," she's leaning toward him, reaching for his seatbelt, "*not* going to touch the yellow car." She grabs his drink, takes his chin, and makes him look at her. "Do you understand me?"

"Yes, Whitney."

I get out and wait at the front of the car. Whitney and Joey

226

come around. "Ready?" she asks.

I'm not sure I'm ready, but Whitney is starting toward the Olds. The blond guy looks up as we approach, checking Whitney out, widening his gaze to include the three of us.

"Tell me that's not your kid!" He half smiles.

"My little brother." She bends toward Joey, "No, stay back. No fingers on the pretty car."

'Pretty car' seems to please the fellow and he shades his eyes, looking up at Whitney.

"You have a beautiful car there. But we—I have a question. How do you get in with no door handles?"

"No handles," Joey echoes and Whitney gives his arm a little shake. "Shhh."

The guy is grinning, and he opens the door and slides out. The tuck-n-roll seats are as immaculate as the exterior. The guy with him gets out and comes as far as the hood.

"So, if I'm just going in to a store for a second, and it's a good area, I usually leave the windows down. He shuts the door, reaches in and pops it open. "It has springs on the doors so they open far enough to get a hold of."

Whitney is taking it all in. "And if the windows are up—maybe it's raining?"

"Well, I have a pickup for rainy days—but..." He shuts the door, moves to the front fender, does something, and the door pops open.

Whitney pushes Joey toward me and peers behind the front wheel. "The ring thingy?"

The guy is totally under her spell and echoes, "Yeah, the ring thingy."

"Can I try it?"

"Be my guest." He closes the door.

She pulls but nothing happens.

"Give it a good tug."

The door pops open and she stands up, victorious.

No Handles shuts the door, but Whitney is not done. "So, can you lock it? How do you know somebody won't see you open it and steal your car?"

"I can lock it, but I don't know if you can be trusted." He's having fun. "For all I know, you stole the TR3." He gives her the *your turn* gesture with one hand.

"You have me there—caught red-handed. Good thing I didn't

227

drive the Rolls Royce I pinched last week!"

He's shaking his head, grinning. "Look, I gotta get to work." He looks at me. "She's a keeper." He bends down and puts out his hand to Joey. "Hey fella, I'm Jason." Joey grins and shakes.

"What kind of wax do you use?" Whitney asks.

"Nothin' but Blue Coral."

The car rumbles to life. "First time anyone walked over and asked."

Whitney watches as the car rolls away, the exhaust producing a deep throb. "Well, *O-K*."

Whitney- Philip

My hair behaves. It's a simple short cut but I don't want it to just hang.

It's gone much cooler, so we're taking Freddy's car. We asked Mrs. Fillmore to let us drive her, but she only said, "You kids don't need me along," and winked.

Mama holds Joey against her legs, hands on his chest. "Honey, Whitney and Freddy have to go. They can't be late."

Joey starts to fuss, "Can I go, can I go?"

Mama gets a better grip on his shoulders. "Tonight is a grown-up night."

"Whitney's not a grown-up. She's just my sister!"

Mama shushes Joey, but I find myself basking in the word *grown-up*. Am I grown up? I don't feel like a grown-up—and yet I realize I've been more comfortable with myself today. Me as I am, and not thinking about standing out—happy to enjoy the people around me.

We arrive and have to use our umbrellas to get to the auditorium. Freddy goes to the piano, and music begins to float through the room. I go back to the lobby and wait for Mrs. Fillmore and take her to her reserved seat. Quite a few of the cast have reserved seats for parents and friends. I wiggle my fingers toward my fishermen in the middle of their row.

I sit while Miss Odegaard does my eyes and puts a little blush on my cheeks. She sits back, takes another few seconds with the pencil, and says, "Just on the eyebrows. Yours are beautiful, but the lights tend to wash us out—so we overdo it a bit, don't you know?" She smells like peppermint.

I stand. "Thank you."

Tucker comes close. "The telephone will be on stage."

I laugh, "Thanks."

Mrs. A herds us up and into the wings. I'm not sure what I feel. It's not nerves. Excitement? Folks have come out on a rainy night, and they deserve the best show we can give them.

I move to my bench, Freddy starts the overture, and the curtain swishes across the stage. We remain frozen, and I know Freddy is at the piano, but I can't see him. My whole body begins to tingle as he slips into my intro.

The show goes so well the cast is ecstatic. We begin the sing-along, and the stage lights go down some. I can hardly take my eyes off

Freddy, but also pick out Mrs. Fillmore *and* Cliff and Jean! They came twice!

After Silent Night, a quiet hush comes over the auditorium as we mingle with the crowd. Freddy finds me and we move through to the lobby, greeting folks.

I'm surprised when Philip approaches. He has a woman who must be his grandmother with him.

"Gran, I want you to meet Whitney. She's the one I told you about that has been helping me with my editing. And this is Freddy. He sits by me, too."

He puts his arm around his grandmother. "This is my Gran, Mrs. Peterson, my dad's mom."

Gran gushes a bit and then Philip joins back in the conversation. "I didn't know you two were so good," he says. "I mean really good."

"Thank you, Philip. That means a lot," I say, and I mean it. I squeeze Freddy's arm. "I had a good accompanist."

My fishermen find me, and Duke introduces us to his wife. Jim is alone, and it makes me a little sad. They promise to see me on Saturday.

We spend a few moments with Cliff and Jean. I surprise myself by hugging Jean and kissing Cliff on the cheek.

"We have our Christmas Concert next Friday. It will be a great show."

"We got tickets on our way in," Jean says, and she kisses *me* on the cheek. "We love to see young, wholesome kids doing well." She looks at Cliff. "Gives us hope for the future." She offers a tender smile.

Cliff's smile has a tinge of sadness in it, and I find myself wondering if they can't have children.

Freddy opens the car door. "So, it's only nine-fifteen. Want to go somewhere, or are you tired?"

"I'm not tired—maybe we could just drive for a bit."

Freddy drives toward the foothills, climbing the gentle curves and slopes. He pulls into a turnout and points the car toward the valley. The lights stretch out in enchanting patterns below.

"We don't have to do anything," he says. "I just stopped here for the view. I thought you would like it."

"It's beautiful." I find his hand, and we sit in silence for several minutes. It's raining again, and I love the patter on the roof.

This time, we kiss longer. Freddy doesn't try any tongue stuff which makes me happy because although I've heard stories, it never sounded appetizing to me. Instead, his lips are so great on mine. Tender, yet firm. It's heavenly.

Freddy- A Sponsor

Kissing Whitney helps me forget about what I am going to tell her. After a few minutes, I am pretty wound up, what with the bubble bath, her lips, her hand on my shoulder, my hand on her shoulder. I pull back and smile. "Wow, you are really something, but let's take a break."

She sits back, a little flushed, or maybe it's the dash lights. "Thank you. For understanding." She pulls my chin so I'm looking right at her. "You know, I'm crazy about you, Fredrick Sanders."

"Not as crazy as I am about you."

But I am not done. I turn forward and reach for her hand. "This thing with my dad may not end well. I don't know what he'll do but if he starts drinking again and tries to hit Mom—I will stop him. But, I'm only seventeen. I don't know what he might do if I stop him —hit him—hurt him."

"Oh, Freddy."

"I'm scared, Whitney. What if he sends me to juvie or something?" I turn toward her. "If I'm in legal trouble—you shouldn't be around me—with me. People will talk. People are probably already talking."

She's quiet but hasn't let go of my hand.

"When he's like that, there is no reasoning with him. The thing is, when he's sober, he's nothing like that." I hate talking about my home life—airing dirty laundry. But for some reason, this girl sitting beside me, holding my hand, seems to be the person I want to tell.

She's quiet, and I'm afraid she's going to bolt.

"What're you thinking?"

"I'm just so sorry."

I turn, facing her, and even in the dim dash lights, her eyes seem transparent. "I don't want you upset, so—is this a deal breaker?"

She puts her hand on my cheek again. "Freddy, even tough times with you would be better than no times with you."

I lean forward, looking at my watch. "Well, speaking of tough times, it's ten-eighteen. If he has been to the bar, he might be home soon."

Whitney reaches for my neck and pulls me into another kiss. "We're OK, Freddy."

232

Dad's truck isn't there, and frustration boils. I find Mom in the living room, watching an old Katherine Hepburn movie. She pats the couch next to her.

"How was it?"

"Good. When did he go?"

"Not till seven."

It doesn't really matter. It's after eleven and he isn't here.

A commercial comes on, and Mom says, "Want to have some ice cream?"

I'm surprised that we would have ice cream. She doesn't splurge, and I give her a questioning look.

"If he can spend money on booze, I can have ice cream."

I'm pleased. I can't remember Mom doing something just for herself.

"Sure. Let's have some," and we sit, not really watching the movie, eating our ice cream.

When I hear the door, I tense and set my bowl on the coffee table, think better of it, and set it on the back of the end table.

Dad comes in and just stands there. "I'm not drunk. I bought two fingers of Maker's Mark and just looked at it. I ended up giving it to Sid."

"Where have you been?" Mom asks.

"I called my sponsor, Tom. We've been at Daisy's, drinking coffee."

Mom puts her ice cream bowl on the coffee table. "Sponsor?"

Dad shifts against the door jamb. "In meetings, we get a sponsor—to help us when we are in trouble. Crisis, some people call it."

I can feel Mom relaxing.

"Anyway," Dad starts again, "I didn't drink. It's only been two weeks, but I didn't drink."

"I didn't know you were going to meetings," Mom says. It's almost a question.

"There are noon meetings. I've been going."

We absorb this information. True to her nature, Mom says, "Freddy and I were just having a bowl of ice cream. Would you like one?"

Dad has already noticed her bowl. It's the kind of thing that can set him off. Get mad about how she spends money. He mulls the idea over and gives her a slow smile. "Sure, let's have ice cream."

The movie is on commercial and Mom says, "We can turn the TV off."

"No, let's finish your movie."

I don't go to my room. Dad sits on the other side of Mom, and for the first time that I can remember, we watch a movie.

I don't really watch but sit thinking of Mom and Dad and Whitney.

Whitney- Seems Disloyal

I try, but can't sleep late. Francie was glad to take the Sunday shift.

I sort of wish we still went to church. Maybe I'll go with Freddy one of these days. After breakfast I tell Mama about my first kiss, and I assure her Freddy is an absolute gentleman.

"Hmmm. Sounds like your daddy and me." She's not tearing up. "We'd been to a picnic with the Wesley Fellowship. He had a tiny Model A pickup, and he took me home and kissed me in front of my house."

I know the story, but know she needs to tell it.

She stops and turns a bit on the couch. "Your daddy was a gentleman, too." She leans toward me. "There is no reason to spend time with a boy who isn't."

"Mama…" It's all I can get out. We sit for several minutes. "Guys—sometimes girls—tease me about the way—I'm built."

She puts her hand on my arm.

"It's hard, Mama." I'm surprised I'm not crying. It's as if I can think of myself in a more matter-of-fact way, rather than an emotional way.

"Freddy isn't like that. I'm sure he notices. It's hard not to notice, but he likes me for so many other reasons."

I think of the night I told him, 'I've been reduced.' But now I realize Freddy has helped me reduce the importance of the part of me I've hated and made it much less than the whole. I turn to Mama. "Freddy helps me believe in all of me."

I begin to ramble. "There are some fishermen at the café who are really nice. And I've been braver. It's possible to see things clearly, to have confidence when your brain is not spending time worrying about what people are thinking."

"Most of the time, people aren't thinking about us as much as we think they are."

"I know that, but when the Mae West remarks come, it's hard to ignore. Apparently, there were even *car bumpers* called Dagmars because of an actress…."

Mama sighs. "I know I haven't been much help, but Honey, we are doing better." She's quiet, staring at the blank TV. "Joey likes Freddy so much. That has to say something. Little kids can tell."

My brain skims over the last few weeks. We moved here to be

near Auntie Barbara, and Mama calls her almost every day. She has coffee with Auntie some mornings before they each go to work, but it's as if Mama isn't walking close to the walls these days.

"I don't know if a seventeen-year-old can really fall in love, but I am pretty crazy about Freddy." My head comes up, alarmed. "Not going to elope or get myself in trouble, but…." I reach for her hand. "I'm just in deep, deep like."

Mama is still quiet, and when I look, I see she's trying to make up her mind about something.

"Say it, Mama." I'm a little scared she's worried about the Freddy thing.

She turns and gazes into my eyes. "I loved your daddy so much. You have no idea. Even though he isn't here, I still love him as much as I ever did."

"I know, Mama. Me too."

She turns back to the blank screen. She's really working on something.

"Whitey, at the store, has asked me out." Her head comes around quickly, searching my eyes. "What do you think? I told him I would have to think about it."

This is one of those moments when your brain is totally shocked and not surprised at the same time. "He's a nice man, isn't he?" I know the answer, but want Mama to have a chance to tell me.

"He really is, Honey." She's thinking again as if there is so much to say she can't decide which things to tell me.

"He came in one time—I was drinking my tea on my break, and he just sat. He knows I'm a widow. It's on the application—who knows why? I was having a hard day, and he asked about Charlie, wanted to see a picture of him."

We're both tearing up, thinking about sharing Daddy with someone in California.

"Freddy asked to see a picture, too. He wanted to know Daddy's name."

"Oh, Honey, that's sweet."

I'm beginning to think Whitey and Freddy are birds of a feather. "So, what do you think?"

"Since that day, he hasn't pestered me or asked any more questions. He has just been—Whitey. He's nothing like your dad. Whitey is—well, more than blond. His hair is white, and has lots of it. He's not tall. About my height." Mama gets quiet. "He has the kindest eyes. Even when we aren't talking, he watches my eyes." She pats my leg. "You can't hide your soul in your eyes. It's right there."

I know all about eyes.

"So, Friday, he asked me if I would like to go to dinner." She gives a little laugh, and I see the young girl in her. "He was so worried. He didn't want me to think it had anything to do with him being my boss—like I was expected to go."

"And?"

"Honey, if it's going to bother you, I won't go."

"You want to go?"

"It has nothing to do with your daddy. Whitey lost his wife five years ago—ovarian cancer." She sits back, taking a deep breath. "I'm not sure why we talked about it that time. I think he wanted me to know he—understood."

"Mama, I hope Daddy is looking down, watching Freddy and me—you and Whitey. Looking with that smile we love. He wants us to be happy."

She turns her wedding band back and forth. "Seems disloyal."

"I think you should go."

Freddy- Concert

I'm just getting started with my spaghetti when Loretta stands near. She gives me a head tilt, and I tell Sam, "I'm gonna talk to Loretta."

We go to the empty table we used before.

Loretta goes through her ritual of spreading a napkin and sets out two tangerines. I know enough to wait.

"So, Freddy, would you say you are ready for the Christmas Formal?"

I'm happy that I know the answer to this one. "Yes!"

One corner of her mouth moves. "So, suit or tux?"

"Tux."

"Corsage?"

"With a ribbon that matches her dress."

Loretta gives me an approving look. "Dinner?"

"Reservations at The Pepper Mill."

Loretta picks up her tangerine and digs at the stem end to get it started. I decide it's time to try the rest of my salad, but I keep an eye on Loretta, in case she's giving me a signal to say something.

"Sounds like you've got things under control." I'm rewarded with a crooked smile that creates one dimple.

I decide a return smile is appropriate.

"So, tonight's the choir concert."

I nod. "I am picking Whitney up at six-thirty." Whitney's mom is going with her sister.

Loretta is sucking in her cheeks, but she hasn't taken a bite yet. I wait.

"Many of the girls will be getting a rose after the concert. Not on the stage, just after the concert. Milly, Laura, Sally, Janice, Kandi." She stops. "You get the idea."

My mind is spinning. There should be rules for this sort of thing.

Loretta takes a bite, chewing calmly, watching me. She knows I haven't thought about flowers, and I talk to my fork.

"Thanks. I'll go by right after school. I have to take Whitney home and then I'll go." I'm hoping they have roses left and look up. "Do they usually have enough?"

"The shop on Third belongs to my mother's cousin. They're expecting you."

238

Whitney is lucky to have such a great friend, and I breathe, "Thanks."

Loretta pops another slice in her mouth, chews, and swallows. "Yeah, well, we wouldn't want Whitney to think she's dating a chump."

"Well, apparently I don't always keep up."

Loretta is back to the subject at hand. "Long stem. Most are getting red. White is OK, too. She's wearing her blue dress, so maybe have them put a blue ribbon on it."

I need to get advice from Loretta more often. "As soon as I take Whitney home, I'll go."

"They close at five. You better get a move on."

"Yes." I feel like a little kid, getting instructions from my mother, but Loretta is not being condescending. She's just a matter-of-fact sort of person.

"So, there will be another order there. I got one for Gail Smith."

Loretta slowly puts the slice she's been holding in her mouth. She's half closed one eye, nodding ever so slightly. "It might cheer her up after Donnie Jacobs started seeing Penny Prather—the twit. Drop both flowers at my house."

She produces a slip of paper with an address. "Two blocks over from Whitney. I'll bring yours and give it to you after Whitney is in the choir room."

Loretta looks as if I've proven trustworthy to carry out this important task. "This way, you won't have to hide it in your car." She offers me one of her lightning winks.

When we stand I notice Loretta is almost as tall as I am, and I wonder if she's still growing.

She comes close. "You're OK, Sanders." She tilts her head toward mine and says, "Whitney's great. Don't goof this up."

I sit in the concert holding Whitney's rose. Loretta and Minnie sit on either side of me, and Loretta has two roses: the one for Gail, and the one I gave her.

She leans in, and says, "Thanks again, Freddy."

I notice that Mrs. A's injured hand is free, and she leads with commanding fluidity. Whitney's eyes never leave Mrs. A. Her concentration and focus make me smile inside.

Whitney's eyes are bright when I give her the rose. "This is lovely!"

Whitney- Well Done

Mr. Sanchez passes back our stories. 'Lovely premise and well written. Don't overdo your tags.' He has circled the second 'said Al' at the end of a piece of dialogue. A+. I automatically hold it over my shoulder.

I sense Freddy leaning closer. "Good job, Miss Tate." He taps my fingers, and I let my paper go and he slips his into my hand.

Mr. Sanchez's writing fills the margin. "Excellent Plot! This could easily become a novel. Great Characters. A+"

There are a couple of editing marks, but I'm reading fast. Freddy has a gift. I hear his characters' voices from their first words, and I'm there in the scene with them. I flip to the second and then third page. By the fourth, he has me misty.

How does he do this? I know my story is good. Excellent. But it doesn't have the heart, the very soul of Freddy's.

I haven't heard a word Mr. Sanchez has been saying, and then realize he's reading about picking apples. I steal a peek at Philip. His head is down.

Mr. Sanchez is such a gifted reader, and the class is hushed. When he finishes, someone claps, others join in, and Philip is purple.

Mr. Sanchez makes it to Philip's desk in four long strides and happily puts the paper down. "Well done, Philip." Philip manages to tip his paper toward me. B+.

He changed the ending, smoothed it, and left us on a heartfelt note—the family eating the first apple pie of the season, a la mode.

Outside of class, Philip is right there. "Freddy, can I talk to Whitney for a second? Not trying anything. I just need some advice."

"Sure." Freddy gives me a wave. "See you later."

He strolls up the walk and meets Ally. She bounces along beside him, and I don't feel one ounce of jealousy. I turn to Philip.

"OK." He's fiddling with his books. "OK—well, first, thank you for giving me edits on my story—three times."

I almost want to reach out and put my hands on his shoulders to help him become still.

"I never thought I could get a B+. I can't remember when I got a B+. Well, except on the poem quiz." His head jerks up. "And I did it myself. But this is writing."

"I know."

"OK, I don't want to make you late, but…" He tucks his books under his arm only to take them out again.

"It's OK, Philip. I'm just going to History. Let's start that way. I think you are two rooms down."

He says, "Oh, yeah," as if he's embarrassed he hadn't thought of it, and we walk slowly.

"So, I saw Ron Packard holding hands with Cindy Caruthers." Philip is really fretting now. "Do you think Loretta would go out with me? I can be a gentleman." His earnest eyes are searching mine. "I will *be* a gentleman."

I'm thinking about the past few days. Loretta is so hard to read. She seems to take everything in stride. We are halfway between our rooms, and the three-minute bell rings.

Philip starts to go, saying, "Don't be late because of me."

"Hey, Philip?" He turns. "Let me do some investigating."

He brightens and says, "Thanks!" He comes back and stuffs a folded sheet of lined paper in my hand.

Whitney- Bummed Out

It's so cute. Philip has made a list. His handwriting isn't getting any better.

1. I wont be a jirk any more.
2. Whitney (he's erased it two or three times, but has it correct) is helping me with English, and I'm doing beter.
3. Mr. Sandchez is tudring me in study skils.
4. Mis Johnsen-well Mrs. Keler now helps me lots she thinks Im lexik
5. I have a job baging ~~groser~~ food at Boys markit.
6. I will take her to the movie of her chois.
7. I know Im a bad speller but im geting better cuz Im working hard now
8. My gran says Im not stupid and I beleve her.

I hold the note close to my heart. This boy has all sorts of troubles. Like me. Like Freddy. Probably like most of the kids in the school.

I can hardly wait 'til lunch and Freddy meets me on the way.

"Freddy—mum's the word, but Philip has a crush on Loretta. If Minnie wasn't babbling about Howard—by the way, they are back on —Loretta might have mentioned she's on the outs with Ronnie."

"You know, I can be quite the matchmaker. I'm the one who got Laura and Jeremy together."

"Yes, Mr. Romance, but I've got this one. See you after lunch?" I grab his arm and pull our shoulders together so quickly we almost step on each other.

"Go to it."

At our table, Minnie has the floor. "So, Howard said we should go to the Christmas Formal. It seems so pedestrian, but my mom got me a dress. It's white and fluffy. I look really cute." Minnie takes a short breath. "Howie—Howard has already gotten a reservation at Guido's. I don't know. I wish you were still going, Loretta."

Loretta leans in. "I'm kind of bummed out. It's not like

Ronnie's all that great or anything, but he asked me way back and now he backed out." She picks up her tangerine only to lay it down. "I mean, *Cindy Caruthers*, for crying out loud?"

This gets Minnie's attention. "Cindy Caruthers! Wait, what?! Ronnie is going with Cindy Caruthers?! A pox on them, I say!"

Loretta tries a smile, fails, and picks up her tangerine. "It can't be helped."

"Come here." I reach across and get Loretta's hand.

"What is going on?" Minnie whines. "I'm in the middle of an important decision!"

I lean close. "Honey, we will be right back, and we both will give our full attention to your dilemma."

Outside, I lead Loretta to a bench. "OK. This is may be good—may be terrible. Do you know Philip Peterson?"

"Yeah?" Loretta is giving me the half-closed eye treatment. "We had History last year," she says cautiously. "Kind of a do-nothing guy."

"Yeah, when I first came, he was cheating. Mr. Sanchez caught him. Big mess."

Loretta nods knowingly. "He's not bad looking, just lazy."

"Well, in the last few weeks, he's kinda turned himself around. I gave him some help with English. Lately, he has been a perfect gentleman—no leering."

This gets Loretta's attention.

"He'd like to ask you out but is scared you won't give him a chance." I look past her shoulders. The day is so clear it seems as if I could reach out and touch the mountains. "If this is a No, please keep this to yourself?" I dangle the note.

Loretta gives me a half smile and holds out her hand.

I wait. She reads. She puts the note on the bench but keeps her hand on it, looking at something far away. She picks it up, reads, and rereads. "Well, he can't spell."

Freddy- Cute

After school I say, "Hey, you want to go on another exciting excursion?"

"Well, I don't know. I don't need any more batteries."

"This is a money maker. But you may need to change."

At her house, she's only gone for moments. She comes out wearing jeans and a flannel shirt she didn't tuck in. I force my eyes to her eyes.

At my house, I lead the way to Dad's pickup, and let down the tail gate.

"Listen, Mr. Hardware Man, I'm not riding back here like a sack of cement."

"No, you'll ride up front with me." I pull open the garage door and point to the Wurlitzer. "But you get to help me load this."

"What a guy, Freddy Sanders. Somehow, when I met you, I didn't think, 'Someday, I'm gonna get to carry a piano for this guy.'" Whitney hefts the end.

"We'll go slo—" I say when Dad interrupts.

"Here, Whitney. Don't let this guy make you carry his piano."

"I'm used to it, Mr. Sanders. I've already had to push his car when it had a dead battery."

Dad and I lift the piano in and tie it down. Whitney hands up the bench. Dad reminds me to take the corners slowly.

At Bill Samelson's house, Whitney slips out and walks up the steps with me, and Bill comes to the door.

"Hey, Bill, you know Whitney, right?"

He smiles. "Yeah. We have typing."

"Bill is the fastest in the class." She gives Bill a smile. "If you play like you type, you'll be great."

"It's for my sister, Annie. She's not here right now." He's apologetic. "Annie tends to get a bee in her bonnet and then sorta forgets about it after a while. This seems like a way to let her start."

Whitney smiles her approval. "That's sweet, Bill. I'm sure she'll appreciate it."

Bill has the garage open. "Annie's birthday isn't until next week, so we are hiding it in the garage." He points to a corner.

Bill and I jump up on the truck, and Whitney says, "Hey, fellas, I'm not helpless. I'm in charge of the bench."

245

Bill hustles it to her and watches her carry it to the corner. I'm not jealous, just happy Whitney chose me.

When the piano is covered with blankets, the bench tucked under the keyboard, Bill hands me two twenties. "Mom says thanks."

"Oh, almost forgot." I get a grocery sack from the pickup. "If Annie decides to take lessons, here are my beginning books."

Bill peers in the bag and then back at me. "Have you thought any more about lessons? Mom was pretty impressed at the Musical."

"Let's see what Annie thinks of the Wurlitzer. But, yes."

Whitney tips her head to my shoulder. "Freddy is very patient."

In the pickup, I say, "I think we're rich!"

"Well, you're rich. I only carried the bench."

"Yeah, but the bench is integral to playing. We couldn't have poor Annie standing!"

Whitney sings, "If you can't find a bench, use a wooden chair," and I laugh. She does a pretty good Elvis.

"So, with forty dollars burning a hole in my pocket, I have a plan."

At a stop sign, Whitney turns her clear blue eyes on me. "I'm listening."

"We take the truck back, and I take you to get the Triumph. Then—and here's the exciting part—you drive us to In-N-Out for burgers and fries!"

Whitney doesn't wear her scarf, and we let the wind blow our hair. It's like she's been driving this car for years. The newspaper says it will be sixty-one today, so after we eat, we drive into Pasadena and down Colorado Boulevard. The little heater almost keeps our legs warm.

"We better start back," she says at a stop light.

Three guys on the corner whistle and Whitney just smiles, and we take off a little faster than we need to. I hear a "Whooo-ooo" from them, and Whitney makes a quick shift, grinning. At that moment, she may have felt as cute as she is.

"I love the way Daddy's car sounds."

Whitney- Trout

Viv let my fishermen in early, and when I come in, I smell fish frying.

"What's going on?"

Steve is at the grill. "You go sit down, Kiddo. You are having trout for breakfast."

Jim is beckoning to me, and I go to their booth. An extra table has been added, and Jim holds my chair for me. He hustles off and is back with hot water and tea.

Steve comes with a platter. "Now, I have breaded and plain."

I'm so touched I don't know what to say and shrug my shoulders.

"Good choice," Steve says with a wry grin. "Nothing wrong with a little of each."

I'm served a plate with trout, fried potatoes, and a fancy garnish. Jim watches me with the sweetest eyes. "Listen, Whitney, you've brightened our Saturday mornings. It's time we brightened yours."

"OK, but you guys eat too." *I'm not eating alone in front of them.*

Steve slips in and lifts his coffee. "A toast to Whitney, a bright part of our fishing days. To your health and happiness, Whitney."

We clink our cups, and I am overwhelmed by the moment.

"Aw, come on, Kiddo," Steve says. "Don't cry on us."

Kindness is like a salve, and I feel like I belong. I belong to California. I belong to Freddy. And I belong to these kind men. I miss a tear that rolls down my cheek.

"Tears of happiness," I say.

The fish is nice and toasty, and I realize Steve has warmed the plates.

"Do you like it?" he wonders.

"I've never had trout before, but this is wonderful." I give Steve a look. "You could hire on to cook here."

My fishermen share a glance, and Steve says, "Aw, Honey, Viv and I own this place."

"What!? Who's Daisy? Why didn't you tell me?"

"Daisy's my mom. She's still around—I keep track of the business end and ordering. Viv didn't want you to be nervous serving the owner."

"Well, now I *am* nervous!"

"Don't be. You're doing fine."

Jim's tea is empty, and I start to get up. "Let me get you some hot water."

"No, Hon." Viv has appeared magically. "I have orders to keep you in your seat until you've finished your breakfast."

And I sit, eating trout with my fishermen.

When we are almost done, Jim says, "There's one more thing. Your tip for your presence today." He hands me an envelope. "Put this to good use."

The envelope feels thick, and I feel very loved.

Oh, Whitney,

You look so good! That blouse is showing your slender self! I know you fuss because it may emphasize your upstairs, but you must believe me when I say, you look lovely. Healthy. Happy. And the blouse isn't like a tent around your waist! Please, please, stop being embarrassed. What Sandra Conners said that time was just jealousy. She was just upset that she had competition.

And Freddy! Look at that hair. Wow. No wonder you fell for him. And your daddy's car has never looked better. So shiny!

I'm so proud of you. What a life you've made! I know you have had troubles, but in two months, you have conquered so much.

I'm sending a picture Mary Ann took when I got my hair cut. She and I are becoming closer. Don't feel bad—I think this is life. I just wish it didn't include me not having you here—but I don't think I would change anything after seeing the new Whitney.

Love and Hugs,

Joanie

248

I cry just a little, but Joanie is right. Life changes. And, someday, I will see Joanie again. You can't kill ten years of friendship with distance.

And, I have a dance to get ready for.

Freddy- Not Going

Mrs. Fillmore makes my tie perfect. "Whitney is with her mother."

Joey is sitting obediently on the couch but blurts, "You look handsome, Freddy!"

Mrs. Tate comes up the hall, looks at Mrs. Fillmore, and then me. "She's having a hard time. She won't come up."

"Should I go down?" Mrs. Fillmore asks.

Mrs. Tate nods, and they go back together.

Joey tugs on my arm. "Freddy, come to my room. I want to show you something."

I sit on the couch and tousle Joey's hair. "I think we should stay here."

I stare at Mr. Tate's picture only seeing his eyes. Whitney's eyes. The clock's hand creeps forward.

"Whitney's crying," Joey whispers.

I've heard, and my heart aches.

Mrs. Tate comes up the hall so quietly I almost don't notice her. Her eyes find mine. "She says she's not going."

Poor Whitney. "Can I talk to her? Through the door? I won't go in."

She gives me a sad smile. "It can't hurt."

I pat Joey and slip down the hall. At the door, I don't hear anything, but I'm not trying to eavesdrop. I take a breath and tap with one knuckle. "Whitney? It's Freddy."

There's a gasp. "Don't come in!"

"No, I'm not. But can we talk?"

I hear rustling and whispering. Mrs. Fillmore cracks the door open, and I move back.

She slides out "She says you can go in."

I put my face close to the door. "I'm gonna come in. Is that alright?"

Whitney's voice is muffled. "No. Yes. I don't know. Yes?"

I open the door just enough to squeeze through and close it behind me. I don't see her and raise on my tiptoes, peeking over her bed. "Where are you?"

Her voice is a whimper. "In the closet."

"Are you alright?"

"No."

"Do you want me to leave?" I take one step backward toward the door and wait.

"No. Yes. I don't know," she wails. "I can't go to the Formal in this dress."

I wait in case she's not done.

"I thought you liked it."

When I don't hear anything, I say, "We don't have to go."

The closet door cracks open, and I see one eye. "Oh, Freddy," she moans. "Your tux is beautiful. I'm ruining everything."

"No you're not." I keep my voice low. "What if you wore another dress?"

She pulls back, and the door closes. She's crying, gulping air. "Mrs. Fillmore—made it for me—from scratch. You made— reservations. She's—good to me. You're so—good to me."

"Whitney, you're good to *me*—you're good to everyone."

After a very long pause, she whispers, "Thank you." She sticks her hand out. "Pass me some tissues, please—by my bed?"

I decide to bring the whole box. "Can I see? It's probably beautiful."

Her voice is muffled from the Kleenex. "It is. It's beautiful." She blows. "Oh, I'm such a mess." A coat hanger rattles. "If I show you, please don't tell anyone about this."

"You don't have to show me. But, what is between us is just for us."

"OK—I think."

There is more rustling, and a hanger clatters to the floor.

"OK." The door opens.

Whitney's in heels, tall and slim. Her hands are on her cheeks, and her eyes are red.

"Nice shoes."

"Thanks."

"The color is perfect."

"Everything is perfect—except...." She sighs and slowly lets her arms go to her side. Her voice is back to a whimper. "Look at me. The dress emphasizes...." She searches my eyes. "Say something."

"Stunning. Tall. Statuesque. Lovely. Beautiful. The girl I know so well."

She gives me a wrinkle smile. "But...."

I hold her eyes. "Whitney, I know how you look." She almost winces. "What's the first thing I said just now?"

"Nice shoes?"

251

"It's the first thing I saw. Honest. Shoes and feet. Pretty feet."

She bends to look at the shoes. "Mama got them for me."

"They make you taller. If anything…." I grasp for the right words. "The extra height—evens you out. I know I'm not saying it right. My eye was drawn to your waist, hips, the way the dress follows your legs."

"But I was covering myself with my arms."

"Whitney, if anything, that makes guys wonder what your arms are covering." I look away. "Sorry. Guys are dumb that way."

"But you're not bad about it."

I look at her, up and down. "You look like Whitney Tate in a lovely gown. And she's pretty."

"Thank you. But look." She steps to the bed and picks up a fuzzy white shoulder wrap, dangling it toward me. Exasperated, she slips it over her shoulders. "I look like a red polar bear in a life jacket. I can't be seen in public in this."

I can't stop a chuckle, but she doesn't mind. "What if you wear another coat? I'll be gallant and let you wear my tux jacket."

She tries a laugh. "We're going to be late." She takes off the wrap and stands in front of me. "Please tell me this is OK."

"It is. Really. This is the way you always look, but now you are elegant."

I start to put my hands in my pockets and take them back out. "I told you before, you could show up in a gunny sack and be the prettiest one there." I take a half step toward her. "But, listen. You have to believe me, you would still look—like you." I give her a crooked smile. "I like you the way you are. But most of all, I like *you*."

She looks in the mirror on the inside of the closet door, turning left and right. "Oh!" She brings her hands to her face, covering herself again. "Mrs. Fillmore is so talented."

"Yes." I want to put my arms around her and comfort her.

There's a tap on the door, and Mrs. Fillmore asks, "Whitney, may I come in?"

"Of course."

Mrs. Fillmore has a hanger with a light jacket. "What about this? It has no buttons."

"Oh, no. That's one of the things you are keeping back."

"Honey, my Gina would want you to go to this dance. If she were here, she would be plowing through her closet until she found something that made you feel right."

Whitney lets her hands go to her sides. "I don't know what to say."

Mrs. Fillmore holds out the hanger. "When in doubt, just say thank you."

Whitney lifts it high, turning it. "So pretty."

"It's a simple cut. That makes it timeless."

Whitney slips the jacket on and goes to the mirror. "Oh, Freddy, look!" She turns to me. "It doesn't splay open." She hugs Mrs. Fillmore. "Thank you."

Whitney turns to her side. "Still obvious—but I feel better." She raises her eyebrows to me. It's a question.

"Perfect."

Whitney looks at her alarm clock. "We're gonna be late!"

"We'll be fine."

She rushes out the door toward the bathroom.

Mrs. Tate joins us and takes Mrs. Fillmore's hands. "I don't know how I would have done this without you. Whitney's daddy was always the one who could—help her during the tough times."

Mrs. Fillmore turns and takes Mrs. Tate's arm, patting her hand. "Not my first time, Martha. Not my first time."

Whitney- Deep Breaths

My face isn't too puffy, but mascara has run to my chin! I look horrible, and Freddy didn't say a word. I wash my face and lean into the mirror. The cool washcloth feels good on my red eyes.

Better. I pat with a towel.

My hand is shaking when I put the mascara brush up to my lashes. I lean both hands on the counter and slow my breathing. *Nope.* I screw the brush into the tube.

When I get back to my room, everyone has gone. Before I put on the jacket, I go into Mama's room to look in her full length mirror. I use her hand mirror to see the back of the dress. It fits perfectly—pretty. *I* look pretty. Normal. Why can't my front side be normal?

I slip into the jacket and it is the ideal complement, and I look again. From behind, it spoils the waist of the dress.

I lay the jacket over my arm and start up the hall.

Freddy- The Way You Look

When Whitney comes up the hall, she's red-flustered but smiles when she sees me. "You are so handsome, Freddy Sanders," she breathes.

"Thank you." I take a moment to really look at her. Her hair is the same, but maybe has a little more "body." I've heard that on commercials.

When I get out the corsage, she is undecided. She slips into the jacket, and I fasten the corsage, enthralled with her cheek and neck.

When Whitney pins on my boutonniere, she's so close my heart is hammering. The wave of bubble bath and the place where her neck meets her shoulder is almost overpowering.

"OK, you two. Stand in that corner with the pictures behind you." Mrs. Tate squints into the camera. "Move to your right. I want your Daddy's picture to show." The flash bulb makes me see more stars than I'm already seeing.

Both Mrs. Tate and Mrs. Fillmore take more pictures, Joey dancing around them.

"Let me take one of all of you," Mrs. Fillmore suggests.

Mrs. Tate hands her the camera, and we gather together. Joey stands in front of us and demands to hold my hand. He squeals when the flash goes off and makes a production of rubbing his eyes.

Mrs. Tate kisses Whitney on the cheek. "Have fun."

Whitney- Close

When we get to the car after dinner, I have another wave of uncertainty. Freddy opens my door, and I lay the jacket on the seat. I can't face him and turn away.

The car would be safe. Going for a drive would be safe.

I look down, not liking what I see.

Across the lot, a motor scooter starts in a cloud of smoke, and a wave of déjà vu flickers.

"Hey, you OK?"

I say to my shoulder, "I may just crawl under a rock and never come out."

"I wish you wouldn't."

The voice. The boy. How could I have not known?

I turn quickly. "My first day—in front of the school. It was you!"

Freddy's mouth lifts at the corner. "You looked so small and sad."

"You saved me that day...."

We check my jacket and go into the ballroom.

Freddy's arm gives me confidence. His voice. His kind words. Caring words.

The room is filling with couples, and our friends have a place for us. I'm getting looks, and I choose to think they are seeing the whole me.

"Dance?" Freddy asks.

"Yes," and we waltz around the outside of the other dancers.

He leans his head toward me. "You know you saved me, too."

I hug him close, and we dance.

About The Author

As an educator, George spent his life stamping out illiteracy in sixth-grade classrooms. He and the kids had a great time, and George learned a great deal. George and Ruth live in an old stone house that was named Graestone long before they came.

George doesn't always wear a tux.

Read more at George's website: graestonewriter.com

About the Publisher

Books from Graestone is pleased to bring you Whitney and Freddy's story. Graestone is a beautiful old stone house nestled on four acres. My writing has blossomed since arriving at Graestone.,

www.ingramcontent.com/pod-product-compliance
Lightning Source LLC
Chambersburg PA
CBHW022032240626
47154CB00007B/2372